THE MURDER OF THE FROGS

AND OTHER STORIES

THE MURDER OF THE FROGS

AND OTHER STORIES

DON CARPENTER

DOVER PUBLICATIONS, INC.
MINEOLA, NEW YORK

Bibliographical Note

This Dover edition, first published in 2020, is an unabridged republication of the work originally published by Harcourt, Brace & World, New York, in 1969.

Library of Congress Cataloging-in-Publication Data

Names: Carpenter, Don, author.
Title: The murder of the frogs and other stories / Don Carpenter.
Other titles: Short stories. Selections
Description: Mineola, New York : Dover Publications, Inc., 2020. | Summary: "The High Sierras, the Oregon back country, Hollywood, San Francisco and its environs provide settings for the two novellas and eight shorter pieces brought together in this uncommonly substantial and satisfying volume by the author of Hard Rain Falling and Blade of Light."— Provided by publisher.
Identifiers: LCCN 2019049271 | ISBN 9780486843438 (trade paperback)
Classification: LCC PS3553.A76 A6 2020 | DDC 813/.54—dc23
LC record available at https://lccn.loc.gov/2019049271

Manufactured in the United States by LSC Communications
84343201
www.doverpublications.com

2 4 6 8 10 9 7 5 3 1

2020

To Martin Lee Fink

Contents

I / Six Stories   3

Road Show   5

The Crossroader   20

Blue Eyes   35

New York to Los Angeles   49

Silver Lamé   69

Limbo   90

II / The Murder of the Frogs   99

III / The Art of the Film   167

Hollywood Heart   169

Hollywood Whore   201

IV / One of Those Big-City Girls   251

About the Author   309

THE MURDER OF THE FROGS

AND OTHER STORIES

I / Six Stories

Road Show

The old Pontiac rattled into the motel driveway just after sundown. Three ragged deer watched from a pen as the dust cloud raised by the car blew slowly away across the deserted countryside. When Carl turned the engine off he could hear the radiator whistling, but he was too tired to get out and open the hood. He just sat there. Except for the word *Vacancy* on the big motel sign there wasn't any light coming from anywhere. "I wonder if anybody's here?" Carl said.

"Blow the horn," Stella said. Her face was covered with white dust, and in the half-light she looked made of plaster. From his place of concealment on the floor in back, Reuben said in a muffled voice, "Do something, God damn it."

The main building was a farmhouse and to the right was a string of dirty-looking cabins. There weren't any cars in front of the cabins, and in fact the only vehicles in sight were a gutted truck on the other side of the deer pen and a jeep parked in the shadows of a tree beside the farmhouse.

Carl got out of the Pontiac and stood for a moment, stretching, and then pulled the seat of his pants out from between his buttocks. He was flexing his fingers when a low shadowy creature came out from under the jeep and rushed toward him, hissing. Carl thought it was a dog and jumped back into the car and rolled up the window. But it was only a goose, neck out, wings raised. The goose honked at him a few times and then turned around and waddled back under the jeep.

"What the hell's going on?" Reuben said from the floor.

"A big bird came at me," Carl said. "I don't think anybody's here." He looked over his shoulder at the word *Vacancy*.

"Here comes somebody," Stella said. "Get out and go over to him."

Carl got out again, keeping an eye out for the goose, and went to the man who had come from around the farmhouse. "Howdy," Carl said.

"You want a cabin?" the man said. He was wearing a dark jacket and pants, and a red hunting hat. Carl couldn't see his face.

"Two cabins," he said.

"Two?" The man went over toward the car, and Carl hurried to get in between.

"My wife isn't feeling too well, and I thought I'd get a room for each of us," he said.

The man seemed satisfied with this explanation and said, "Follow me," and led Carl up the steps and into the farmhouse, turning on lights as he went. The office was in the parlor. The man got behind a small paper-covered desk and rummaged around, coming up with a motel register, which he handed to Carl. Carl could see his face now, washed-out eyes behind silver-rimmed glasses, a big red nose and a thin mouth. It was a country face, and Carl did not like it, any more than the motel-keeper or whatever he was liked Carl's thin sunburned city face. Carl signed two forms, one in his name and one in his wife's name, and handed the pad back to the man.

The blue eyes looked out the window at the darkness. "Be six dollars," he said. "In advance. For each room."

Carl gave him twelve dollars, a ten and two ones. The man looked at the money, and then back out the window. "Pet the deer for fifty cents," he said. "Apiece."

"I beg your pardon?" Carl said.

"*I say you can pet the deer for fifty cents,*" the man said loudly, still looking out the window.

"Oh. No, thank you," Carl said. They left the building, the man turning out lights as they went. Carl stopped him before he got to the car. "Could we have our keys?" he said.

"Don't need any keys out here," the man said. "Pick out your cabins and move in." He went back around the building out of sight. Carl got in the car and turned on the motor. He drove slowly to the last cabin in the row. The cabins were built in pairs, with enough space between each pair for a car, and so Carl pulled in between and parked. "I'll go in first," he said. He reached into the back seat for the two suitcases and was struggling with them when Reuben said, "Come around and take them out the door."

"Okay," Carl said.

Inside the cabin there was a layer of dust on everything, including the bedding. The bed, the chest of drawers and the chair were all bolted to the floor. Carl put down the suitcases and checked the two doors in the cabin. One led to a bathroom in the back, with a toilet, a sink and a roll of paper towels, and the other led to the duplicate room on the other side. Neither door had a lock, and neither would shut tightly. Carl turned the light back off and went outside. "Okay," he said. The back door of the car opened and Reuben came out crouched over and ran into the cabin. Then Stella got out and said, "You better get some water for that radiator."

"Okay," Carl said. He got the rest of their stuff out of the trunk of the car and took it into the cabin, and then made several trips with their thermos jug, filling the radiator. When he was finished he went back inside and sat on the bed. Stella and Reuben were both in bathrooms washing themselves. Carl lit a cigarette and waited. There was a Spam can lid for an ashtray.

Reuben came in from the other cabin in his tee shirt and shorts, carrying a nearly full bottle of whiskey. He was a large thickset Negro, and his freshly washed skin gleamed in the light from the naked overhead bulb. "Drink time," he said. He sat down in the only chair.

"Where are we going to eat?" Carl said.

"Looks like we don't," Reuben said. "We'll hit a town tomorrow morning sometime."

"I sure would like to eat," Carl said.

Stella's voice came through the bathroom wall: "I have a couple of Mounds in my purse."

The two men were eating candy bars and washing them down with whiskey when she came out of the bathroom, still wearing her slacks and blouse. She sat down on the bed next to Carl. "Is there any left?"

Carl handed her the last little bar and she made a face and began eating it. She was a blonde in her early twenties, and with her face washed she looked young and pretty. She was a vocalist; Carl was a master of ceremonies and comedian, and Reuben was a piano player and singer. They were on tour, taking whatever bookings they could get. Their last booking had been a week in Winnemucca, Nevada, and their next was in Burns, Oregon. Right now they were about halfway between the two places in the area called the Great Basin.

Carl and Stella were not actually married, but they seldom had enough money to afford three rooms, and so Carl and Reuben had been sleeping in one room and Stella in another. In Winnemucca it had not been possible to register Reuben in a room at all, because he was a Negro, and so he had slept in the car. They had been told, in fact, that this would be the way it was all through the desert and basin country. They hadn't known this when Carl registered himself and Stella as man and wife in Winnemucca and he had been afraid to try to change things, and so he and Stella had shared the same bed for a week, while Reuben stayed in the car and pointedly did not comment on this new arrangement. They had all been strangers to one another when the tour started six weeks before, in the booker's office in Los Angeles, but when the original bookings had given out, they had decided to stick together and make their own way. It was better than hanging around Hollywood waiting for a break, they reasoned, and it was giving them professional experience and a chance to see the country. Now they were right in the middle of it, and the tensions were beginning to show.

Carl had somehow gotten the idea that because he was the master of ceremonies and owned the car, he was the leader. Reuben put an entirely different light on it. "You think because you're white you can boss me around," he said once. "Don't try it," he added.

"Oh, you men," Stella had said.

And then there was Stella. Carl was not very good at making advances to women, and even during the week he slept in the same bed with her, he did not try anything funny. She had made it clear to him that she was not cheap. This made it difficult for Carl to get to sleep. He was afraid that in his sleep he might touch her or grab her, and he also hoped that she might snuggle up to him, but neither happened. Anyway not while he was awake.

Reuben knew nothing about this, and from little things he said they could tell he thought they were making love. It did not make him any easier to get along with. Both Stella and Reuben had taken to giving Carl orders, as if he were incapable of doing anything without their advice. He took it, because it was easier to do what they said than to stop every time and put forth an argument.

What bothered him most was that he was falling in love with Stella, and was beginning to think it would be pleasant to marry her. That week in Winnemucca had proved that they could get along together in close quarters, and in his eyes, at least, she was growing more beautiful every day. What he dared not hope for was that they marry and return to Los Angeles and a career for him in television. She could stay home and have children and keep house. Actually, she had little talent, and when this job came up she had been working as a cocktail waitress. She could go back to that while Carl established himself. Reuben, on the other hand, did have talent, both as a singer and as a piano player, and Carl thought he was foolish to try to become an actor. There weren't that many jobs for Negro actors, anyway. But he couldn't mention any of this. If Stella found out that he thought Reuben was more talented than she was, Carl wouldn't have a chance with her.

He did not like the way Reuben was sitting there in his underwear. Show people, he knew, were informal, but this bordered on arrogance, especially since Reuben must have thought he and Stella were lovers. Maybe he thought of himself as a friend of the family, or maybe he was showing off. Either way, Carl didn't like it. But he was not going to be the one to say good night. If he did, they might expect him to go into the other room, and he had no intention of going back to sleeping with Reuben. Reuben snored and thrashed around in the bed, and more than once Carl had had to take Reuben's arm off his chest. The arrangement begun in Winnemucca should continue, he thought, but he did not know exactly how to suggest it.

Reuben saved him the trouble. "We better get to sleep early," he said, "so we can get up and get on the road." He stood, stretched, and went into the other room. The door did not quite shut behind him.

Carl said, "Dirty," and went into Stella's bathroom. He spent a long time washing, and when he came out he was in his underwear, carrying the rest of his clothes over his arm. Stella was in bed, the grimy covers pulled up to her chin, both pillows behind her head. She was watching Carl. He put his clothes on top of hers, on the chair, looked around and then sat on the floor to take off his shoes and socks. "Everything is so gritty," he said. He stood up and turned off the light.

"You're not going to sleep in here," she said.

He went over to the bed and kneeled down and whispered, "I love you."

"Don't give me that," she said clearly. "Go in the other room."

"But I love you," he whispered. He reached under the covers and took hold of her arm. Her skin was soft and warm. "This is different," he whispered. "I love you. I've loved you for a long time. Please."

"Carl, I'm just not interested," she said. "Go in the other room."

He stood up, his face burning. "All right," he said. "If that's the way it is."

"That's the way it is."

He could hear the bed in the next room shaking on its springs. "I have to turn the light on," he said. He had a hard time finding it in the darkness, but finally switched it on. He did not look over toward the bed, but got dressed facing the chair. "I'll sleep in the car," he said. He did not know which of them he hated more, Stella for refusing him or Reuben for overhearing it and laughing. He went out the front door, carrying his shoes and socks, and pulled the door tightly shut.

It was cold and the sky was full of stars. He got into the back seat of the car and put on his socks and tried to get comfortable. It was impossible. He sat up and lit a cigarette and tried to think, but that was impossible, too. All the time he had been deluding himself into thinking she cared for him. She didn't. He could hear the words of her refusal, over and over again. She hadn't even been polite about it. She hadn't even bothered to whisper. He couldn't understand why. All that week in Winnemucca they had gotten along so well. But now, thinking about it, he could remember little things. Maybe they hadn't been getting along so well after all. She had bossed him around all the time. She would never let him watch her undress when they were alone, even though the three of them often had to change together in the one dressing room of the various clubs. And now, as he began to remember things clearly, it occurred to him that she had never once said anything nice about his performances, and the only time she had given him her big beautiful smile was on stage, in front of an audience. The car was filling up with smoke so he opened the back door and dropped out his cigarette. It seemed even colder now. He shut the door again and curled up on the seat. He wondered how Reuben stood it, sleeping in the car for a week. But he did not care, and viciously he hoped Reuben would have to sleep in the car in Burns. Of course they would have to get two rooms from now on.

After a while he knew he would not be able to sleep at all. It was just too cold. His whole body ached. He climbed out of the car and stretched his muscles and then went into Reuben's side. Maybe Reuben would be asleep and not hear him come in. He undressed as quietly as he could, in the darkness, and climbed carefully into the bed. He could not feel Reuben. He lay there wondering where Reuben was, and then jumped out of the bed, found the light and turned it on. The room was empty, and the connecting door was open. He dashed into Stella's room, and in the half-light saw the two of them lying there side by side.

"So that's it!" he shouted.

"Don't you know enough to knock?" Reuben said. "You interrupted us."

With a scream of fury, Carl jumped for the bed, trying to strangle Reuben. He got his fingers on Reuben's throat and squeezed. Reuben's hands were under the covers, and in his haste to get them out he knocked Stella on to the floor. Carl was growling and squeezing when Reuben finally got him by the shoulders and began shaking him. He shook Carl until he felt the fingers loosen from around his throat, and then, still lying on his back, he threw Carl back and heard the crash as Carl went off the end of the bed and knocked over the chair. Then he jumped out of the bed, ready for anything.

"What happened?" Stella asked.

"I don't know," Reuben said. He found the light and turned it on. Carl was lying on the floor, an expression of terrible rage on his face. His eyes were open and his head lolled on his neck.

Stella came around the bed. Both she and Reuben were naked, and she held her hands over her breasts, looking down at Carl. "He's dead, isn't he?" she said.

"It looks like it," Reuben said. He kept staring at Carl's open eyes, and then with a low cry he ran for the door and threw up. After a while the cold air cleared his head and he went back into the room. Stella was getting dressed.

"We have to get out of here," she said.

"I killed him," Reuben said.

"We don't have time to worry about that," she said. "We have to get out and take him with us. Hurry up and get dressed."

"I didn't mean to," he said. "He was trying to strangle me. I just defended myself."

"I know it," she said. "Get your clothes on."

"They'll hang me," he said. "They won't listen, they'll just hang me. We got to get out of here!"

"They'll do the same to me if they find out what's been going on. *Now get dressed!*"

Reuben dressed in a hurry, and by the time he was done, Stella had everything packed and ready except the body and Carl's clothes. "We have to dress him," she said. They did this together, and then got everything in the car. They didn't have room in the trunk for the body, so they put it on the back seat, curled up.

"You drive," Reuben said.

"I don't know how," she said, and got into the right-hand seat.

"Oh, God," Reuben said, and went around the car. They got away from the place and headed up toward Burns.

"We have to think," Reuben said. "All this trouble."

'We have to get rid of the body," Stella said. She was smoking rapidly. "We could just bury it out here someplace."

"We don't have anything to dig with," he said. "They're going to catch us, I just know it."

They drove on for fifteen minutes, and didn't see a single car. "Pull over here," Stella said. They were in the middle of nowhere. "Drive away from the road as far as you can," she said. They drove nearly a mile off the road, until there was a slight rise between them and the road. "Okay," she said. "We have to leave him here. We have to bury him some way."

Reuben got out and rummaged through the trunk. All he came up with was a tire iron, but that gave him an idea, and he pried loose a hubcap. He showed it to Stella. "I'll dig with this," he said.

"Get me one," she said.

They dug in the sandy dirt for an hour. The first place they tried had solid rock only a few inches below the surface, but they finally found a place where they could dig down about three feet. Both were sweating and covered with dirt and dust by the time they had the hole deep enough. They got the body out of the back seat. It was perfectly stiff, and Reuben had to break the rigor before they could get the body out and lay it in the grave. It only took twenty minutes to cover the body and pat the dirt down. The extra dirt they scattered by kicking at it.

They got back in the car, both of them panting with their mouths open.

"Let's go," she said.

"We're not going to get away with this," he said.

"Can you teach me how to drive?"

"Not quick enough."

"Then let's go."

"Look at us, we're filthy dirty."

"We can clean up in a gas station. Let's go."

They drove back to the highway and continued on north. They each had a pull at the whiskey bottle, and for a while neither spoke. Then Stella said, "We gas up at Burns and get ourselves clean. Nobody will be looking for us for a while. Then I think we can get as far as Portland if we drive all day. That's a big town. We'll be safe."

"Are you kidding? People know who we are. What happens when we don't show up for the booking in Burns? What happens if we go back to Hollywood? They catch us. Nobody's going to believe me, especially now. You know damn well." He looked over at her. "You could turn me in and get away scot-free," he said.

"I know it," she said. "Don't think it didn't occur to me."

"Well, are you going to do it?"

"No."

"Why not? You could get away. There was never anything between us anyway."

"I guess not," she said.

"It wasn't worth it."

She didn't reply.

"Don't tell me you're crazy about me," he said. "You're not crazy about anybody but yourself."

"I don't see how you can say that," she said. "After what we did together."

"Oh, come now," he said.

They were silent the rest of the way into Burns. It was full daylight when they pulled into the Standard station, gassed and cleaned up. They were well on their way to Bend when Reuben said, "I can't live with it. We have to turn ourselves in. I can't stand it. I keep thinking about Carl."

"Carl's dead," she said. "It was his fault. If we tell the police they'll put us in jail. You know what they'll do to us."

"I guess you're right," he said. "But I feel so bad."

"I feel bad, too," she said.

"I'll bet. The way you treated him."

"He asked for it," she said.

"You're a very hard woman."

She sighed and lit a cigarette. The hot flat countryside rolled past slowly.

1967

The Crossroader

Nobody ever did find out where he stayed while he was in town. Some thought down among the Indians on the other side of the river, but that wasn't likely, because the Indians didn't like Negroes, either. Not many Negroes came to town, and the one or two families of them in eastern Oregon lived farther north, in Bend, and didn't travel around. Once, a couple of years back, the U.S. Air Force made a mistake and assigned a Negro to the radar station out on top of Raincloud Butte, but he got off the bus at the depot around eleven o'clock one night and got on another one before noon the next day and went back to Tacoma, after the mayor and the chief of police drove up to the station and explained things to the major in charge, and the major telephoned to his headquarters there in Tacoma and explained things to them. That one solitary Negro Air Force man wouldn't have been happy stationed here because he would have had to stay on the station and not come to town. Not because anybody would say anything to him, just that nobody in the bus depot would serve him and he wouldn't get waited on at the barbershop and there would be no seats left at the movie. Things like that.

So when the other Negro showed up and stayed around for three days, everybody wondered where he slept and ate. Nobody saw him do either, and there weren't any strange cars in town, and besides, he was seen to get off the bus from Bend with his two little pieces of luggage, one a faded-brown canvas overnight bag and the other what looked like a black leather fishing-rod case, although nobody around here had ever seen a fishing-rod case that looked quite like it. He was slim and small, this Negro, and looked almost white, a lot whiter than the Indians, but with that kinky hair. Most of us first saw him when he came into Bud's Billiards on Walnut Street, but we had already heard about the overnight case and the fishing-rod case, and he wasn't carrying either of them. So he must have put them down someplace, and wherever it was, he must have slept and ate there, too, and probably counted his money, because nobody ever saw him do that, either, and from time to time that money needed counting. And putting away.

Nobody quite remembers how it got that way, but Bud's Billiards is about the only place in town where the Indians can come and go as they please, and maybe that's why this Negro just didn't get the cold shoulder right away and leave town; but anyway, he didn't. We all saw him come in, and after a while we all looked away from him, not forgetting him at all, but just not looking at him, and pretty soon Otis Cranmer said, "He's back there playing pool by hisself," and some of us turned to see how good he was. You couldn't tell. He would just put the balls out on the table and shoot at them like anybody else, sinking a few and missing a few, walking around the table slow and easy, not worried, just passing the time.

He played and played and time passed and some of us went to dinner and came back and he was still there playing by himself and it was almost ten at night before anybody thought to play a game with him just to see what would happen. We only have three good pool shooters in town, and it was one of them, Lew Bagge, who got up from the horseshoe bar and went back there and challenged the Negro to a game of rotation. Lew worked out at the lumber mill, used to be a logger but got his leg broken some time back and now limped a little, favoring the hurt leg more and more as the evenings passed and he got more liquor inside him; not a bad man, just a little mean, not from the accident but always just a little mean, a tall thin man with reddish-yellow hair and red skin, and right where you would expect a big nose hardly any nose at all. He had a wife and five children but he never spent any time with them as far as anybody could tell. He was in Bud's every night, and you sort of wondered where those five children came from. But not out loud.

Some of us moved over by the pool tables to watch the game, sitting at the two poker tables that were empty at this time of the month and would be empty until tomorrow night, when the mill and most of the ranches paid off.

"Tom, you rack those balls," Lew said. The Indian had been letting the Negro rack his own, but when Lew called out to him he came over and slapped the rack triangle down on the table and asked what game.

"Ro-tation," the Negro said, and he almost smiled while he said the word, as if it was a joke. He and Lew tossed for the break and played. It was easy to see after the first couple of games that Lew was no match for him. They started out playing for fifty cents a game, and then Lew raised it to a dollar, his face all red and his mouth tight, and by the time they were playing for two dollars a game Lew wasn't winning any of them. He drank all the time he played and got to limping more and more as he went around the table, and finally, he just went broke and couldn't play any more. He just stood there at the end of the table, leaning on that cue of his and staring at the Negro, who just waited. "Tom," he said finally, "you just put that on my bill."

"That's all?" the Negro asked.

That was all. Lew left, and the Negro kept on playing by himself and nobody came up to challenge him. When it was time to close most of us left together and nobody saw the Negro leave. One minute he was there, and the next he was gone. Bud said later he paid his time and walked out about the same time as the rest of us, but we didn't see him. Lew was outside, sitting on the bench in front of the bus depot on the corner, and he asked a couple of men where the nigger was, but nobody knew.

He was back the next afternoon. It was payday, and after a while all the poker tables and pool tables were in use, and the Negro just sat in a chair out of the light and watched. He didn't ask to get into any of the nine-ball games, he just sat. And nobody asked him to get in, until Lew showed up a little after dinnertime. Lew was drunk, and he stood over by the door to the men's room, leaning against the wall, and watching one of the nine-ball games that had his two fellow good pool shooters in it, refusing to get in the game, and just laughing or drinking out of his glass as he watched.

"Come on, Lew, get your stick," Billy Hagstrom said. He was probably the best pool shooter in town, a little fat man who worked in the hardware store, and he and his wife raised chickens. He hadn't been there the night before, and hardly ever came in except on payday or Saturday nights. But he couldn't help but know what had happened the night before.

"No, you go ahead," Lew said. "You and Fergis win all the money. Then we'll see." He looked over toward where the Negro was sitting in the dark and laughed. "Maybe later we'll get up a good game."

Fergis had been there last night. He said, "You mean, he beat you, and now you're gonna watch while he beats us."

"That's right," Lew said.

"Who?" said Billy.

"The little man who wasn't there," Lew said. "You'll see."

Fergis said, "Well, I won't see anything. One more game and I'm going home."

"You ain't goin' noplace," Lew said.

"Mind telling me why?"

"You'll try him," Lew said. "You got to."

"I saw you and him last night, remember? I don't have to drink poison just because I saw you do it."

That got to Billy, and he walked right over to where the Negro was sitting, "Well, you're so good, why don't you play? You want a special invitation?"

"I'll play," the Negro said.

Lew laughed. "I'll get my stick, too," he said. "Let's us just play three-handed."

The game was for a dollar a nine-ball. Billy shot first, then Lew, then the Negro. It wasn't long before everybody could see what was going on: Billy was shooting as well as he could, but if he didn't see a chance to make the ball, he'd shoot badly and leave a good shot for Lew. If Lew couldn't make the ball easily, he just shot safe, to leave the Negro where he couldn't make a shot at all. It was the old whipsaw. By all rights, the Negro didn't stand a chance. He lost eight or ten dollars before things changed, and by this time Billy and Lew were too far in to get out. Or maybe they were too stubborn, or maybe, since they had made up their minds to cheat the Negro, probably deciding on it before either of them got to the pool hall that day, couldn't back out because when you cheat you're supposed to win, otherwise there would be no point in cheating. At first, Lew made it look like he was really trying to win, so the Negro wouldn't catch on that he was being cheated, but after a while, after the Negro started winning his own money back, and then some of Billy's and Lew's, he even stopped that and just plain shot safely without ever trying to sink a ball, and the hell with what the Negro thought.

The Negro didn't seem to notice anything, or if he did, he didn't let on. He just kept playing, and no matter where Lew left the cue ball, the Negro would move around the table, slow and easy, sighting the balls and the angles, and finally come up with a shot that would either sink the ball he was after or leave Billy so bad he couldn't even make a bad shot, let alone sink a ball. It got to be a pretty ugly contest, with none of the players saying anything. When the Negro won the game he would break for the next game, and that sometimes meant he would just run all nine balls and break again, and after a while, he had won a considerable amount of money, always picking up the bills and tucking them in his shirt pocket. After a while the game was over and he had all the money.

"What'er you gonna do with all that money, nigger?" Billy said. He looked mad, and his skin was white all around his mouth.

"All what money?" the Negro said. "This few dollars?"

"Around here, boy, a few dollars is still money," Billy said.

"I reckon I'll get in this-here poker game, if you'll let me," the Negro said.

"Go ahead," Lew said. "Let him in the game. It don't matter. Let him win all the money he wants." Lew was grinning again, and I doubt if there were two people in that room who didn't know what Lew meant. Some of us looked pretty uncomfortable, and after the Negro sat down at the stud table and bought chips, a lot of us left, not just not wanting to see what happened, but not even wanting to be around when it happened.

We heard later how the poker game turned out. There was no cheating, Bud wouldn't allow that, but it didn't matter, because they never had any intention of letting him get out of there with the money anyhow. He won a good deal of money playing poker, some said over a hundred dollars and others said closer to two hundred, but a lot, anyway. "We should of known," Billy said the next day, behind the counter at the hardware store. "When he cashed in his chips we should of known he wasn't dumb enough to come out the front door and walk right into us. No, all he did was say something about washing the grime off his fingers and got up and went into the toilet and didn't come back out. He must of noticed the window earlier. Some of us waited around nearly a half an hour, and Lew I don't think got any sleep last night at all, but spent the whole night roaming around town lookin' for the nigger. He even went over to the Indians, but they said they hadn't seen any strangers."

But sure enough, there he was again, Saturday afternoon. Ready to play pool again, or poker, or anything anybody wanted to play. That was the funny part. We all thought he'd have enough sense to get out of town now that he had won so much money, but here he was back again, fooled people twice and going to try it for the third time. But this time nobody was going to let him get out of any men's-room window or anything of the kind, in fact, nobody was going to let him get out of sight. Nobody would play him any more pool, since he had beaten the experts even when the experts were trying to cheat him, and so he sat down at the stud table and played poker all afternoon. When people came back from dinner he was still there, still playing, and still winning. Pool is one thing, you can win at pool if you have more skill than anybody else, but poker is another game entirely. How he continually won at poker was a real mystery. He couldn't have been cheating, because everybody watched him so closely. One thing was certain, just having him at the table upset most of the players, and they were so busy watching him that they might not have had time to play good poker against him. And he would talk in that Southern accent of his, and that was pretty irritating. Anyway, he kept winning all day and most of the night. Lew and Billy were both there at night, but neither of them played. They sat together at the bar and drank and talked quietly together and waited. Because sooner or later the Negro would have to make his move. He would have to try to get out of there and get out of town with all that money. It was close to five hundred dollars by now, pretty nearly every loose nickel in this part of eastern Oregon. Not very many of the regular hangers-out at Bud's Billiards felt like letting him leave with the money, and a good few of them probably would have liked to lynch him. But nothing like that ever happened here and wasn't likely to. So they waited, and while they waited the Negro just kept on winning all the money.

And it was worse than that. Nobody is trying to make any excuses for this town, or at least for some of the men who hung around Bud's; it's here in the telling, the way we behaved when we were put off balance by that Negro coming to town and winning all that money; but it was worse. Somebody talked to the chief of police, Bob Dickey, and what was going to happen was that Bob was going to find the Negro after the men got through with him and put him in jail for vagrancy.

But he saved us. Not Bob Dickey, he was probably willing to pretend to himself that he was doing his duty by putting the Negro in jail after he caused so much trouble. No, it was the Negro saved us. At least, you could look at it that way.

You see, he had a real problem. He not only had to cash in his chips, which would be a signal that he was getting ready to go, he also would have to get out of the place, go to wherever he hid his bags, and then go to the bus depot. Because there just wasn't any other way for him to get out of town. So he couldn't just cash in and then make a run for it, because no matter how fast he ran, he would have to end up at the bus depot, and that was not as much as a block away. Besides having to wait for a bus—any bus—leaving town. That was his problem. And he sure couldn't get police protection, and he didn't have any friends waiting around for him, or we would have noticed. He was all alone. It was quite a problem. Some of us probably even hoped he would get away, and save us from what we thought we had to do. Because it wasn't just Lew and Billy and the boys who lost to him in poker, even though it started out that way. It was all of us, counting our police department. That was the worst part. We knew it, we felt it, and even felt smug about it. We were protecting ourselves from that one outsider, Negro or not, and if we lost, if he saved us, it was through no fault of our own. He did it by himself, and we could see then how a small thin fellow like that, Negro or not, could manage to survive in the dangerous business he was in, of coming into small towns like ours and collecting all that loose money and getting out again. There must have been times when he didn't make it, when the boys of whatever town it was caught him, beat him half to death and got that money. And towns where they took the money from him right in the jail. So maybe the reason he pulled it off was because he had the practice and we didn't. That and even the courage to try, or if it wasn't courage, the hatred, because even that was possible; the hatred and the ability to hide it.

It happened so quick that it was a couple of days before we understood how completely we had been taken, before all the facts and suppositions got themselves straightened out and fell into place. At first it was just confusing.

He got up from the table and cashed in his chips at a little after midnight, and that left him only four minutes or so to catch his bus, only we didn't know this last part. He tucked the money into that shirt pocket and instead of going to the toilet or heading toward the door, he came over to the bar, to where Billy and Lew were sitting drinking. We were all watching by now, but nobody was close enough to hear what it was he said to them. We all saw Billy and Lew get up, Lew kind of smirking, and we all saw the three of them leave the bar together, and when the door closed there was a kind of universal sigh, because we knew now that whatever was going to happen, we weren't going to have to do it. Not actively participate. Billy and Lew, being the first and worst stung, would do it for us.

It was over twenty minutes before Billy and Lew came back into the bar, and by that time the Negro was fifteen minutes at least out of town. The first thing Billy said was, "Where is he?" He looked all around the room. "Where the hell did he go?" Then we began to understand, as Billy and Lew stood there, tall and thin, and short and fat, with their faces frozen in unbelief. Understand not how, but what. It was quiet for a minute, and then Lew began to swear, and he and Billy and a few of the rest of us poured out of the place and down the street to the bus depot, to find out what we already knew. The woman at the depot, Mrs. Callisher, said yes, he had the little brown overnight case and the black leather fishing-rod case with him when he got on the bus.

Back at Bud's, Otis Cranmer said to Billy, "Well, what did he offer to sell you? The Empire State Building?"

"He didn't sell us nothing," Billy said. He finished his drink and went home. Lew was already gone. For a while, some of us thought he might have offered to divide up the money with them, but that wasn't it, either, because that didn't explain how he went one way and they went the other way, just as soon as they got outside. Finally, though, it came out.

"It sounded too good to be true," Billy finally said. This was on Monday, and Billy was behind the counter in the hardware store. He didn't look too pleased. "He just asked us if there was some place out on the edge of town, some secluded place, he called it, where he could start up a little crap game."

"Just the three of you?" Otis asked. He could ask that because he doesn't gamble, and didn't have anything to do with anything.

"No," Billy said. "Anybody who wanted to play. I told him we could play out in my barn, and he said that would be fine. This was all right there at the bar."

"Well, how did he convince you two to escort him outside?"

"That's the hard part," Billy said. "It was our idea. He said he had to go get his bag, that had some more money in it, and had his dice in it. So we said we'd go with him. He didn't like that, but he let us come with him anyway."

"He let you," Otis said.

"Well, we thought—never mind what we thought. You didn't hear him. You weren't there."

"So the three of you were going out to your nice lonely barn and shoot dice," Otis said. "With the chickens."

That was all we could get out of Billy, and Lew wouldn't talk at all, just limped around town as if he had a wooden leg, and so we mostly had to guess at the rest, supplied with a few hints, what you might call tangible evidence found in the alley back of the pool hall, and a few other ideas, as to how, once outside and in the dark of the alley, the Negro must have explained that he didn't want anybody to know where he kept that bag and that fishing pole, and that, so nobody would think he was trying to cheat anybody, he would give them something to prove his good intentions, and the guesses ran that he must have slipped the bundle to Lew, taking it out of his shirt pocket in the dark and putting it into Lew's hand—not Billy's, because Billy would have taken it out into the light and looked at it—and disappeared into the dark. Because that must have been the way he did it, preparing that wad of cutup note paper beforehand, maybe even before he came to town, and then when nobody happened to be looking exchanged the wad of money from his shirt to his pants and that wad of cut-up note paper from his pants to his shirt, so it would look natural for him to reach into his shirt pocket and put the whole wad into Lew's, not Billy's, hand—a man in that kind of business has to be a good judge of human nature—knowing Lew would slip it fast into his own pocket and already be trying hopelessly to figure some way he could cheat Billy out of his half. And that would make it Billy who demanded that they wait for the Negro to come back with his bag, because Billy didn't have the money yet, and wanted the Negro to get it back so the two could take it from him together. It must have happened that way. There is just no other explanation for all those pieces of note paper, all rumpled and wrinkled, scattered around the alley back of the pool hall that more than one of us happened to notice the next day, Sunday, on the way to church.

1964

Blue Eyes

We called her Blue Eyes not because she had them but because she liked them. She would go outside with anybody, but any man with the right color eyes had the best of it with her, so they all said. I don't remember when she got the name. Blue Eyes was half Modoc Indian and her family lived across the river with the Klamaths and claimed they were Klamaths to get the government subsistence grant. There weren't supposed to be any Modocs around, and since the Modocs under Captain Jack held off the U.S. Army for so long that time and even then didn't lose but were talked out of the lava beds and then shot and hanged, there probably wasn't any government grant for Modocs, especially since they didn't have any land the government wanted even if they did exist, which, as I said, they didn't. Not officially anyway.

Her father was the Modoc. His straight name was Jim Weeks. No one but the Indians knew his Indian name but everybody called him Runner because when he was young he used to go out into the desert and run a lot instead of just hanging around the camp or the post office waiting for the grant money. He had a lot of ambition and could read and write. He used to read those Western magazines and one of his money-making schemes was because of those magazines. He knew a place out in the desert where there was a big outcropping of obsidian and he brought a lot of it back to the camp and tried to make genuine Indian arrowheads out of it. He was going to put an advertisement in the back of one of the magazines to sell the arrowheads by mail. But they were too hard to make, and when the time came he went to work at the lumber mill like everybody else.

But before that, somewhere late in the 1920's, the girl who became the mother of Blue Eyes came to town, on the back of a stolen motorcycle, already pregnant by the fellow who stole the motorcycle, and got dumped in town by him, while he went off to be a cowboy, and went to work in the hotel restaurant and had her baby off somewhere and came back. She was young and blonde and did have blue eyes, and must have met Runner on the street somewhere because Indians didn't go into the hotel. There was a story that she went outside of town a few miles to jump off a butte and kill herself after she had her first baby and Runner happened to be out there and saw her jump and break a leg and an arm and carried her back to the camp to heal in his family shack, but that's probably just a story. Anyway, the next anybody saw of her she was around town again and pregnant again, living over across the river with the Indians.

Two or three times she would come to town at night and get drunk but Runner was always somewhere around in the shadows waiting for her, and so when she would finally pass out all we would have to do would be to leave her out in the street and he would pick her up and carry her back to camp. The last time she did that she was well along in her pregnancy, and the next anybody saw of her she was back in town working at Tom's Café and living out in back and not seeing the Indians at all. They didn't go into Tom's, either. She was flat again and only worked at Tom's a few weeks before there was an accident with the shotgun Tom kept down back of the counter, and the Indians came and got her from Dr. Wilson's place and buried her.

Blue Eyes started hanging around outside the Wagon Wheel right after the end of World War II. Runner had left four or five years before to work in the shipyards in California and never came back and so she must have been raised by the Klamaths, because by that time Runner was the last of the Modocs, at least around here. I remember her from then. She was a slender girl, tall for an Indian. She let her hair grow long but didn't braid it, and she wore Levis and plaid Pendleton shirts and no shoes. Money and work were scarce again, even with the price of beef up, and so maybe her people talked her into doing what she did. Waiting outside the Wagon Wheel until some man would come out and take her into the bushes for three dollars. A lot of men did, and pretty soon we all knew how she felt about blue eyes.

The Harkins family moved here from Portland a couple of years after the war, and Edward Harkins, the father, bought up both hardware stores and closed one and built the other one up into a sporting-goods store with hardware, and either he knew something nobody else knew or he was just lucky, or it was a coincidence that what he wanted a lot of people from the cities wanted, because almost as soon as he opened the store a lot of out-of-towners were coming here in the hunting seasons and bought gear from Harkins. The whole town was changing anyway. All the logging for miles around had been logged, and most of the cattle ranches were run together, and there just wasn't anything else, so a lot of people went into the tourist business for the hunting seasons, and the Wagon Wheel would be full of men in the big wool coats swapping stories about how many Roosevelt elk they had gut-shot from five hundred yards, and the poker game over in the corner went from ten-cent ante off season to dollar ante in season, and the few cowboys and mill hands left would get into the game on Saturday night for about ten minutes and leave all their pay for the hunters to take back to the city with them, and about the only person in town who didn't own a hotel, a cabin, a store or a bar who made any money off these people was Blue Eyes.

There were a couple of weeks when the police got the bright idea to stop the gambling and take Blue Eyes off the street but it was pointed out by several of us that hunters had plenty of places to hunt besides around here and that maybe it wouldn't be too good an idea to clean the place up too much.

But it got cleaned up partly anyway because of Eddie Harkins, the son of Hardware Harkins. Eddie was only sixteen or so when his family moved here, and he didn't seem too happy about the idea of leaving his city high school and going to our union school, where all the boys and girls went together. Eddie's big success those first couple of years was starting the school basketball team with the five boys who didn't just quit school and go to work as soon as they were old enough. With just the five boys, including Eddie, they still managed to win the Eastern Oregon Conference. The way it worked was that when one of our boys fouled too much and got sent out of the game, the other team would have one of their players just stand there on the court with his hands behind his back and not play, so it would be four against four, or three against three, or whatever. This was Eddie's idea, and I saw the game against Prineville—everybody in eastern Oregon saw it—where we won the championship with four Prineville players standing around the court with their hands behind their backs and an Indian boy named Sim Hoxie won us the championship playing alone against a Prineville boy at least six inches taller than he was, while Eddie Harkins stood out of bounds with tears running down his face.

He was a funny kid. That night, late, he brought his whole basketball team into the Wagon Wheel and demanded that they be served whiskey, including the Indian boy, and the way Eddie did it, not being pushy or anything but just going right up to the bar while the other boys hung back and telling the bartender in a voice you couldn't hear from two seats away, you could tell he really meant it and wasn't trying to be smart or anything, and so they all got served a couple of drinks apiece and went home. When they left, Blue Eyes was standing out in front of the bar waiting for a customer, and a couple of minutes later she was gone again, so maybe all of them didn't go home. I think Eddie must have seen her and then walked down the street with his friends and then sneaked back and got her.

Because a few days later he took her to the movie, and after that you could see the two of them together on the street holding hands, or in the bowling alley at night while Eddie bowled and Blue Eyes just sat there watching him. And when Eddie was given his gold basketball at a dinner, we all knew, without really knowing but just thinking about it, that she would end up with it, and she did. She wore it around her neck on a gold chain, and that's when Eddie's father blew up. Nobody knows what really happened between the father and the son, or the mother and the son, because she must have been there, too, crying and carrying on while the father and son shouted at each other, but everybody was in on what happened next, because Eddie made it public by moving into Blue Eyes' shack over on the other side of the river. He lived there with her for three days and then Eddie's father sent Bob Dickey, our policeman, over in his police car to bring him home under the shotgun if necessary.

It wasn't. Eddie came along. He was a nice-looking boy, with light-colored hair and blue eyes and a good smile and a lot of real humor in his face. But after that he looked different—mean, the way only a kid can look mean—and so when he was seen by Bob Dickey at the bus station at two o'clock one morning Bob didn't try to take him home but checked back when the bus came and saw Eddie get on and then drove out to the Harkinses' house and told his father. He didn't have to wake Harkins. He was already up, had been up. He took the news quietly and thanked Bob Dickey and Bob left, and we didn't see Eddie again for five years.

What he did was enlist in the Navy. He was too young but they took him anyway, or maybe he had his father's permission; nobody knew because Harkins never said. Anyhow, he was in the Navy for two years and went to college down in California for three more years, and then came home. He brought his wife with him, a girl he had met at college, and they rented a little house and he went to work for his father in the store.

You will want to know what happened to Blue Eyes. Well, for those three days Eddie lived in her shack she stayed there with him and didn't come up to the Wagon Wheel, but all the time he had been taking her out before that she would show up after he had gone home. And the day after he was taken away in the police car she was there, and she was there every night all through the five years he was gone except for the nights she was sick, and now that he was back with his new wife she was still there, only Eddie probably wouldn't have recognized her if she hadn't been standing in the same place. She was very fat by this time, the way Indian women get, weighing at least two hundred pounds but still wearing Levis and a Pendleton. She still wore the gold basketball, too, only under her shirt.

She didn't get much business. There was a regular whorehouse outside of town now, for the hunters and anybody else with five dollars, and so Blue Eyes' price went down to a dollar and then down to fifty cents, and still there were a lot of nights she didn't get a single customer. When that happened she would come into the bar and walk up to men at the poker table and not say anything but just wait there until somebody gave her some money. Anything would do, above a dime. Then she would leave.

By 1960 that's all she was doing, begging. Nobody had gone out with her for years, but she still stood in front of the bar all night and waited for the time to come in and stand by the poker table and get her money. We kept a glass on the table and threw a nickel a pot into the glass for her, and some nights she made as much as ten dollars, but we all knew she was splitting with Colvin, who owned the bar. Nobody minded, because if anybody said anything Colvin would have made her go away, and it had been years since any of the Indians would talk to

42   DON CARPENTER

her, and even more years since the government stopped giving the government money to the Indians, so that was her only means of support.

If she recognized Eddie Harkins or if Eddie recognized her nobody said anything about it, and gradually we all forgot about him living out in her shack for three days. After all, the man had three children by now and was an important man, considering that someday his father was going to die and Eddie would own not only the sporting-goods-and-hardware store but a good share of the bowling alley and half the Ford agency.

That fall the government finally paid off the Klamath Indians for their tribal lands—termination, they called it— and every member of the tribe got fifteen thousand dollars including Blue Eyes even though she wasn't a Klamath. It was a government mistake but nobody pointed it out to the government because nobody could prove it and nobody cared enough to try. Anyhow, one day the town was swarming with young government people in white shirts and neckties, filling up the cabins and motels that would have been empty until hunting season and holding meetings in the hotel dining room where Blue Eyes' mother used to work years ago, and calling the Indians in one at a time to sign papers and listen to talks on financial responsibility, and then one day all the Indians were called in together and talked to and when they lined up they were all given checks from the government. The Indians filed out of the hotel and walked two doors up the street to the bank and went in, and even though it was five minutes to three when the first one got to the window with the others right behind him and ignoring the other windows, the bank stayed open to accommodate them, hoping that they would open savings accounts. Once the manager of the bank came out on the sidewalk with his coat off and looked at the line of Indians coming out of the hotel and rubbed his chin and went back inside. The Indians all wanted cash. Of course the bank did not have that kind of money around the premises and had to send all the way to Portland for it. The Indians waited in front of the bank all night and all the next day and then went back to their shacks across the river and waited, leaving a couple of men to watch the bank, and the money finally came on a Friday and the Indians came in and cashed their checks. By now everybody knew what they were doing and storekeepers with anything to sell were waiting in their stores and a lot of strangers were hanging around town and going across the river to talk to the Indians. But we should have known. We should have known because on that first day the three Indians who got paid before the bank went broke all took a bus out of town. But we couldn't believe that they would all do that. But they did. When they showed up at the bank they all had bundles and packs, and when they left the bank with their cash they went straight to the bus depot and stood around and waited for the Portland bus and got on.

I think Eddie Harkins was the most disappointed man in town. Ever since the termination began he had been busy getting up a committee to protect the Indians from people who would take advantage of them, working with the government people and the local Lions Club and making personal calls on a lot of the strangers who had come into town. I heard some of the talk that was going around. It was Eddie's idea that with all that money acting together the Indians could buy themselves a good piece of land and build decent houses on it and have automobiles and their own school and raise corn and pigs. It could be done. Eddie had been talking about people raising corn and pigs for a long time, because of something he had read somewhere, and he had even gone out to some of the logged-off hills and planted corn to see if it would work, and it would. So when the Indians all left and took better than half a million dollars with them, Eddie must have been pretty disappointed. So were a lot of other people.

The only Indian who didn't leave was Blue Eyes. I don't think the other Indians wanted her along. She lived by herself across the river with all those shacks and rusted-out cars, and the night of the day the Indians all left she wasn't out in front of the Wagon Wheel. She didn't show up until almost midnight and then came inside as always and went over to the poker table. There wasn't any glass of money for her but I don't think she expected one. She stopped right beside Eddie Harkins and took fifteen one-thousand-dollar bills out of her hip pocket and put it on the table in front of Eddie.

"I give you this," she said.

Eddie just stared at the money. We all did.

"You come stay with me," she said. Then she walked out of the place, leaving the money there on the green table top in front of Eddie.

Eddie's face was a picture. Somebody said, "Hot damn!" and we all laughed and things started to move again, but Eddie just sat there, and after a bit he reached out a finger and touched the money, using his fingertip to fan it out. They had been brand-new bills and now they were wrinkled and bellied from having been in her hip pocket, but they were still one-thousand-dollar bills. Eddie was already too important a man for us to say the kinds of things that were occurring to us right about then, so after a bit the talk and noises fell off and the room was quiet again while Eddie stared at the money that all he would have to do to get would be to throw his life away. He could still have the store and the share in the Ford agency and the bowling alley and he would still be an important man around town but he would have to get rid of his wife and their children and forget about ever doing anything political the way we had heard he was thinking, and not even have to move across the river but have her move over on this side and into his house. He couldn't have had much of a home life anyhow or he wouldn't have spent most of his evenings in the Wagon Wheel. But it was impossible and he knew it and we all knew it, and so maybe what he was thinking about was not How can I get hold of this money, but What must she have been thinking about all these years? Or maybe he was remembering the three days he did live with her ten years before, when she had been tall for an Indian and beautiful and only sixteen years old, and he had been full of city-boy ideas and a boy's passions and hopes, and had even left home because of it, because of *her*, and gone away to see the world and find out about himself and then come home defeated—he must have been defeated because there couldn't be any other reason for coming here if you have a chance to go someplace else—anyway, remembering something and thinking about something looking down at that money that wasn't enough to buy his life and was too much to just let go of; and finally he pushed his seat back and took hold of the money and stuffed it into his shirt pocket and walked out of the place. The whole room sighed with either relief or just from everybody having been holding their breath, and somebody said, "I guess he went to take it back to her," and somebody else said, "Or something," and we had our last laugh out of it and the game started again.

She doesn't come into the Wagon Wheel any more. Eddie's life goes on the same way, except next year he is going to run for mayor, and nobody knows where the money is. We do know she doesn't need it to live on because most of the money she made in her life from either whoring or begging she saved and put into the

BLUE EYES   47

bank, that much we got out of Cauldwell, the banker, that she had money in the bank and had had it all along and that she did not make any fifteen thousand dollar deposit and neither did anybody else. So the money just disappeared. The other Indians, the ones who got on the bus and went away, nearly all came back and their money had disappeared, too, and they went back to living on the other side of the river and some of them working in the mill or on ranches or as pin boys in the bowling alley, with only a few newer rusted-out cars to remind them of the termination of the Klamaths.

Of course we have our guesses and I have mine. My guess is that Eddie has the money, put away somewhere. She gave it to him and he tried to give it back to her and she wouldn't take it, and he didn't have the strength to force it on her or just leave it with her, the way she did with him. So he has the money, probably in his safe-deposit box, those same hip-creased fifteen one-thousand-dollar bills, and every once in a while he will go into the bank and open his safe-deposit box and look at all that money that was too much and yet not enough, and dream about corn and pigs. That's my guess.

1968

New York to Los Angeles

Warren Stebbins and Cay Sharman got off the flight from New York to Los Angeles at a little after ten in the morning. Warren's leg was bothering him from the long session in the reclining seat and he felt like dragging his leg whether anyone took pity on him or not, but Cay immediately noticed the limp and moved around to his other side and took his arm. She was exactly as tall as he was, in her heels, and he smiled painfully into her eyes and said, "Stiff." They walked that way through the airport to the baggage carrousel. She left him standing by a post while she made some telephone calls, and he watched the baggage come up through the opening. There were a lot of blue Navy and green Army duffle bags stacked in several piles around the room, and Warren smiled to himself as he watched a young soldier try to lift his bag in a military manner and throw it over his shoulder while keeping hold of an overnight bag, an orders jacket and a cardboard accordion folder. Other men were picking up their gear and heading out through the glass doors to a line forming at the bus stop, where Warren could see a sergeant and two natty young officers in conference. By this time the first young soldier had dropped his glasses, and, stooping over red-faced to pick them up, lost his cap, the huge bulky bag swaying on his back and then finally clumping to the floor. Two airport porters watched from a distance, like Warren, not offering to help. When the soldier's cap hit the floor, the round rubber grommet bounced out of it, and the soldier either didn't notice or no longer cared, because when he finally got the rest of his gear together he left without the grommet. It lay there, looking both forlorn and a little obscene, until Warren, unable to help himself, walked over and picked it up. He was careful not to limp as he went outside into the surprising fresh morning air and tapped the soldier on the shoulder and smiled and handed him his grommet. "You dropped this," he said.

Warren knew just exactly how the soldier felt. He was humiliated, frightened, embarrassed, angry, and, most of all, confused. His glasses were steamed up, and he did not have enough arms as it was, without having to trouble with his grommet. Warren smiled and lifted the boy's hat, inserted the grommet, and replaced the hat on the boy's head. He knew that by doing so he was adding to the boy's discomfort, but there was nothing else to do. He could hear the other soldiers' laughter as he walked, not limped, back into the baggage room.

Most of the baggage had already come up by now, and men and women were picking out their luggage. He could not see Cay Sharman anywhere, so he moved over to the line and tried to determine, unsuccessfully, which suitcases were theirs. He settled on a suite of gray plastic airplane luggage and was about to move toward it when a tall woman said, "That's us," and directed her husband to pick it off the line. Warren gave up and lit a cigarette. He could see a military bus outside at the stop, and all the green-clad men climbing aboard with their duffle bags. He watched, still able to get some comfort from knowing he was not going to have to get on that bus, or any like it, ever again. Cay came back and beckoned to a porter and pointed out their luggage—his turned out to be pale-blue plastic and hers white plastic—and they went outside.

Cay went over to the limousine kiosk and asked some questions and came back. "Our bus comes in fifteen or twenty minutes," she said. She smiled at the porter and said, "Thank you very much," and handed him two quarters. The porter sneered a greasy smile, not so much, Warren thought, at the tip, but at their clothes, too old and shabby to be packed in such nice new luggage, and gave Warren a wink and a salute and went away.

"I could have handled that," he said to her. "My leg doesn't hurt any more."

"Oh, I'm sorry," Cay said. "I'm so used to traveling by myself I forgot." She smiled. "The masculine prerogative."

"Let's take a cab," he said.

"In Los Angeles? Are you kidding?"

"Well, how much does the limousine cost?"

"Two-fifty apiece." She frowned and wrinkled her nose, as she nearly always did when they talked about money.

"I'll bet the cab ride doesn't cost much more."

"Don't they charge by the person?"

He knew she knew better and was just arguing, so he waved to the lead cab driver across the street and he hurried over to help with the luggage. Cay appeared to sulk all the way to the hotel, but Warren didn't care; he was too busy getting his first look at Los Angeles. From the freeway, everything looked only a little less awful than he had been told to expect, but after they got off and were driving through West-wood, Warren was pleasantly surprised by the number of expensive houses and small tight green lawns, the trees and the flowers, and the way everything looked so well cared for. He was surprised, too, by the jagged rim of hills they were driving toward, clustered with houses and dimmed by the light smog, but still hills, and hills with open country on them. He was feeling better and better. He always liked to see new places, especially places he had heard about all his life, and he especially liked the way Los Angeles was surprising him. He would go walking in those hills, all by himself. He looked over toward Cay. She was not even looking out the window.

He thought he knew Cay, and after their first look at the Beverly Hills Hotel in all its gaudy splendor he expected her to react with sarcasm and invective, to complain about the obvious expense of all that luxury, the palm trees, the pinkness, and all the other things that did not fit into her New York Lower East Side concept of life. He deliberately did not look at her while they followed the bellhop down the path to their cottage, and almost protectively moved quickly to tip the bellhop two dollars before Cay could give him fifty cents, but he needn't have bothered. When the bellhop left he saw that she wasn't even in the room. He went into the bedroom and saw her sitting on the bed. She was a beautiful girl, but she looked frumpy and unattractive, sitting there. He had only seen this in her once before, at the Colony, when they had moved over to Mick Shannon's table, and then he had believed her story that the food had given her gas. It occurred to him that she was frightened, the hotel was frightening her. As if to warn him that he was right, his leg began to throb.

There was a sun-filled private patio off the bedroom and living room, surrounded by greenery. He slid open the glass door and stepped out into it. He could hear birds in the shrubbery, and a distant pock of tennis balls. The patio was hot, and he wanted to take off his clothes and lie in the sun until his leg stopped aching. But he looked back into the bedroom and saw her sitting there, very much alone, and knew he could not do anything with any pleasure in it. He went in to her.

"Honey. What's the matter?"

"Nothing. I have gas, that's all. The trip."

The telephone rang, and he answered it, sitting beside her on the bed. It was his collaborator, Stephen Wenk.

"Are you all settled in? They give you the VIP treatment?"

"We just got here."

"We?"

"Cay's with me. You know that."

"Oh, yeah. Listen, Warren, she's not going to talk a lot, is she? I mean, my old lady's here, you know."

"Don't worry about that. Hey, I like Los Angeles."

"You can afford to. Listen, you guys have to come to dinner tonight, my place, okay? We can start work right away, over the eats. Hollywood-style."

"Just tell me how to get there and when to come."

"Oh, that's right, you don't have a car. Why don't you rent one? Or did you?"

"No."

"You can rent one right there at the hotel. That's some hotel, you can do or get anything just by picking up the phone."

"Maybe I'll buy one," Warren said. He was not looking at Cay. She had gotten up from the bed and seemed to be standing in the middle of the room. "I've never owned a new car," he said to Stephen Wenk. "That's a good idea; I think I'll buy a car."

After he had gotten his instructions and hung up, Cay said, "Don't expect me to go with you. I despise that man."

"Honey, you're making things tough for both of us. What's the matter? Why did you come, if you didn't want to be here?"

"I wanted to be with you," she said. She looked right at him, and he got to his feet. "I love you and I want to be with you. I don't think either of us should be here."

He didn't have an answer for that. "You should take a nap. You're tired. I have a lot of things to do this afternoon. We could eat lunch right in here and then you could take your nap while I get a car and some other stuff."

"All right, but I don't want anything to eat."

He left her in the bedroom, shutting the door gently behind him, and plopped down on the long couch. It was just another of the decisions he could not make, that did not seem worth making. To get rid of her coldly and deliberately was simply beyond him, and he half admired the men and women who could do it. To be honest with her would not work because they had always been honest with each other, as far as possible: she had told him she loved him but did not like him or the life he seemed to want to lead, and he had told her that he loved her but that he was not sure that what he felt and called love was love at all. He had told her that his mind worked that way: he never knew whether what he felt was genuine or not, or whether he simply overanalyzed his emotions to the point where nothing seemed real. Even with pain. He could remember the shock and then the pain, the agony, of being shot in the leg, and the terror of thinking he was drowning in the paddy, and then the leaden hopelessness of being certain he would bleed to death full of morphine and not even caring, but even then, even while these dramatic things were happening to him, he was wondering if the pain he felt was the pain other men felt, because, after all, he did not scream or cry, and had not thrashed in panic as he lay in the muddy water or moaned on the stretcher; all the time it was all happening to him he was *thinking.* The only time his mind had been jarred into thoughtlessness was during the actual fire fight, which he now could not remember at all. He had been honest with her about all that because she demanded that they have a dialogue of honesty and he agreed; but then she had told him that he did love her and everybody suffered the same confusion of emotions if they had an imagination, and he had assumed that she was probably correct. So honesty wouldn't work. Nothing would.

Warren left the automobile agency on Wilshire Boulevard without buying a car after all. The ones he had looked at were all sleek and powerful and the salesman was discreet and didn't try to pressure him, but somehow the fun of buying an expensive new car for cash was diminished by the thought of Cay back in the hotel brooding. Driving up in a Porsche or a Jaguar wouldn't please her; she would see none of the adolescent fun of it, wouldn't want to go for a ride or even just sit in it grinning. She did not see the transition that way at all. In fact, more than once Warren had thought unkindly that she couldn't get any fun out of their new wealth unless she could continue living in the same ugly flat on Second Street. There it would have been real to her; it would have expressed itself as slightly better cuts of meat and slightly more expensive furnishings at the Goodwill, and, of course, small loans to her friends. Warren hadn't really minded any of it; in fact, all the time his play was running he continued to share her flat and her friends, even though he was earning better than five thousand dollars a week, and it wasn't until the Hollywood offer was accepted that he moved out. And, of course, she came with him. Unwillingly. He could not understand how she managed it, not wanting to come and coming anyway even though he could not remember having asked her.

He walked down Wilshire, enjoying the sun and the attractiveness of the people. It was so unlike New York, where the rich and poor were all jammed in together; here was a city that did not seem to have any poor people in it at all. Beverly Hills. Where we don't have to see them, he thought. His own home town of Indian Wells, Washington, didn't have any poor people, either, but that was different because everybody was more or less poor. Everybody, or so it seemed, had lived in shabby warped houses with dismantled rusted-out cars in the front yards. A really poor person would have been kicked out of town before sundown, by Officer Tipton, and a rich person, or even a well-to-do person, would not even stop in the town, because there was nothing there. Not even a motel. Just people who worked at the brewery eighteen miles away. There weren't even any Indians in Indian Wells.

Warren stopped in front of a real-estate office, and looked at the pictures of the houses in the window. Some of them, white remote houses with red tile roofs, looked big enough to house the entire population of Indian Wells. He saw himself in the glass, squinting, and beyond his reflection a man standing at a desk, his fingertips on the glass top. The man had curly black hair and a mustache, and he saw Warren looking at him and broke the eye contact by sitting down. Warren smiled, looked at himself smiling, and went into the place.

A really lovely blonde girl who ought to have been in pictures smiled up at him from behind the counter and asked him if she could help him. Behind her, the man was busy with some papers.

"I want to look at some houses," he said. "To rent."

"I'm sorry," she said. "We don't have rentals."

"Well, maybe I'd like to buy," he said. The man beyond sighed and got to his feet. As he approached the counter the lovely girl went back to her typing.

"Anything particular in mind?" the man said. Then his face did a funny kind of twisting and he smiled, holding out his hand. "Name's Cuttler, Fred Cuttler."

"Stebbins."

As they shook hands, Cuttler said, "Warren Stebbins?"

"Yes."

"Well, of course. I recognized you from your pictures. Pleasure to meet you, Mr. Stebbins." The girl stopped typing, and while Warren did not look at her, he knew she was looking up at him.

"Thank you," he said. They went back to Cuttler's desk and sat down.

"I read in the *Times* a couple weeks ago that you've been signed to work on the picture," Cuttler said. He leaned back and took out a package of cigarettes, gave one to Warren and to himself, and lit them both with a thin gold lighter. "Fact, my wife and I saw *All the Money in the World* last year in New York. Vacation. You can't imagine how tough it was to get tickets, but this fellow I know has some connections in the picture business and he got them for me." He grinned at Warren. "Hell of a fine show."

"Thank you," Warren said.

"Going to make a hell of a fine picture. In fact, I read the other day they cast Mick Shannon for it. True?"

"True."

"So you're out here to work on the picture. Well, of course you'll want to lease a place."

"The girl said you didn't have any place for rent."

"No, but we can get them. There's open listings. We don't like to handle rentals because frankly it's a headache, but we're sure glad to be of service to you."

"Maybe I'll buy a place," Warren said. "I already like Los Angeles."

"Sure. Lots of our clients maintain a home here and an apartment in New York. I suppose you'll be doing a lot of traveling back and forth."

Warren shrugged, and the conversation seemed to die. Finally, Cuttler got out his black loose-leaf books and they began to look at houses, Warren sliding his chair around so that they both could see. He was no longer very interested in buying or even renting a house, although he was sure Cay would feel better out of the hotel, but he could not think of a way to back out. They went through the book, looking at the pictures and reading the specifications of the houses, and Cuttier explained what the figures meant.

"This one here," he said, "they're asking ninety and the loan outstanding is for fifty, so you can figure an offer of something in the neighborhood of seventy-five would be respectable. That's a nice house, I've seen it. Good pool, private, good road. Let's look at it this afternoon." Altogether, they pulled the specifications of ten houses to look at, and before Warren could think of any excuses, Cuttler had taken him out in back and seated him in his Pontiac. Warren sat back and relaxed. It would kill the afternoon, and it would be a good way to get another look at Los Angeles, or at least Beverly Hills. Maybe they would even see the homes of stars.

Two hours later, in the hot middle afternoon, Cuttler said, "Listen, let me take you to one more place. I'm not suggesting you'd want to buy it, but I think you'll be interested. Only a mile from here." Warren didn't care. He had seen enough houses by now, but all, it seemed, through the eyes of Cay Sharman. He had immediately recognized at the first house that it would be impossible to take a place without getting one and probably two or three servants. The places were simply too big. He could imagine Cay with servants. Himself, for that matter. And he truly did not think that such houses could properly be furnished by dozens of trips to local Goodwills. In fact, he did not suppose Beverly Hills or Hollywood would even have any Goodwills.

Cuttler and Warren were driving up the winding Laurel Canyon road, through the strangest collection of houses Warren had ever seen. Yet after a while the houses did not seem so strange; there were trees and the heat of the sun, and once Warren saw a hovering hawk, and the houses seemed to fit somehow into the canyon. Cuttler turned left on Mulholland Drive (Warren had heard of this road; it was supposed to be where all the neckers parked) and then after a few twists and turns, left Mulholland for a smaller road, and then a smaller one yet, climbing all the time, until at last he pulled up in front of a huge shaggy hedge and parked the car. They were at the top of one of the peaks, and to the south Warren could see Los Angeles under its blanket of smog. As they got out of the car, Cuttler said, "Now, prepare yourself, Warren. This is really the strangest thing I've seen in all my years as a realtor."

The lockbox was on a large red wooden gate with wrought-iron hinges and a new-looking brass lock. Cuttler got out the key and opened the gate, gesturing for Warren to enter ahead of him. "Now, remember," Cuttler said, "I'm not showing you this as a property you might be interested in." Warren went through the opening and came out on the graveled approach to what had been a half-acre of rolling lawn. Now it was yellow-brown uncut hay, with a few dusty green weeds here and there. The path wound up to the entrance of a castle of gray stone. At least it looked like a castle at first, until Warren noticed all the large windows and the several wooden decks with torn faded awnings dripping over them.

The front door was built in a moorish arch. It was not locked. They went into a large tiled entry hall, with two stone staircases leading up around a stained-glass window. On either side of the hall were other moorish arches. High above them in the gloom was a chandelier with at least fifty light posts made to look like dark-yellow candles, but there were only a dozen or so of the flame-shaped lights. But of course it was the tiled floor that caught Warren's eye. It was covered with old garbage. Papers, letters, magazines, sacks with discolored stained bottoms bulging with cans and papers and milk cartons, used TV-dinner trays, dirty conical filter papers half filled with coffee grounds, broken eggshells, and so many bottles—milk bottles, soda-pop bottles, whiskey bottles, beer bottles—armies of bottles, upright and fallen over, whole and broken, the bottles even stacked on one of the staircases up as far as the fifth or sixth riser.

"Something, isn't it?" Cuttler said. "You should've been here yesterday, before we opened the windows. The smell would've killed you. The place just came on the market yesterday. We'll get a crew on it to clean it up before we show it. I'm not really showing it to you. We may even have to put a few thousand into it. I don't know. It's up near the limit. Some of these houses get to the point that you can't charge more than a per cent above what a lending institution will go. It doesn't even pay to fix them up."

Warren bent over and picked up a torn and faded paperback book. *Are Flying Saucers Real?* was the title. The author's name was torn off, but up in the left-hand corner, written in green ballpoint ink in a tiny spidery hand were the words *Mesta six and the cool problem.* At least, that's what it looked like to Warren. He bent down again and replaced the book on the tile.

Even though the windows were open, the place had a musty, damp smell, a smell that was somehow familiar to Warren. As Cuttler led him through the many rooms of the place, Warren tried to remember the smell, but couldn't. The whole house was the same. In some rooms there were books, hundreds of them, stacked sideways against the walls. Warren looked at several titles, and then gave up. They were the kind of books you found moldering away in the dim back rooms of all the cheap bad secondhand bookstores. And in one of the large bathrooms on the second floor, in the sunken marble tub, there were perhaps two dozen books and as many magazines, all torn in half. Many were scorched, as if someone had tried to start a fire in the tub. The kitchen, downstairs, was garbage from one end to the other, and the smell of rotting fish filled the room. There were perhaps a dozen dead plants in pots lining the counter, and next to these a stack of unopened and opened letters. Warren picked up one of the letters. On the envelope was written in the same green spidery hand, "Oh, you go to hell!!!" The letter was from the Famous Artists Institute, and was addressed to Mrs. Nancy Porcoe Wissen. Cuttler grinned at Warren while he opened the letter. Inside was a bill for $346.57, long past due, and a letter from the Institute explaining to Mrs. Wissen that they were going to turn the account over to their lawyers. Warren dropped the letter and looked at some of the others. One was a stapled set of long-distance telephone charges. Long, incredibly long, calls had been made to places like Fargo, North Dakota, and Coral Gables, Florida. Many were to New York. The total bill ran to over a thousand dollars. Warren dropped it, and saw that all the letters, opened and unopened, were bills. Some from banks, some from finance companies, two from a karate institute, at least a dozen from the Columbia Record Club. Many had the green writing on them, but Warren could no longer read them. He turned away. "Let's go," he said.

Cuttler grinned. "Kinda gets you, doesn't it? But I haven't showed you the best part. Or best parts. Come on."

Warren followed him, no longer wanting to see, embarrassed for the poor debt-ridden woman, down a narrow flight of stairs, hearing Cuttler say over his shoulder, "This was the playroom down here, bath, dressing rooms." They stepped out into a long room with leaded-glass windows. Many of the panes were broken. The floor was carpeted, and in a corner of the room the carpet had been torn away and folded over. It looked scorched. The large stone fireplace was full of TV-dinner trays and papers. The room was still partially furnished with overstuffed chairs and a couch, and, at one end, a snooker table. Someone had attacked the furniture. The cushions were on the floor, torn and shredded, the stuffing everywhere. In front of the couch, beside a torn cushion, was a broken and rusty pair of shears, the tip of one blade broken off. The snooker table was covered with stacks of newspapers. The room reeked of insanity.

Even Cuttler was silent in the face of it. The two men stood and looked at somebody's last mad attack, and then Cuttler waved for Warren to follow him out a door. The sun was surprising. A mockingbird was singing somewhere. In front of them lay a stone terrace, and beyond it a large swimming pool with only a few inches of water in it. It must have been rain water, Warren thought. He wondered when it had last rained in Los Angeles. They crossed the terrace together and looked down into the pool. It was full of water-soaked clothes, all men's clothes. Warren saw a shadow move quickly across the pool, and looked up, in time to see a hawk disappearing over the rim of a canyon. It was really a spectacular view: from this side of the property you could see down the hills to the San Fernando Valley, and, even through the smog, see the mountains beyond, still with some snow near the tops. The mountains looked a thousand miles away. Warren turned from the pool, and started back around the house to the gate. Cuttler followed.

"The bank's asking a hundred thousand, just to get their money out," Cuttler said. "I think that must be the firm price. Get a crew of men up here and in a day or two you wouldn't recognize it."

Warren was walking on a stepstone path between rows of calla lilies. He stopped, surprised. On one of the broad leaves a brilliant emerald-green tree frog sat, no more than an inch and a half long. Then Warren saw another one, and then another. The third one wasn't green, but a deep reddish-brown. They looked like jewels. He looked into the white flower of one of the lilies, and saw two frogs looking up at him, nestled in with the yellow stamen.

"Frogs," he said to Cuttler. "Look at them."

"They'll spray the place," Cuttler said. He looked at his watch. "Well, let's go."

"Can you drop me at the Beverly Hills Hotel? On your way?"

"Sure. Don't you want to talk?"

"I'll call you," Warren said. He did not speak again on the trip back to the hotel.

"What's the matter?" Cay said. She was wearing a black one-piece bathing suit, and Warren could see droplets of sweat on her temples. She had a towel in her hand.

"Did you go swimming?" he asked. He thought about the pool he had seen that afternoon.

"No. Just sat out there and got some sun. I think I'm getting a headache. But what's the matter with you? You look half dead."

Warren sat down and took off his shoes and stockings. His leg was throbbing badly now. He worked his feet, and kneaded his leg with his fingers. "I went house hunting," he said. "I didn't get a car."

"About fifty people called here. I finally had to tell the girl not to put through any more until you called in."

"We have to go to dinner," Warren said.

"I told you, I'm not going with you," she said.

"I can't go without you."

"I'm going to have dinner with some friends of mine. I promised."

He looked at her. "I didn't know you had friends out here."

"I have friends everywhere," she said.

Warren picked up the telephone and asked for his messages. None of them seemed important. He asked for room service and ordered a bottle of whiskey and some ice. While they drank, he tried to tell Cay about the final house, the castle on top of the hill. He half expected her to sneer, but she seemed fascinated. After he told her about the frogs and what Cuttler had said, she smiled and bit her lip.

"I'd like to see the place," she said. "Can we call that man and go see it in the morning? Early? Before you have to go to the studio?"

"Well, sure," he said. "I guess so." He really did not want to go back there, but Cay looked so interested. And all the earlier depression seemed to have lifted from her. "Sure," he said.

"We ought to have a house," she said. "This hotel's too expensive."

1967

Silver Lamé

The house was a couple of blocks west of the library on Throckmorton Street, in the older part of Mill Valley, set back from the road on a level lot shaded by a number of redwood trees; one of those old brick-and-white-shutter houses, unusual for northern California. It had a garage instead of a carport and a flight of outside stairs on the side, leading to what must have been servant quarters above the garage. There was no garden to speak of but it looked as if somebody regularly cleaned out under the trees, and there was a stack of fresh-cut wood on the porch. I rang the bell and waited for a while, and then tried the brass knocker. I knocked pretty hard, thinking that the old woman might be hard of hearing. It worked, and the front door opened.

"You're Mr. Gorman, aren't you?" she said. "I'm Hallie Rhodes. Come in. I was out in back sitting in the sun. We'll go out there and talk, if you don't mind."

I followed her through the dim house out to an old moss-grown loose-brick patio surrounded by trees but open to the sun. She was small and slender but with a figure more like that of a girl than an old woman. Her hair was straight and sun-bleached and hung down to her shoulders, held back from her face by a yellow bandeau. Her jacket and slacks were yellow and her sweater dark wine. The light tan of her face made her teeth seem bright under a strong nose and a pair of brilliant green eyes, the first truly green eyes I had ever seen. We sat down and she offered me a bottle of beer, pulling the bottle dripping from a bucket on the other side of her chaise. I had expected a much older-looking woman. I knew she was supposed to be about fifty-five, but she looked ten or fifteen years younger, especially her eyes. I smiled at her and took a pull at my beer.

"I like beer in the morning," she said. "It seems fresher and brighter. But you want to talk about real estate, don't you? Mr. Rhodes left me the property, and I haven't done anything but pay taxes on it for the past twenty years. I didn't even know I was doing that until my attorney told me. I think it's time to sell, don't you?"

"This would be a good time to sell," I said. The property was a ten-acre parcel of land on Middle Ridge, open fields and copses of oak and madroña, surrounded by expensive homes. It was probably the largest parcel of good undeveloped land in Mill Valley, and worth a fortune. I had only been selling real estate for about a year, and the prospect of getting this land as a personal exclusive tightened my stomach and made my palms sweat. I didn't even dare compute the probable commission.

Simple building lots in that area were worth ten or fifteen thousand dollars apiece.

"Do you have any particular plans, or do you just want to sell it?" I asked. "It might take a while to find a buyer for the whole parcel."

"Is it nice?" she asked. "I've never seen it."

"Would you like to drive over and take a look at it?"

"Not particularly. You've looked at it, haven't you?"

"Yes, and I've looked it up for zoning and everything. It's a fantastic piece of land."

A large bright-blue Stellar's jay flew into one of the trees and began fussing, and we both looked up at it.

"That's Aleister Crowley," she said. "Hello, you old devil!"

"That's an odd name," I said.

She looked at me and smiled. "You're too young to know who I mean, aren't you?" The bird flew away with a squawk. "Well, it doesn't matter. We have to decide what to do with my fantastic piece of land."

I wanted to ask her why she had chosen me, but didn't. We talked instead about the various possibilities for her land, from selling it outright to subdividing, and I of course made my pitch for subdividing as strong as I could. She listened to me and drank her beer and smoked cigarettes and said little, and when there was nothing more for me to say, I shut up. We sat quietly for a few moments, listening to the wind in the trees.

"My husband was a stupid man," she said. "He built this place, tried to bring New England out here. After the market crashed he came out here with what he had left, bought that land we've been talking about, built this house and tried to retire. He was only about forty. He wanted to be a writer. He always wanted to be a writer. He sat up there in his study for five years, trying to write musical comedies." She laughed. "I came to see him once, in about 1932. He was completely crazy by then. We sat up all night and he read one of his plays to me, sang all the songs, danced. He even made me sing the love duets with him."

I couldn't think of anything to say, so I stood up. We walked around the house together, as far as the mailbox. The mail either hadn't come yet or she didn't get any, and she stood by the box while I got into my car, and then said, "I'll think about what you've told me, and give you a call."

When I got back to the office, a little after noon, Tom Breeden asked me, "How did it go? She really want to sell?"

"I don't think so," I said. "I think she just wanted somebody to talk to. God damn old women, anyway."

"That's half this business," Tom said.

During the next two weeks I had a lot of business but no sales, and I didn't hear from Mrs. Rhodes, but I did find out how she happened to pick on me. She had come to the office and talked to the boss about selling an apartment building she owned in Sausalito, seen me talking to a customer, and asked my name. The boss also told me she had a monthly income of around two thousand dollars, and certainly wasn't thinking of selling off her land because she needed the money.

"You know," he told me, "her husband bought that land for about fifteen dollars an acre, back in the Depression. A real case of blind foresight."

"What makes you say that?"

"Oh, he was an old nut. I knew him, saw him around. A real pre-beatnik."

"What ever happened to him?"

"I dunno. I went away in the Marines, and when I came back he was dead and gone. *She* didn't move in till about five years ago. Some lawyer managed the property, kept the house rented. I wish to hell she really wanted to sell that land, though. Not that I could afford to buy it."

So at the end of two weeks I was surprised when she telephoned.

"Can you come and see me, after dinner sometime tonight?" she asked. "I've been thinking all this time, and perhaps the best thing would be to subdivide, as you suggested."

I made an appointment for eight and hung up. Tom looked up from his desk, across from mine. "Mrs. Rhodes," I said.

"Eight o'clock?" he said. "Woo woo." We both grinned and he said, "Well, though, you can't really say no, can you? What if she really wants to sell?"

"Subdivide," I corrected.

"Now, that's what I call *bait!* She must have run out of gold-plated Boy Scout knives."

I went to my apartment in Sausalito after work, showered and changed into a sweater and slacks. There was nothing else to do around there, so I went to a bar I liked and had a couple of drinks and thought about dinner. I didn't eat breakfast, and lunch was easy because there was always somebody from the office to eat with, but dinner was a problem. I don't cook and I hate to eat alone in public. I can't get over the feeling that people are watching me. I was on my third drink when a couple of people I knew came in and sat with me, and at about seven-thirty the three of us went over to the fish-and-chips place and ate. I just had time to wash my hands in the gas station across the street, get in the car and drive back to Mill Valley. I was ringing the bell at exactly eight o'clock.

Hallie Rhodes was wearing a shapeless gardening outfit and glasses. She looked older than she had the other day, but not old enough. I followed her into the living room. The whole place smelled funny, sweetish and cloying, a smell I recognized but couldn't identify. I thought maybe it was incense.

The room was disordered but not dirty, as if she had not gotten around to cleaning up for the last day or two. She sat in a large dark comfortable-looking overstuffed chair and put her feet on a matching ottoman. On the table beside the chair her cigarette sent up a curl of smoke, and beside the ashtray was a glass half full of a pale-greenish liquid. I went to the windows and looked out at the trees in the twilight, conscious that she was watching me. I wished she would say something, but she didn't. The fish-and-chip dinner sat heavily on my three whiskies and I was not feeling at all like the bland real-estate salesman I was supposed to be. I went over to the mantel and looked at the three framed photographs on it. One of them showed a much younger Hallie Rhodes, with shorter hair, wearing a long-sleeved blouse, jodhpurs and lace-up boots, holding the arm of a man dressed in a shooting jacket and slacks. The man was about thirty. He was smiling, but his eyes were in shadow.

"Is this a picture of Mr. Rhodes?" I asked her.

"No," she said from her chair. "I don't have any pictures of him. Lost them, I guess. That's a fellow named Salisbury. Would you like a drink?"

I turned and smiled. "I thought you'd never ask."

"What would you like?"

"Whatever you're having would be fine."

She laughed. "Are you sure?"

"What is that stuff? Absinthe?"

"Ab-*sonth*," she said. "No. All the Americans used to ask for ab-*sonth*. But that's not what I'm drinking. In fact, I forgot you were coming over. I would have dressed. I hope you'll forgive me." She got up. "I'll get you a brandy."

While she was out of the room I went over and took a sniff of her drink. That was the funny smell. When she came back with my brandy she wasn't wearing the glasses any more, and I could see that her eyes were darker now, almost brown, and sleepy-looking.

"Do you really want to subdivide?" I asked her. I sat down on the couch, after moving some newspapers.

"It would be something to do," she said. "If you want me to, I will."

"What do you mean by that?"

"What do you think I asked you over here for?"

"I don't know. Just to talk, I suppose." It was full dark now, and the only light in the room came from the bridge lamp beside her chair. She sat in the light looking at me, her legs crossed, a cigarette in one hand and her pale-green drink in the other. She looked like a child dressed in man's clothes.

"You're not much of a salesman, are you?"

"I guess not." I wanted to say something cruel, but didn't, and I thought about going back to Sausalito, back to the bar or to my apartment and the television.

"Well," she said, "shall we talk? Why don't you tell me why you became a real-estate salesman in the first place. Was it to make money?"

"Yes," I said. "Is there any other reason?"

"I don't know. But if you want to make money, you've got a very good opportunity to do it here and now. If you like."

"What was it you expected me to do for you?" I said.

"You could start by calming down. Look at me: I'm perfectly relaxed. You're all tense. You should have another drink, and then, another one, and meanwhile we could talk about anything. Then, when you're not afraid of me any more, we could talk business. But as friends, not as a couple of wary strangers."

"I'm sorry," I said. "I asked for that, didn't I? All right, let me have another drink."

She laughed. "That's better. Take it easy, you'll be rich in no time. Then you can have anything you want." She got up and left the room again.

By midnight I was thoroughly drunk and we had decided not only to subdivide her property but also to develop it ourselves. I remember having felt smug about learning all her secrets while keeping my big secret to myself, and laughing in the car on the way back to my apartment about the foolish woman who was going to make me rich because she was lonely. It seemed then that I was actually putting something over on her by simply doing my job as a salesman and real-estate developer. In the morning, naturally, everything seemed different, and I wasn't so sure it would all work out. I had, after all, laughed at her and called her a fool.

This was when I had learned what it was she was drinking. I followed her into the kitchen, carrying my glass (I had switched from brandy to bourbon) and seen her pouring from something that looked like an old-fashioned beer can, with a raised top and a screw-on cap.

"What the hell's that?" I said.

"My favorite drink," she said. "Can you keep a secret?" She handed me the can. It was ether. I handed back the can.

She grinned at me, and added bottled lime juice to the ether. "I've tried it all," she said, "and my kick is ether."

We went back into the living room after I made my own drink. "Doesn't it make you pass out or anything? Good God!"

"You have to be careful," she said. "There're people in Europe and New York with bad ether habits. It's all they do, lie around drinking the stuff. But not me. Once in a great while, that's all. Of course the best kick in the world is cocaine, but after a while it destroys your mind. Avoid cocaine."

"I promise," I said. It was on the tip of my tongue to blurt out my own secret, now that I had discovered hers, but I didn't. It was not much of a secret, only that I wanted to buy a sloop and live on it, go sailing when I had the time, not just in the bay, but ocean sailing. "You're a fool," I said.

"Do you really think so?" she said. "Do you hope so? I learned to drink ether from Manchester Salisbury, and he learned it in medical school in Boston. But it wasn't his favorite drink. He liked grain alcohol, codeine and raspberry cordial. He called it 'Red Death.' "

"Is that what killed him? He is dead, isn't he?"

She laughed. "Of course he's dead." She waved at the mantel. "They're all dead. Do you know what Chet

Salisbury told me once? He said, 'Always add limey juice to the ether, not to cut the taste, but to keep from accidentally blowing yourself up.' And that's exactly what happened to him. He blew up. Poum. In Spain." She stood and went over to the mantel, to look at the picture. "That was thirty years ago," she said. "Four wars and thirty years ago. Good grief."

"Are you going to cry?"

"No. I'm going to have another drink."

I waited until eleven to call her. The telephone rang several times before she answered it.

"I'm sorry," I said. "Did I wake you?"

"I was outside enjoying the sun," she said.

"I wondered if I should start doing the paperwork. We did decide to develop, didn't we?"

"Yes, we did. You'll have to meet my lawyer, you know. Why don't you come to dinner tomorrow night. He'll be here. Then we can get all the preliminary details settled."

"You certainly know how to hold your ether," I said. "Doesn't it give you a hangover?"

"I hope you're not blabbing that all over," she said.

"Come about six, all right?"

Her lawyer did not like the idea at all. His name was Gifford, and I never learned his first name because she called him Giff. He had a tight wind-burned face with a large nose and white eyebrows. His hair was white and longer than most men's and his eyes were sharp and blue.

He was taller and thinner than I am and his hand was rough to the touch. He stooped, like a man used to dealing with smaller people and perhaps embarrassed by his size. He was dressed neatly but not conservatively in a rich dark-brown suit with a vest. We had drinks in the living room before dinner, and he hardly spoke to me.

Hallie wore a burnt-orange cocktail dress and for the first time I noticed a broadness across her lower back, a flatness that was out of harmony with her figure. She made drinks in the kitchen while Gifford and I sat in silence. Gifford sat in her chair and I sat on the couch, and when Hallie came out with the drinks on a tray, she sat down next to me, put the tray on the coffee table, and Gifford had to get up and lean over to pick his up.

"Thank you, my dear," he said.

"Cheers and victory," she said. We drank.

"Did you read that Foremost prospectus I sent you?" he said.

"Yes, but let's not talk business. Not yet. I want you two to get to know one another."

Gifford and I looked at each other. I'm sure he wanted to say, "I already know all about this young man I'd care to know. Why don't you let me handle this thing?" But all he did was smile faintly and then look back at Hallie.

She said, "Giff's real old San Francisco. His grandfather was here for the gold rush. What did he do, desert a ship?"

Gifford smiled, but not much. "Everyone did. They left the ship in the harbor to rot. Off to the gold fields."

"But not his grandfather," Hallie said to me. "He didn't rush off to the mountains with the rest of them. He opened a store. Isn't that wonderful?"

"It wasn't that simple," Gifford said. "You oversimplify everything."

"Your grandfather sounds interesting," I said.

He did not look at me. "Warren Howell is after those diaries again," he said to Hallie. "He thinks we can get fifty thousand dollars from some university for them. Of course I'm not selling."

Hallie said to me, not to him, "The diaries cover his sailing trip—the grandfather's—and his first year in California. There are twenty little books, and Giff keeps them in a safe-deposit box. I think he's afraid somebody will find out his grandfather couldn't spell, or something."

"Light destroys old paper," he said stiffly.

"Do you think I should sell *my* old diaries?" she asked him.

"I didn't know you kept any."

"I could write some."

"I'm sure you could."

"Giff has been protecting me for thirty years," she said. "First he protected me from my husband—"

"Charles and I were close friends," he said.

"And then from my husband's sister and her family, and now from you. But we've only known each other for five years. You don't want me to sell, do you?" she said to him.

"I wouldn't say that," he said.

"But you would rather conserve the estate."

"I'm only your lawyer," he said. "But as a friend, I would ask that you allow me to investigate this matter thoroughly before proceeding."

"I'd want you to," I said. He looked at me as if he was surprised that I was still there.

"I should think you would," he said.

Dinner went about the same way. We ate in the dining room, served by a Negro woman I hadn't even known was in the house, and the conversation was mainly about whether Hallie should invest in the Foremost Milk Company. We went back to the living room with coffee, and I decided to make my statement.

"All right," I said. "It's time we talked about the project, don't you think?" I stayed on my feet, and explained that I had gone over the maps and felt that we had thirty-four buildable lots on the parcel, and that in that neighborhood and with the kind of land we had, the houses should be built to sell for forty-five thousand dollars or perhaps a little more.

"How much would this cost us?' Hallie asked, at one point.

"Nothing," I said. "Beyond the cost of organizing the thing. We get one-hundred-per-cent loans to build, and you already own the land. The first few houses will appraise at more than it cost to build them, and you can change from high-interest building loans to relatively low-cost mortgages if you want, but I don't think you'll have to. They'll start selling immediately. We start on the property bordering existing streets and sewer lines, and then, as the capital mounts, go into the interior."

"I assume you would want an exclusive on the development," Gifford said to me.

I looked at Hallie.

"What does that mean?" she asked.

Gifford said, "That means this young man and this young man alone would have the right to sell your properties as they were developed."

"Not just me," I said. "My company. I'm just a salesman, not a broker."

"Oh," Gifford said. "I thought you were the principal."

"He is," Hallie said. "The development is his idea, and I think he should be the one to sell it."

"It's not that simple, my dear. Anyone can look at a piece of land such as yours and say that it should be subdivided. It's obvious. The thing is to subdivide intelligently, to put up properties that *will* sell, and that will be worth the money. After all, you wouldn't want to have any part of erecting a potential *slum*, right in the middle of Mill Valley."

"Why do you dislike him?" Hallie said. "You don't even know him."

Gifford gave that little smile of his again and said, "I don't necessarily dislike Mr. Gorman, my dear. I'm simply explaining to you that this thing can be complicated, and requires experts. Mr. Gorman may well be the man we're looking for, but he doesn't have any actual vested interest in your property simply because he suggested a subdivision. After all, we've been holding the property with subdivision in mind for over thirty years. Before this young man was even born."

"You don't like him because I picked him," she said.

"I'm getting a little sick of this," I said. "You people should work these things out between yourselves. If you want me you know where to find me, and thank you for the dinner."

"Oh, good God," Hallie said. "This isn't what I wanted at all."

"Perhaps that would be best," Gifford said. "Why don't you give me your business card?"

"He's not leaving," Hallie said.

"I'm not staying to argue," I said.

"There will be no more argument," she said.

"Then I shall have to leave," Gifford said.

"Why don't you give me one of your business cards," I said, and Hallie laughed.

"Serves you right," she said. "You seem to keep forgetting that the property is mine, not yours."

Gifford stood up straight, his white eyebrows jumping angrily. "It is *not* yours, and you know it!"

She laughed at him. "Go away," she said, "and don't come back until you're in a better mood."

"You'll see!" he shouted. We heard the front door slam, and then in a minute heard the engine of his car racing as he backed out of the driveway. We were both still standing in the living room.

"Well," I said.

"This calls for a drink," she said. I followed her into the kitchen. The Negro woman was gone, the dishes washed and put away. Hallie got ice and whiskey and made us each a drink.

"No ether this time?" I said.

"I honestly had forgotten you were coming over, that other time. Ether is not a very social drink, as you may have noticed. It satisfies everything. You don't need anybody else. It's like taking dope. I never could understand why dope addicts would get together in those places, just to lie there and look stupid."

"You've certainly been around," I said. We went back to the living room and sat.

"For an old woman, you mean," she said.

"I didn't mean that at all."

We drank, and kept drinking, and got drunk. She played the radio and the rock music and the braying voices of the announcers seemed terribly out of place in the dim room. While we got drunk, we talked.

"What did he mean, you don't own the property?" I said.

"Oh, that's sort of complicated. It seems that my husband, Charles, left everything to his family, and Giff forged a will, one of those handwritten things, leaving everything to me."

"Why on earth would he do a thing like that? It sounds like something out of a murder mystery."

She laughed. "Or a romance. He did it, he claims, because he fell in love with a photograph of me, and with what Charles had told him, he knew he'd have to have some sort of hold over me. Isn't that silly?" She laughed again, this time at the look on my face. "Don't you think it's possible?"

"I don't know," I said. "I don't know much about law, but isn't it impossible to cut your wife out of a will? Can't that be broken?"

"Oh, Charles and I were never actually married," she said.

"What?"

"You poor darling, you just don't understand, do you? He wanted to marry me, but I wouldn't. I never married anybody. I call him my husband because he called me his wife. He felt strongly about it, especially after I left him. We only lived together a few months, in New York. And I came out here to see him that once, before he died. But that was all. The rest is Giff's terrible plot. Giff is a romantic of the worst sort. Rides around in a sailboat all weekend. Forges wills. Hatches plots."

"But my God, if the property isn't yours, how can you sell it?"

"But, darling, the property *is* mine. Giff didn't forge any will. I'm sure by now he believes his own story, but it just isn't true. I saw Charles write the will. Right in this room. I've never mentioned it to Giff because it would break his hold over me." She winked at me. "I'm his secret mistress, the one he'll die for. I think he liked it better when I was living in Europe, and all he had was the picture and my postcards. When I decided to move out here I think he was upset. It's one thing to have a secret mistress, and quite another to actually have to take possession, especially so many years after the photograph was taken. Poor Giff! His sweet distant young creature turned out to be a middle-aged woman with ether on her breath."

We both thought that was terribly funny, and had a hard time stopping our laughter. "Poor Gifford!" I said. "He's afraid that you'll sell the property and move away."

"Oh, no," she said. "He'd like me to move away. But the property, *oh the property!*" She got up and began dancing to the music from the radio.

"What would you do if he claimed the will was forged?"

Her eyes were closed. "I'd have him jailed for conspiracy to defraud," she said, "along with Charles's sister and her husband. I'd jail the whole lot of them. I'm a tough little cookie, I am." She moved around the room turning off the lights, until the only light came from the hallway, beyond the stairs.

"What are you doing?" I asked.

"I want to show you something, and it looks best in semidarkness," she said. "Make yourself another drink, if you need it, and I'll be back in a little." She went up the stairs.

I thought I had gotten up and walked out the front door and gotten into my car, but I hadn't. I was still sitting on the couch in the dark room waiting when she came back down the stairs. I could barely see her in the light. Something was flickering in the light, a silvery shape coming toward me. I knew it was her but it looked like a ghost shape coming toward me and I held myself stiffly in the chair. I wanted to get up and sneak out but I couldn't. I could hear her humming now, over the sound from the radio. The silvery thing was right in front of me and I stared up at it. I could not see her face, only the outline of her head.

"I couldn't get it on," she said. "I wanted to. But I'm too big across the middle." She turned and went to the radio, shutting it off. I saw that she was holding a silvery dress up to her body, that otherwise she was naked, except for silver shoes. I closed my eyes.

I heard her voice, somewhere above me. "You look so much like him," she was saying, "so big and young and pretty."

I didn't know who she meant, one of the three men in the photographs or her husband or some other man she had known at one time or another, but it didn't matter. I opened my eyes. The silvery dress was gone and she stood above me naked. I reached out and touched her on her hip. The skin was soft.

"I can't," I said. "You're too old. You're old enough to be my mother, for Christ's sake. Go away."

She laughed, and the sound of it made my skin crawl. "You poor thing," she said. She went to her chair, picked up her drink, and drained it, turning toward me still holding the glass. "You can't expect me to make you rich, now, can you?"

"Is this what I have to do for it?" I said.

"Yes. Exactly. And with great style." She laughed again. "You old bitch."

"I'll be upstairs, in bed, waiting," she said. After she had gone, I turned on the lamp beside her chair. The silvery dress was lying in a heap beside the radio. I went over and picked it up. It looked so small. I took it upstairs with me.

1967

Limbo

The billiard ball was on a spot in the middle of a ten-inch circle at one end of a strip of green baize simulating a billiard table. Dave thought there was probably nothing under the felt but a piece of wood, although to be a billiard table and let the balls work right it should have been slate. He had been practicing on a regular billiard table in Quinton, but he was sure he could do it out here. There wasn't much of a crowd; this wasn't a popular concession. Anyway, most of the sports were still at the race track on the other side of the Fayette Fairgrounds. Dave squinted in the late-afternoon light and chalked his cue. The man in the straw hat put the fifty-cent piece on top of the billiard ball and said, "All the boy has to do is knock the four-bit piece out of the ring and it's his to keep. Easy for the few, difficult for the many."

Dave had heard the pitch plenty of times; this was his favorite concession because he was sure he could beat it. He lowered his head and arched his fingers into an open bridge—open so the pitchman wouldn't think he was a professional pool shark—rested the cue on his bridge and began to stroke, not letting the pitchman or anybody else see that he was going to use dead-high English, but stroking as if he was going to hit the ball low. Better miss one, he thought on impulse, and did stroke low.

The cue ball ran down the felt and struck the object ball, stopping dead from the reverse English. The fifty-cent piece dropped well within the circle. The shots were three for a quarter, so Dave had two more before he had to pay again, and he thought about missing both times to keep the pitchman from thinking he had practiced. But when the cue ball was returned to him and he bent down again he knew he had to try for it this time, and make sure he could do it. High English, so that when the cue ball hit the object ball it would continue on through, striking the dropping fifty-cent piece and knocking it out of the ring. He stroked, keeping his wrist stiff, and heard the *ting!* and looked up in time to see the silver flash of the coin as it flew up and into the pitchman's hand. Dave felt good.

"The boy books a winner," the pitchman said. "Next customer please!" He handed Dave the fifty-cent piece and fished another one out of his vest pocket and built the setup again. "See how easy it is? Even a kid can do it."

"I have another turn," Dave said to him. He looked around. There were quite a few farmers and clerks watching now, and he could see in their eyes that they knew he was going to be cheated. It had never occurred to him before that the pitchman would cheat him. But of course he would. This game was too easy. "I have one more shot," he said, and took the cue ball in his hand.

He and the pitchman looked at each other. The pitchman was thin and his straw hat didn't fit him. It probably wasn't even his hat, Dave thought. He was probably wearing a costume. When he wasn't working he probably dressed like everybody else. Even the toothpick in the corner of his mouth was probably part of the costume.

"Okay, kid, you got my number," he said to Dave. "Shoot. Break me."

Dave made five dollars before the pitchman stepped in and begged him to quit. The crowd was large by now and Dave felt an obligation to quit. He really was breaking the man. What the hell! But just for fun (and because people were looking at him with something like respect) he stuck around and watched others try the game. They should all win, he thought; they saw me, so they know the trick. But he was surprised to find that nobody really had understood at all, and in fifteen minutes the pitchman had earned back the whole five dollars and still had customers lining up.

Dave wandered off down the midway. It was almost sunset, and he could hear the sounds from the track over the music and machinery noises of the concessions. But it was no use pretending he was just wandering around. He knew he was going over to the girlie show and watch the girls come outside. It was a popular event with all the men, and Dave was no exception. But he got there early and had to walk across to the orange-juice stand and have a drink, so people wouldn't see him waiting. He was not the only man at the orange-juice stand waiting, and it was funny to watch them gulp their juice down and move away when the pitchman—this one small and square with a striped coat—got up behind the ticket box. Dave was the last one to cross, and by the time he got there the three girls were already out on their platform in front of the curtain.

They were amazing. It had something to do with the late-afternoon light, the way it struck their faces and body makeup and the way it made their costumes look. They looked the way Dave imagined movie stars would look if you saw them on the street. They glowed. They were different. Maybe it was just the make-up, but they looked different from any girls Dave had ever seen. Especially the one on the right, the young one, wearing a green-and-silver harem costume, slit so that her legs were bare, and cut low enough for her breasts to swell out pink in the light. He could even see her belly, all pink and glowing. She was probably no more than seventeen or eighteen and with all that make-up on her eyes and cheeks and lips she looked like a goddess.

"I come to see hair," a farmer joked, "but I ain't seen hair yet." Everybody laughed. Dave had heard that remark every day for almost a week. The pitchman as always pretended not to hear it and went on with his sales talk about what could be seen inside for only ten cents. Dave was again tempted to go in and again when the time came and the girls had vanished behind the curtain he walked away. He took his five-dollar winnings home to his trailer house in the park across the creek from the fairgrounds and put it under his mattress and then made himself a baloney sandwich and went back outside and sat on his lawn chair and ate. He could see and hear the carnival through the warm night and he was sorry it was going away in another week and he would be left without much to do but work. Since his father had died six months before, he had done almost nothing but work and come home, go to the movies or hitchhike over to Quinton and sit around the pool hall. He wiped his mouth and lit a cigarette. An old couple went past, ignoring him. Most of the people in the trailer park were old, except for the married servicemen who lived there and worked at the air base five miles away. His father had been a chief master sergeant in the Air Force, and his mother had been dead for years. They had lived lots of places, so Dave was used to being by himself. It wasn't that. It was something worse.

At last he got up and went back to the carnival, leaving the five dollars at home. For days he had been scheming and practicing that billiard-ball trick, and now it was over with, and he didn't want to play any more, even if the pitchman would let him. He didn't go near that concession. Instead he went around by the girlie-show tent and got there just in time to see the girl, the young one, slip out of the back of the tent in a cloth coat and walk rapidly across the midway.

He followed her. He knew it was the young one even though she had no make-up on and her hair was different. He followed not to talk to her or catch up or anything, but just to see where she was going. Wherever it was, she was in a hurry, and so Dave was surprised when she left the carnival area entirely, crossed the bridge, went past the edge of the trailer park and up a dirt road Dave knew led nowhere except up into the hills. He kept following her, but at a distance. He was beginning to be pretty excited but he didn't want to think about why. He followed her for more than ten minutes. At last she stopped in a grove of trees, sitting down on a stump and lighting a cigarette. He could see her face in the light of the match. He hid behind some trees and waited with her.

When the farmer in overalls showed up, Dave moved in closer to see and hear better. He didn't have any feelings; everything was too intense for that. He just watched and listened.

"I didn't think you'd come, little lady," the farmer said. He had his hands shoved down inside his bib, and Dave could not see his face.

"Gimme the five dollars," the girl said. "We got to hurry. They catch me out here, they'll kill me."

"Nobody gonna kill you while I'm here," the farmer said.

"Well hurry up and give me the money."

"Three dollars be enough for you," the farmer said. He held out something. She took it. The farmer let down his overalls, and the girl stood up and took off her coat. She didn't have on anything under it but a brassière. She laid the coat on the ground and got on it, holding her arms up to the farmer.

"Hurry up," she said.

"Nope," he said. "Not that way." He got down still wearing his shirt and Dave couldn't see what he was doing.

"Hey, cut it out!" she said sharply. "I told you cut it out! I'll call the cops!"

"Whore like you don't call no cops," he said, and Dave saw his hand go back and heard the sound of the fist hitting her. He jumped up and ran down to them, pulling the farmer to his feet and hitting him, knocking him back and down.

"Get out of here!" Dave was panting. He had never been in a real fight in his life, but he wanted one now. He wanted to hurt the farmer. But the farmer just grabbed his overalls and said, "You God-damn pimp," and went off through the trees.

"Thanks," she said. "What were you doing? Peeping Tom?"

"I guess so," Dave said. He didn't look at her. "What was he trying to do to you?"

She laughed. "He tried to give me the old farmer fuck. You know, up the ass. I wasn't going for it at all, but I guess I would have had to if you didn't come along. You want a free fuck? It's worth it to me."

"No," Dave said. "I guess not."

"Strictly a watcher, huh?" She was up and had her coat on and Dave turned to her and looked at her face. She was even younger than he thought. She was younger than he was. She didn't even look upset.

"You're just a kid," she said. "Haven't you ever got fucked?"

"Hell yes," he said.

She laughed. "Okay. Listen, thanks again. I'll see you later maybe."

"I'll walk you back," he said.

"Okay, but don't worry about that creep. He's halfway back to the farm and his God-damn pigs by now."

They walked silently through the trees and down the road, and suddenly Dave said, "Come to my trailer. I have a trailer in the camp. I live alone."

"Aha," she said. "Got your nerve up, huh?"

"I have five dollars I can give you," he said.

He took her into the trailer and they made love on his bed. Afterward he got the money out from under the mattress and gave it to her. "I won it over to the carnival," he said.

"Easy come, easy go," she said. She lay on the narrow bed looking up. "You live here all by yourself?"

"Yes."

"You go to school? Work?"

"I work. In a lumberyard."

"Jesus. This isn't a bad place. Dirty as hell, but nice anyway."

"Where do you live?"

"We got a trailer, too, but there's the three of us in it. Crowded as hell."

"Do you all do this?"

"Turn tricks? Sure. Why not?"

"I don't know," he said. "I come over and look at you every night."

"Now you've had some. Nice, huh?"

"Thank you," he said.

She smiled at him. "You're just a dumb kid," she said, "but I like you. How about one on the house? A nice free fuck, only not so fast."

"No thank you," he said.

"Okay," she said. "I get it." She stood up and put on her coat. "See you around the midway, kid."

"No," he said. "Don't leave. I want you here."

"Stick it up your ass," she said. And then she was gone.

1967

II / The Murder of the Frogs

One

They came to this lake every summer for the whole summer and lived in the cabin Walter's father had built for them, and that year his older brother, Teddy, did not come with them, for the first time, and Walter was glad of it. Later he would recognize what his brother had been trying to avoid, but at the time he only thought that Teddy wanted to go someplace where there were a lot more girls, like the Russian River, Carmel or even just over the mountains to Lake Tahoe, and Walter was convinced that his brother was betraying something by not coming to the lake. As a twelve-year-old boy Walter did not see the lake as it was but only as it was supposed to be, which is to say, as his parents and the other families on the lake saw it: a retreat from the city, a wonderful and educational place for children during the summer, and an evocation of the rough frontier past Americans have a right to be proud of; a small lake, arrived at by traveling five miles over a rough dirt road, high in the Sierra Nevada Mountains, with a small public campground at one end and otherwise surrounded by eighteen private cabins and a Girl Scout camp. Every summer they could come here and forget about the Depression and later World War II, and the changing social ecology of the San Francisco Bay area, with its floods of Negroes, Mexicans and hillbillies all come north and west for the war work; they could come here and pretend that none of it, indeed none of the twentieth century, had happened and they were safe. There were no rich people at the lake—it was not that kind of place—and no poor people, either, unless you counted the family that ran the little store or the orphan girl who worked for one of the families (she was the only servant on the lake, and instead of raising the prestige of the family she worked for, she lowered it, as if the family had violated an unwritten code), and so there they all sat for their full summer, all except the fathers who had to work, and even they came up on weekends and for the full term of their vacations, and then they, too, sat, content and comfortable, listening to the everlasting wind in the trees and waiting for autumn and the return they must make.

Of course there were rules and regulations; no community, however harmonious, could last without some regulation; and so they formed a community council, on which every family had a seat and Walter got to see democracy in action at the community level. He attended his first meeting when he was ten, and it was the one at which they decided that firearms should not be allowed on the lake. This motion was brought before the council by Evan Crosstrees, the plump man whose family had the orphan girl for a servant, and even though nobody liked him the majority agreed with his motion and were about to pass it without debate when Fred Koller stood up, his face darkening even under his new sunburn, and began to object. The meeting was being held out in back of the Crosstrees' cabin where the family had built a modern-looking and much-despised patio with fireplace, and about half the men were sitting on garden furniture and half on log sections that Koller's boys had sawed for Crosstrees at fifty cents an hour. Their cabins were next door to each other, and Koller began his speech with the remark that such a resolution could be aimed only at him because he and his boys were the only people on the lake with firearms, and by God there was no law against firearms, only against hunting, and that such things were under the control of the state through the Forest Service (this was slightly inaccurate, since the Forest Service was federal, but everybody knew what he meant) and that the council had no right to pass resolutions on matters of that sort. He sat down on his log section, furious, his sandy hair raised up from passing his hand through it, and before Charlie Gorman, whose cabin was across the lake next to the Girl Scout camp and who had firearms of his own, could speak, Evan Crosstrees replied as legalistically as Koller by saying that the council could rule on anything that did not actually *go against* the Forest Service, and he sat down to a murmuring of assent from most of the others, and before

Charlie Gorman from across the lake could get his mouth open, Fred Koller said a dirty word and left the meeting, and Charlie Gorman, even Charlie Gorman, knew enough not to interrupt the shocked silence that followed. It was Crosstrees' place to do so, and he did. "All in favor of the motion to ban firearms signify by saying aye." Everybody said aye, even Charlie Gorman. Walter had been watching Mr. Gorman and had expected him to try again, but he didn't, said aye with the others, and somehow Walter felt betrayed. He had been taught how to shoot out behind the Gorman cabin, with Charlie's .22 target pistol, and he had been looking forward that summer to trying out the Koller boys' .38 pistols. The meeting went on to calmer matters and was about to break up when Fred Koller strode back into the center of the circle, his hair still up.

"When you say 'at the lake,' in reference to this firearms business, what, exactly, do you mean?" he asked the group. No one answered, and he looked around at the group with a triumphant gleam in his eyes. He even winked at Walter, who was sitting on the ground behind his father's chair near the fireplace. "I assume you mean 'in the general cabin area.' Correct? Because if that's so, then you can go ahead and pass all the resolutions you want, because my boys and I *never* shoot in the general cabin area. We always go out, as you damned well know, to that place about a hundred yards back of our place where there couldn't possibly be an accident, and you know it."

"Earshot," Crosstrees said without getting up. "We meant out of earshot."

"What the hell's earshot?" asked Koller.

Crosstrees said, "We should amend the resolution to state that no firearms can be fired off within hearing of the lake. Don't you agree?"

"You don't have the power to do that," Koller said. "Your authority doesn't extend beyond the general cabin area."

"He's right," said McQueen, the English teacher.

Crosstrees changed his tactics and began a lecture on the danger of firearms, and so Koller changed his and began talking about the dangers of swimming, fishing and hiking, but even Walter could see what was going to happen, that Mr. Koller was going to lose, and Walter got very excited because another legalistic point had occurred to him and he waited for it to occur to Mr. Koller: that if Mr. Koller resigned from the council he wouldn't have to obey it, since the council had no way of enforcing its decisions; but it never happened. The final vote was taken and Mr. Koller swore again, but there was no more firing of firearms within earshot of the lake.

There were other regulations. You could not run a motor-boat on the lake. This affected Walter's family most, because they were the only ones with an outboard motor, a little quarter-horse Johnson that Walter wanted very much to clamp on to the back of their rowboat, the rowboat that his father had made in their garage in Berkeley, from plans taken out of a magazine, and that was the fastest one on the lake, and just try it out, just once, to see what it would be like. The outboard was used only to power the Cannons' barge, and only then when building supplies had to be carted from the big pier down by the public camp to one of the building lots. The barge was a deck of one-by-sixes lashed to six large oil drums, and all through the thirties and early forties when people were building their cabins it was in use nearly all the time. Walter could not understand why the regulation permitted this, when the regulation said that the oil scum left by the outboard killed the fish and that was why he could not use the motor on the rowboat.

But he did get to use it, in the late summer of 1945, when he was fourteen years old and an entirely different person. By this time all the cabins had been built, all the lots occupied, and his family's barge was anchored permanently out in the water in front of their cabin for swimming and the motor lay under the cabin wrapped in a greasy old tarp. He rowed down to the store to get the milk, bread and mail, looking neither left nor right but watching the cabin at the far end of the lake get smaller and smaller until his peripheral vision told him it was time to turn the boat sharply and increase his stroke so that his boat was pointed toward the small beach where other boats were tethered, and going fast enough so that he could ship the oars and stand up and face the shore, guiding the boat away from others by tilting his body, and then, by pushing down sharply, raise the bows so that the boat slid half its length onto the shore and he could step out on to dry land. He clumped up the steps and into the store, where everybody was excitedly gathered around the big Zenith radio Matty, the storekeeper, had been using for the past few days, since they got the news of the big new bomb, and Walter found out that the war had ended, the war that had been going on nearly all his life, the war that determined everything, his future, his brother's life, everything. Walter went back out on to the porch without getting any of the things he had come for, thinking: The war's over. It's over. What can I do? Finally he thought of it, rowed back home fast enough to make his callused palms hurt and got out the old Johnson quarter-horse engine and clamped it to the back of the rowboat, mixed the fuel, dug around under the cabin among the spiders and finally found the pull rope and went out and started her up. The motor made a satisfactory sputtering noise, and Walter slid the throttle bar all the way to the left and felt an actual thrill as the bows lifted and the engine's noise deepened and he could see the twin waves widen behind him. He cruised all around the lake, about twenty or thirty feet from shore, and when people came out to see what the noise was, he shouted at them, "The war's over! The war's over!" When he went past the big pier, the oldest Koller boy, Clyde, ran out wide-eyed and waving and yelling, "Pick me up!" but Walter grinned and pretended he could not hear him. Finally it got old and he cruised up to the beach in front of the store, moving fast, and lifted the motor's tail out of the water until the boat slid up the shore, and then tilted it all the way in and clumped into the store again, where old man Matty bawled him out in front of everybody for breaking the rule. This so surprised Walter, this and the look of righteous outrage in every eye, that he blurted out, "Fuck you!" and left.

Clyde Koller, who was eighteen, was awaiting for him grinning. "Let's take it out again," he said.

"We can't," Walter said, and rowed home with the motor tilted into the boat. That night his brother and Clyde Koller and old man Matty's son Lew went to Lake Tahoe in Teddy's '32 V8 roadster and didn't come back until the middle of the next day. Tahoe had been wild, they told him, and grinned at each other and lit cigarettes and wouldn't say any more. Walter was sure they would have taken him along if only he had broken the rule with the motor just one more time, but now, watching their arrogance and superiority, he was glad he hadn't, glad he was not included.

In the summer of 1943, the year his brother got the car and hadn't come to the lake, Walter had been glad for a different reason: Walter considered that he was no longer a child, and not having a big brother around would make it easier for him to impress this fact on everyone. When he took his sleeping bag up into the rocks behind the cabin out of earshot of the lake this time he was alone; this time he would make camp for himself, not under the direction of his brother, and things would be laid out the way he wanted them: the wood here, the fire here, the bag here, the orange-crate shelf here, the fishing gear here, and it would all feel and look like his camp. It took him an hour to make the camp, and he was purposely slow about it, almost finicky, cutting and laying the fir boughs for his bed, selecting and placing the small granite rocks for his fireplace, gathering wood, and, last, going back down to the cabin to eat supper and get his pail of water from the lake. His mother said, "Why don't you catch some trout for us now your brother's not here," and so he got his bucket of water and went back up to his camp for the fishing gear and went out for the first time that year to fly-cast for trout, standing up in the boat with a small mosquito tied to his line, the water calm and windless in the near twilight, insects cruising the surface, occasional bats and whippoorwills fluttering down darkly onto the surface and trout rippling the lake. He stood in the boat, his line out, slowly drawing it in with his left hand, watching the mosquito, feeling as completely happy as he ever had in his life, and caught four trout big enough to keep, four, on his first June night out, and cleaned them in the lake's edge, throwing the guts into a pan and then cutting off the heads and throwing them into the pan, and placing the cleaned fish bodies in another pan just slightly overlapping each other and took them to his mother to cook. When it was all over, that part of his life, he knew finally that being a child was good, too, and that although he had come to the lake thinking he was no longer a child, he still had been, had been right through that beautiful lonely first night and on into the days that followed, still young enough to believe that you could do these uncomplicated things, you could still stick your thumb down the neck of a living, strangling trout, and snap its neck with no thought but the pleasure of having caught the trout, and could still feel pleasure from making camp and pretending to be alone in the wilderness and part of nature; things he knew now were real to a child only because a child couldn't think or feel or know any agony but his own.

On Saturday night the families of several cabins in a row staged their first big cookout of the year, among the rocks directly back of the Koller cabin, the huge fire built against a ten-foot granite ledge where over the years many layers of the sheeted granite had crumbled loose from the heat, giving the blackened surface a concavity several inches deep at the base. Each family brought its own food and the Kollers provided a rickety old table to stack it on, and earlier the children of all the families had gone to the lake's edge to cut willow poles for weiner and marshmallow roasting. It was full dark by the time the fire was lit, and as always with the Koller fires, enormous amounts of wood had been piled on and set ablaze, snapping and crackling and sending thousands of sparks upward into the starry black sky; always, when the cookout was at the Kollers', something nearby got ignited by the falling sparks, and always they built a fire so large that for a long time it would be impossible to get close enough to it to begin cooking anything, with the Koller boys, Clyde and Billy, always first to try, with ridiculously long willow poles, their faces lit yellow by the heat and flames and the rest of the people back well past the table in the zone between the heat and the sharp cold of the night, not a drinking crowd, talking, holding paper plates and coffee mugs, waiting for the fire to die down, someone inevitably making the joke that he (or she) hoped the food on the table wouldn't all be cooked just sitting there on the table. This year Walter isolated himself from it all by sitting on a rock far to the left, next to the path to the Kollers' privy. If Teddy had been there, Walter knew, he would have been the third to try cooking something, always competing with the Kollers and always coming in third, because Teddy was smaller than either Koller boy, although Billy was a year younger; no, not always, Walter remembered with some pleasure. The year before, Clyde Koller and his brother, Teddy, had gotten into a fight over something, at the parking lot back of the big pier, and Walter had been out at the end of the pier with the rowboat, waiting, and had heard the shouts, the sharp explosive profanity and the metallic sound as somebody's body had been slammed against the side of a car, and had then seen Clyde come out from between the cars, his dark face furious but at the same time comical because his nose was white with zinc ointment, and for a moment Walter thought Clyde was coming after *him*, but then his own brother streaked out from between the cars all dusty and yelling and grabbed Clyde and picked him up and threw him in the lake. Clyde was at least three inches taller and ten or fifteen pounds heavier. When Clyde surfaced and took hold of the side of the boat, he waited a few moments before speaking and then said, "I'll get you for that," and Teddy said, "No you won't." Teddy looked so absolutely confident that Walter realized for the first time that even with the competition between them Teddy had always known who would win a fight, and then, from the look of sheepishness on Clyde's face Walter guessed that Clyde had always known, too, but had lost his temper and now wished he hadn't, because there wasn't going to be any fight, and now all three of them knew it, and so when Walter said, "Let me help you into the boat," the tension broke and everything was all right. But the competition went on.

This year the Kollers had a guest, a great hog of a boy named Witzger with crooked teeth and thick dirty glasses, who was now trying to compete by getting as close to the heat of the fire as the Koller boys, and Walter watched happily, glad he was no longer a child and didn't have to do that kind of thing any more. Bob Witzger was a school friend of Billy Koller's, and Walter had seen them earlier out in the lake in the Kollers' big flat-bottom rowboat, side by side, each with an oar, trying to see who could row the fastest, making the boat waggle through the water. Of course, they were directly opposite the Girl Scout camp float, where the beautiful counselors could see them.

Walter snickered in remembrance, and just then the bugle sound of taps came through the air and everybody became quiet to hear it: the crack of the fire and the distant sweet sad sound of the bugle. Mr. Peebles, whose family was here by the fire, was in the Navy and far across the Pacific Ocean, and even the youngest children seemed to know enough to be quiet now and listen to the bugle call and think about the war for a moment, and when the adults began to talk again, after the call was finished, it was in a quieter tone, and about the war.

The fire had died down enough for Walter and the others to begin cooking their wieners and for the next hour eating was just about all anybody did, and when Walter finally quit, his stomach bulging and his mouth covered with the sticky sweetness of marshmallow, he noticed that Billy Koller and Bob Witzger were gone but didn't think to wonder where, and so when it was all over, all the singing, the talking, the word games, the ritual of getting the buckets of water and putting out the fire, and Walter went alone with his five-cell copper flashlight across the rocks to his private camp, he was completely stunned by what he found: his camp destroyed, his little fireplace scattered, his sleeping bag filled with dirt, everything thrown around viciously, as if by some animal like the wolverine who destroys what he cannot use. It took him an hour to fix things up enough to allow him to go to sleep, and he had to rebuild the fireplace first because his flashlight began to dim as he was shaking out the sleeping bag. He heard them, too, in the distant trees, giggling, but he knew they wouldn't come out this late and do anything else, so he just went ahead with his work and finally lay down in the gritty bag and waited for it to warm up and watched falling stars, not even planning his revenge because his stomach hurt so badly he could do nothing but try to keep from crying. It was a long time before he went to sleep. All he really wanted, he told himself, was to be alone, and it didn't look like they were going to let him. Not just the two boys, but everybody. Even at the cookout people had kept coming over to his rock and asking him did he enjoy hot dogs and did he miss his brother and how was he doing in school, and he knew they didn't care, they were just asking him polite questions to be polite and there was no feeling behind it; it was one of the things he hated about them all, the way they talked and talked and didn't listen, didn't hear what you had to say, a thing he later recognized as middle-class manners and learned how to do well but which now, nameless, irritated him when it was supposed to do just the opposite. But Sunday would be another day and Monday after that still another, and because most of the men would leave Sunday night the social activities would drop off and he could be alone more, because, he reasoned, they couldn't bother him if they couldn't find him most of the time, could they?

Walter had laid out his camp so that the sun wouldn't hit his sleeping bag until it was fairly high in the sky, but because of the vandalism of the night before, he had moved the bag, and so awakened early, hot, burying his face in the bag but knowing it wouldn't do any good because pretty soon the bag itself would become heated, and so he got up and stood naked in the morning air, blinking, feeling the grit all over his body. He thought about taking a dip to clean himself and then shrugged and put on his clothes, sitting to lace up his boots. Down at the cabin his parents weren't up yet and so he ate a couple of slices of bread with salt and pepper on them and took his rod and creel and rowed out into the lake for some early-morning fishing.

Two

Walter could not believe his luck. She was sixteen years old, sixteen, and she seemed to prefer his company. She was even an inch or two taller than he was but it didn't seem to make any difference to her. She didn't call him Walt or Wally or Wall-ter; she called him Walter and she did not seem to think there was anything funny about his name but on the contrary said it as if it tasted pleasant on her lips; nothing like the way she said *Clyde,* for example. She seemed automatically to agree with Walter's private feelings about Clyde Koller; things he had never said to anybody about him she appeared to understand without saying, and she was the first person, male or female, adult or young, who had Clyde Koller completely buffaloed. Nearly a week had gone by, and Billy Koller and Bob

Witzger had made the only kind of apology they were capable of, when they were sure Walter had not told on them, by inviting Walter to go fishing with them at the meadows, an all-day trip with packed lunches, and he had gone, but not because he really wanted to, only because they had asked and he did not want to refuse the apology by refusing the trip, and that had taken care of one day.

On another day clouds blew up heavier than usual and the temperature dropped fast and it began to snow thickly, turning the green lake water black and silencing the entire world, even the wind in the trees gone, and at first it had seemed exciting to have this freak snowstorm to watch, but the snow kept falling and tulle fog formed on the lake surface about two feet thick and everything was turning white except vertical surfaces like the sides of the cabin or the trunks of trees. Walter's mother watched from inside the cabin while Walter went out in his jacket and threw a few snowballs, but finally she tapped on the window and called him back in and said, "We better get some more firewood, the two of us."

"Why?" he said. "This won't last." He was a little irritated with his mother for looking so serious.

"I've heard stories," she said. "We could be snowed in."

"You mean the road?"

"Yes."

"We can't look for firewood *now*. It's snowing."

"We can't wait for it to stop."

So he and his mother bundled up and went into the woods east of their cabin and gathered and brought in several loads of broken branches. On his last trip, when his hands and feet were cold and his mouth tasted sour from fatigue he could faintly hear the distant muffled sound of an ax hitting wood coming from the direction of the Koller place to the west, and so he knew that his mother was not the only one concerned. In fact, they had been getting wood for better than an hour and the snow was heavier now than before. She built a fire in the fireplace while he made the last trip alone, and he had completely stripped and put on dry underwear and was standing with his back to the fire when he remembered his camp.

"I have to go back out," he told his mother. He put on a fresh pair of brown cotton socks with white heels and toes and tugged on his wet and smelly boots and his leather jacket over a sweater and went out the back door and up the granite slopes past their privy, the snow easily a foot deep and almost dry, and he could not find his camp. Everything had changed. He knew the camp was in a sort of trench directly east of a copse of lodgepole pines and he could find the trees but they didn't look the same and he couldn't tell in the storm which was east and he began to be frightened. He couldn't see their privy, either, through the falling snow, and a sense of real isolation came over him and he began to tremble, his hands shoved down into his Levis' pockets. He could feel snow gathering on his eyebrows. My bag will be ruined, he thought, and he repeated the thought several times to keep from thinking anything else, and began to walk around kicking at the snow. Finally he saw the upright orange crate high-piled with snow and he knew where he was. He found the corner of the sleeping bag with the tip of his boot and then knelt down and lifted the bag and shook the snow off it, leaving a rectangle of dead boughs exposed to the snow, and by the time he had gotten the bag somehow rolled up and found his flashlight the boughs were covered with a fine powder of snow, and pretending that he was not lost he just walked under the weight of the wet bag in the direction he knew even in the dark was the way to the cabin and it was and he was safe.

It was a freak storm and everybody around the lake talked about it for years. Shortly after Walter made it safely back to the cabin from nearly a hundred yards away the snow stopped falling and they could see clear across the lake from their front windows. The fog was still on the water, but Walter could see the outline of their boat, surrounded by fog and filled with snow, even the indrawn oar blades topped with mounds of snow, and not long after that the clouds broke or moved on and the sun came out, and Walter had to put on his sunglasses to even go out on the porch and look at the snow scene. Great hunks of snow were falling wetly from tree limbs, and Walter barely missed getting a great mass of it dumped on him from their roof, and he laughed and walked through the brightness over to the Koller cabin, where a great snowball fight was going on, and joined in, and before five o'clock in the afternoon there wasn't a bit of snow to be seen anywhere except up on the mountains to the south, and there had been a lot of snow on them even before the storm. It was warm enough to go swimming before sundown. That was another day.

The day Marilyn Pettigrove arrived from the Midwest to spend the summer with the Peebles, Walter had been away and so missed the spectacle of combined gallantry and boorishness that established forever the relationship between Marilyn and Clyde Koller—to the great relief of Mrs. Peebles, who was taking care of the girl because her father and Lieutenant Commander Peebles were aboard the same ship in the South Pacific and were good friends. And while Mrs. Peebles was on good terms with her next-cabin neighbors the Kollers, neither she nor anybody else had any doubt that Clyde Koller and to a lesser extent his younger brother, Billy, were ruffians and troublemakers, and what followed when the girl got off the mail truck from Jackson and came shyly into the store to ask, of all people, Clyde himself, where the Peebles' cabin was and how could she get there (Mrs. Peebles had not expected her until the following day, but even so she was usually at the store for the arrival of the truck—the major social event of the morning—but this morning missed it for some reason), both justified Mrs. Peebles's feeling about Clyde and calmed her fears. The slender pretty blue-eyed blonde-to-white-haired girl who stood nearly a foot shorter than Clyde Koller could take care of herself nicely.

Clyde, Billy, Bob Witzger and Lew Matty were standing talking in front of the slot machine by the door when she came in, and when she asked Clyde for directions his face stiffened into a bantering grin (or what he probably supposed was a look of amused nonchalance) and he began kidding her, not taking into account that she was over a thousand miles from home, tired and among strangers and not interested in being kidded. This made it impossible for her to answer in kind, and so she just blushed, and Lew Matty, who at twenty was already a wounded veteran, said politely, "I'll take you there. Do you have stuff on the truck?" and in one motion held open the screen door for her to go out ahead of him, and behind her back shouldered Clyde out of the way, followed her and let the screen door flap into Clyde's reddening face.

Lew distributed her baggage on one of the rental boats and put her in the back and began to row her the half-mile to the Peebles' cabin, and when they were in the middle of the lake the Koller boat approached, with the three other boys in it, Billy rowing, Bob Witzger in the back and Clyde standing up in the bow. All three boys were wearing the bathing suits they kept on under their regular clothes, and when they got close enough Clyde leaped rather than dived into the water and came up at the stern of Lew's boat and took hold of it, his hair plastered down by the water, shook his head and spat, and then grinned up at Marilyn, who was half-turned looking down at him.

"You ain't afraid of the water, are you?" he said. His hands were at the corners, and he rocked the boat slightly. The other boys in the Koller boat laughed, and Lew Matty stopped rowing and waited to see what would happen.

"Please don't," she said.

"You're not afraid, are you?" He rocked the boat again, a little harder.

"My things," she said.

"Your *things!* Oh ho *ho!*"

He did not rock the boat this time, but waited for her to react to this *double-entendre*, but she didn't; instead, she changed the subject, forever.

"There's something coming out of your nose," she said, and when he let go of the boat with one hand to wipe guiltily at his upper lip and whatever it was stuck to his hand, she laughed at him, not an encouraging laugh, not a laugh between friends, but the kind of laugh a well-mannered young girl might make at the antics of a child. Clyde let go with the other hand, flustered, still with the something stuck to his fingers, and Lew dug in with his oars and their boat pulled away from the others, leaving them in the middle of the lake, where Marilyn could have seen them if she had turned around; but of course didn't.

Walter got back from his day about four in the afternoon but his mother already had the story, which must have been transmitted by Lew Matty, since nobody else would have. He didn't care; Clyde Koller and some girl. Walter himself had been through a strange day and the only thing that had brought him out of the mountains was hunger. He had gotten up early again and hadn't felt like fishing and so after breakfast he packed himself a lunch and went off alone, south, over the meadows trail. He did not know where he was going or what he was going to do; if he had known he wouldn't have done it, because he did not like either hiking or mountain climbing. It just happened.

The meadows trail goes through woods for a little over a mile and then breaks out into the open at the edge of the highway, with the Caples Inn another mile down the road to the left, and the meadows themselves directly ahead; a small grassy valley rimmed by low but sharp mountain peaks, the valley cut by two meandering creeks. It was a good place to fish, even though a small herd of cattle was pastured there in summer. To the left of the valley as you look southeast is a long giant hump of volcanic rock called Sunset Mountain, because it can be seen from the west end of the lake and at sunset it lights up bright lavender and gold. Its lower slopes are covered with ponderosa pine, loose rock and brush, and for some reason Walter had never been on top. He did not think he would climb it today, although there was an easy trail around the north end and nearly everybody around there had been on top at one time or another, and he knew that older boys, such as his brother and the Kollers and Lew Matty, had climbed the perpendicular face, which was ridged by chimneys and fissures, but by the time he was ready to eat his lunch he was almost to the top of it, climbing slowly by wandering around in the shady parts at the north end, more or less looking for the supposed ice caves Lew Matty claimed he had found up there but which no one else had ever seen. He didn't find the ice caves, but after he ate he went out onto the loose rock at the base of the cliffs to explore the chimneys and when he found one that looked very easy to climb, he climbed it. Halfway up he came face to face with a small fox deep in a ledge-like formation and the fox bared its teeth at Walter and Walter almost fell off, and became so frightened at the thought of falling that he closed his eyes until the dizziness went away. When he opened them the fox was gone, and after hesitating (he did not think he wanted to try getting down the way he had gotten up this far) he continued to climb. After he got to the top of the cliff it was just walking, so of course he had to walk to the highest point, but it was farther away than he had expected. The whole top of Sunset above the cliffs was domed, and so Walter kept on walking thinking that the highest point would only be a few dozen yards away, but the top kept on being just that far away and he was terribly hot and sweaty out in the open like this and couldn't quit, and so lost his temper and walked along with his head down until he sensed that he was gradually walking down rather than up, and had to stop, look around, turn back and return to the high point he had already passed.

There was a small lake near the top of Sunset, its waters half-clogged with reeds, and Walter walked over to it after a while and sat down on a fallen tree, in the shade of an old juniper. The water looked inviting, and there wasn't anybody around, so Walter undressed and went slowly into the water. This snow lake was different from most of the others in the area; the larger ones were ice-cold, and the smaller ones usually had bottoms of silt, but this one was on solid rock and had a sandy bottom except on the other side where the reeds were, and so it was almost like taking a bath. In order to get wet all over, Walter had to sit down in the water, and it was far too shallow to swim, but he could play around and splash like a little kid. He was cool now and the sweat was gone, and he got out of the water and up onto the rock in the sun to dry off. This is when it began to get strange. The erection was not unusual—he had been having them every morning for months—but the feeling that came over him as the gentle winds dried his body was completely new, as he imagined getting drunk might feel, or going crazy, or having an epileptic fit, like a boy in his class who would be dreamy-eyed for hours and then go nuts. Walter did not really think he was going nuts, but he had certainly never felt like this before. He did not want to put his clothes back on; he wanted to run around naked, and for a while he did, his feet getting hotter and hotter from the rock until he had at last to go stand in the lake water and cool them, and then the feeling gradually went away, to be replaced by a dull aching in his testicles. He dressed slowly, feeling a little guilty, and sat on his fallen log in the shade and tried to think. He wondered what people would think if they knew he liked to run around naked as a baby, and at the same time he wondered if he could come back here tomorrow and do the same thing, if it would feel the same, or if it had been an accident. Or if he could do the same thing other places. Then he got hungry and had to go home. That was another day.

This new morning was quiet and hot, and except for the mosquitoes and the fullness of the lake almost like a day in August. It seemed impossible that it had snowed heavily only a couple of days before. In defiance of Marilyn Pettigrove Clyde organized a party of young people to hike up to the Sentinels, which were the three odd-shaped volcanic crests overlooking the lake from the top of the mountain directly to the south. It was an ordinary hike, one which even the adults often took, except for the rock-climb to the tops of the peaks, and it was probably here, at the base of the dangerous-looking climb, that Clyde hoped to humiliate Marilyn. The three boys from the Koller cabin, Marilyn, and Kent and Winifred Sommerlade, who lived at the end of the lake and were seventeen and fifteen, made up the party. Kent and Winifred seldom did anything with the Koller boys; they were thin serious-looking young people who went to private schools, and Clyde only invited them along because they happened to be standing out in front of the store when the rest of them came by, and they only went along because they had nothing better to do that day, no nature hike with their mother, no guitar lessons, no painting session, no summer studies (their mother was in bed with a sick headache), and Lew Matty did not go along because that day he had to go over to the Girl Scout camp and work on a gas-operated generator that was on the blink. Walter was not invited because nobody thought of him, and he did not even know they had gone until most of them were back.

Walter had on his bathing suit and an old pair of tennis shoes without socks. He rowed out beyond the shallows in front of their cabin and pulled the oars in and drifted, thinking about whether he wanted to swim or not. It was not time for the little girls at the camp to be out swimming yet, but when Walter looked over toward their camp float about two hundred yards away he saw one girl pulling herself up out of the water onto the float, a girl with a white bathing cap and white suit, her shining skin dark in contrast. She looked too old to be one of the campers, so Walter assumed she was a counselor. They were older, sixteen or seventeen. The little girls were Walter's age and younger. The girl saw Walter and waved to him and took off her bathing cap and shook out her long dark hair, but instead of waving back Walter eased himself off the seat and down into the bottom of the boat, not hiding from her, merely ignoring her and getting himself out of the breeze, which even on such a hot day was enough to raise goose-pimples on his skin. Down here it was hotter, and

Walter just let the boat drift eastward, listening to the slap of the wavelets against the side.

The hiking party, led by a fierce brooding silent Clyde Koller, trudged up the dirt road toward the branching trail that led up back of the Sentinels. Everybody was having fun but Clyde; Bob Witzger seemed to think Marilyn was interested in him and he walked beside her talking about everything that he could think of, and Marilyn walked along with her head tilted slightly in his direction listening, and Billy Koller brought up the rear listening to the Sommerlade children explaining to each other what each flower, rock, bird, insect and tree was, and he grinned to himself thinking that they would not be so talkative when it came to climbing the peaks with the wind trying to throw them off the cliffs and burning their faces to the color of his. Like his older brother, Billy had a complexion that reddened quickly under the sun and wind and stayed red rather than tanning off, but unlike his brother he could never bring himself to wear the zinc oxide on his nose, and so most of the summer his nose ached and itched; but he did not really mind; it was part of being in the mountains. The Sommerlades had good mild tans and fine pale hair, and Billy did not like them a bit, never learned to like them. He expected them to get tired and whine about resting, but they never did. The party left the road and went up the steeper trail, resting twice in the shade of trees (not because the Sommerlades asked to but because Clyde ordered rest stops, like any good leader), and finally came out onto the ridge where the wind blew all the time and they could be seen from the lake below if anybody was looking, and at last reached the base of the first of the peaks, where they sat down on the dark volcanic rock and Clyde lit a cigarette. He offered the pack of Luckies around but only Billy and Bob took one.

When they put out the cigarettes Clyde stood up and said, "Okay, let's start the climb."

"What climb?" said Kent Sommerlade.

Clyde pointed up. From where they were sitting the knobby peak looked impossible. Kent smiled and said, "No, thanks. We have to get back for lunch."

"Well you guys go ahead. We're gonna climb it," Clyde said.

"All right," Marilyn said. "Thank you for inviting me." She turned to Winifred and said, "Do you want to go now, or shall we rest some more first?"

Bob Witzger grinned badly and scratched the top of his head and, not looking at Clyde at all, said, "Let's go now, and stop at the store for some pop."

"Go on!" Clyde said. His lips were almost white from anger. "All of you! I'll climb these God-damn things by myself!"

"I'll stay with you," Billy said stupidly, but his brother just glared at him and so they all went down together leaving Clyde by himself.

Walter felt his boat drifting into the reeds at the end of the lake and sat up. He had almost fallen asleep. He got up onto the seat and began rowing back out of the reeds. He felt strange. Not quite the same way he had felt yesterday on top of Sunset, not free, but isolated without being actually lonely, distant from himself; hot but not really uncomfortable: strange. He rowed around the edge of the lake to the entrance of the small bay that had the island in it, and then rowed in. The bay was surrounded by trees and was much quieter and hotter than out on the lake. The island was a hump of granite with a couple of trees on it, and he pulled the boat up and got out, into the shade of one of the trees, and sat feeling strange, looking out past the almost yellow water of the bay to the dark blue of the lake itself, hearing only the wind in the trees. He felt even stranger now. When he was cool he got up and walked around the island. Behind it the water had a clear channel of about seven feet between the island and the really thick reeds that edged the bay; the water was only three or four feet deep, and, he knew, much warmer than the regular lake water. The only trouble was, the bottom was oozy silt, yellow on the surface but black underneath, and if you went wading in it you could sink in almost like quicksand, and get the black mud all over your legs, and when you got out of the water it smelled awful, unless you sat down in the rocky part and carefully rubbed all the mud off your legs; so Walter did not want to go in, even though nobody could see him.

He got back in the boat and slowly rowed around to the back of the island, and pushed the boat into the reeds, using one oar as a pole, sitting on the stern seat of the boat. The reeds made a slow hissing and snapping noise as he pushed the boat in deeper, leaving a trail of reeds bent toward the boat, some of them slowly snapping back upright out of the water. He stopped pushing and put the oar back in the oar-lock, and sat. The air was full of gnats, but there were no mosquitoes. It was too hot and still for them, perhaps. There were lots of dragonflies. Walter got down on the bottom of the boat and put his head under the rowing seat in the shade, and stuck his feet up out over the back of the boat.

They all came out in front of the store with their soft drinks and walked down to the little beach and looked up at the Sentinels, trying to see if Clyde would be visible on top of one of the peaks. It had been Billy's idea to look. Bob Witzger was still murmuring into Marilyn's ear but the rest of them, including Marilyn, were looking up when the rockslide started, and when Marilyn went tense suddenly Bob looked up, too, and saw the streak of white appearing on the face of the mountain and drawing itself rapidly down toward the timber line and then, just as the first of the roaring started, the streak of white cut through the trees and they could see great sections of tree flying in the air, looking tiny at this distance, and then the roaring got stronger and they could actually hear the snapping sound of the trees, and then the streak disappeared behind the intervening granite hills and the sounds were beginning to echo and a great cloud of white dust rose up from behind the granite and rose almost as high as the Sentinel peaks before it began to blow slowly east.

Three rescue parties started out at once: Billy, Bob and Kent Sommerlade, leaving the two frightened girls to go into the store by themselves and wait; Lew Matty, from the Girl Scout camp, his hands black with grease, starting out at a dead run right up over the granite; and McQueen, the English teacher, who saw the whole thing from his porch and ran down and jumped into his canoe and paddled across the lake alone and forgot to tie up the canoe and had to go down to the east end of the lake later that afternoon in a borrowed rowboat and fetch it out from the reeds. Lew got to the raw scattered wreckage first and knew at once it was hopeless, with the same certainty that he knew those fool kids had been skylarking around and slipped and fallen and been ground to pieces; and then saw them coming with white faces and counted them and said, "Where's Clyde?" and got only the white-faced looks for a reply.

Clyde was at the store when they got back, drinking a Lemon Kist and playing the slot machine. He claimed he had had nothing to do with the rockslide and pretended he couldn't see what the fuss was about or why so many people were mad at him, but the one who hit him was his own brother, Billy, who cried out and hit him right in the face and ran out of the store. Clyde later admitted to Lew that he had been pegging rocks around and started the slide that way. The white scar remained on the face of the mountain for two years and finally weathered away.

Walter had been killing some frogs when he heard the echoing sound from the mountain, and he rowed back out into the lake in time to see the cloud dissipating. He rowed home and put on his pants and shirt and walked over toward the store to find out what had happened, and was there when Clyde came in alone. He watched Clyde and old man Matty alternating on the slot machine for a while and then walked back to his cabin and made himself some lunch. His mother was visiting Mrs. Koller, and he had the cabin to himself for a while. He went out on to the porch and got on one of the cots and took a nap in the shade. In the late afternoon he went on over toward the Kollers' place and heard all about the whole thing. He saw Marilyn down in front of the Peebles' cabin with Mrs. Peebles but he did not meet her until the next day.

Three

Walter did not want to be alone any more. He got to the Koller cabin before they had finished breakfast, and so after his own breakfast of scrambled eggs, bacon and toast he joined the Koller boys and Bob Witzger in pancakes and coffee eaten out among the rocks back of the cabin. For some reason they were all wearing hats that morning, Walter with his old battered red felt hat full of holes and trout flies and the other three boys wearing new straw cowboy hats. They talked about yesterday's rockslide but nobody mentioned Marilyn Pettigrove, and by now the joke was on the grownups. Nothing was said about Billy hitting Clyde and crying, either, but Walter had heard about it from his mother. It was agreed between the boys that a trick must be played on Lew Matty to get even for some of the things he had said. Walter's mother would not give him coffee but Mrs. Koller would and Walter loved it; no morning seemed brighter with promise than this one after two cups of black coffee, and he still felt the same way when, instead of doing anything that was fun, the Koller boys went right to work splitting wood. They had a wood stove as well as a fireplace and had to spend a lot of time on wood, and unlike the Cannon boys, each Koller had his own double-bitted ax. They would go out into the woods and find a nice big old dead gray tree and saw it down with a big double-handled timber saw and then Clyde would climb up on the fallen trunk with either a trimming ax or a sledge hammer and knock off all the limbs that hadn't snapped loose in the falling. The limbs would be broken and chopped into suitable fireplace lengths and the trunk sawed into rounds about twenty inches deep. The worst part was hauling the rounds back to the Koller cabin, and often this part would take a couple of days of grudging work. Out in back, where they were just finishing breakfast, the rounds made a huge untidy pile. One of the biggest was always selected for a chopping block, and the others would be placed on top of it one at a time and wedges driven into them to split them in half, and then quarters. The quarters were reduced into sticks with the double-bitted axes, and the trick was to drop the ax blade into the top of the section with just enough force to lift the section and then bring the whole thing down with a *thwack* on to the chopping block and make the two split halves fly off. Before this year Clyde had done all the axwork and Billy had done all the picking up, hauling and stacking, but this year they split the axwork and even gave Bob Witzger a crack at it, and gradually over the morning the pile of rounds got smaller and the breastwork of split wood got higher and longer. Walter helped out by stacking the split wood, and by late morning he was hot and sweating and dirty, covered with fine splinters and pitch, the coffee exhilaration gone but replaced by the pleasures of the work itself, and when they decided they had done enough for one day and it was time for a good swim before lunch, Walter was given all the split wood he could carry as his reward for helping, and he staggered home under the load, put on his bathing suit and came back. They were all out in front but nobody had gone into the water yet, and the girl, Marilyn Pettigrove, was there with them, wearing a pale-blue one-piece satin-looking bathing suit, a pale-blue cap, and escorting the two younger Peebles children, who were bulky in red life jackets, button-eyed and tugging at her arms.

Walter put his towel down on the rocks where they usually sunbathed after swimming and dived into the water at the deepest place. As usual the water was shockingly cold but, on seeing the girl, Walter knew he couldn't enter in his usual way, an inch at a time, his arms hugging his body even though he was sweating in the sun; he couldn't do that in front of a girl because that was how a girl entered the water, and when, still under water, he heard the tumult of somebody else jumping in he assumed it was Clyde and turned around before surfacing and found himself face to face not with Clyde but with the girl. Her eyes were shut and she was coming straight for him and even though he automatically dodged and came to the surface, breaking water with a toss of his head, her arms touched his legs, and then she surfaced, coming up high out of the water and back down right in front of Walter, and opened her eyes and smiled at him beautifully and he grinned at her. On shore, Bob Witzger stood with a tugging child at the end of each arm. The Koller boys had jumped in by this time and as usual were swimming as hard as they could for the other side of the lake. They always did this, Walter explained to Marilyn, and their mother had once swum the length of the lake and back without stopping, the boys going along beside her in the rowboat. She laughed.

"Did you ever swim across?"

"No," Walter said, "I'm a weakling."

"See you later," she said, and without even the advantage of a running dive, which the Koller boys always took, she started swimming easily across. Walter got out of the water and shook himself and Bob Witzger said, "Here, take these kids, will you?" and Walter said, "Sure thing," and jumped back in the water. It seemed warmer now and he swam out a ways and tried to tread water with his hands out. No luck. Then he went diving to the bottom, keeping count, to see if he could stay under four minutes, and when he felt his lungs would burst kicked against the grassy bottom and surfaced with a wild splash. When he got the water out of his eyes he could see the three small distant heads over toward the opposite shore. Turning, he saw Bob Witzger up to his knees in the shallow part, holding on to the two splashing children. Bob did not look happy. Walter came ashore and got out of the water and let the sun dry him off, sitting on the granite, watching the older kids swim back toward him. They arrived together and climbed slowly up out of the water and she took off her bathing cap and shook her head and they all sat down by Walter and she took her big striped towel and put it over her shoulders and looked out at the water calmly, still breathing deeply, and Walter fell in love with her.

Bob Witzger did not ask her to take back the children; in fact, he seemed to be enjoying himself helping them splash each other. When they started bawling he brought them up out of the water patiently and tenderly and smiled at Marilyn as a father to a mother, and she said, "They'll get their feet all dirty; would somebody help me carry them back?"

Clyde said, "Billy," and Billy and Bob each took a child and began to walk gingerly over toward the Peebles' cabin.

Marilyn went with them, her towel still over her shoulders, and Walter watched her until they were out of sight among the trees.

"God, I'd like to fuck her," Clyde said. He grinned at Walter and said, "I guess you don't know anything about that, yet."

"I bet you don't, either," Walter said.

"I know *about* it," Clyde said. He sat with his arms hooked over his knees. After a moment he said, "Geez." There was something about the way he said it that made Walter know, absolutely know, that Clyde didn't have a chance with her, not only the thing he had mentioned, but at all. Walter almost felt sorry for Clyde.

After a while Billy came back and sat with them, putting his arms around his legs and his chin on his knees.

"You know what he's doin'?" he said.

"What?" Clyde asked, after a moment.

"He's tryin' to *date* her. Take her for a *walk*."

"He's too young for *her*," Clyde said.

Bob and Marilyn came back together, talking, and sat down, and after they had all taken another dip, Walter had to go home for lunch. He assumed that Bob and Marilyn would probably be together all afternoon, not because she would want it but because Bob would not have sense enough to leave her alone, so he was surprised, when he rowed down to the store in the middle of the afternoon, to see her there alone, talking to old man Matty and his wife. They all smiled and said hello to him and he walked over to the big Coca-Cola cooler and opened it and dug around in the ice for a bottle of creme soda, uncapped it and put his nickel on the counter. Old man Matty in the meantime had gotten the two letters for Walter's mother out of their box and put them on the wooden counter top, picked up the nickel and walked around the end of the counter. Walter watched him get two cherries and a lemon on the slot machine, and then put the three nickels in one at a time and lose them all, while Marilyn still talked to Mrs. Matty. Then it was time to go, but Walter did not want to go. He said, "I have a boat. Do you want a ride back?"

She said, "Oh, that would be good, thank you," and picked up her mail and they went outside. When they were in the middle of the lake, facing each other as Walter rowed slowly, she said, "Those Mattys have relatives where I come from. But I don't know any of them. Their name isn't Matty, though. I forget what."

She was wearing a yellow sweater and fawn-colored slacks and sandals. Her hair was neatly combed and she had on fresh lipstick. To Walter she looked like a movie star and he wanted to tell her so, but of course he didn't. Instead, he said, "You going to be up here long?"

"All the rest of the summer. My mother's in San Diego, and you know my dad's in the Pacific somewhere. He's an officer on a ship. Communications officer. I don't know what that means. I guess it's important." She leaned back and trailed the fingers of one hand in the water, a thing

Walter liked to do when he was sitting in the back. She said, "How come you didn't go on the hike with us yesterday?"

"Oh, I was doing something else," he said.

"That Clyde is such a baby," she said. "He thinks he's Huckleberry Finn or something. He's my age and he acts like he was about twelve."

"I'm twelve," Walter said, "but I'll be thirteen before school starts."

"I know," she said, "but you act older. You don't show off all the time."

"Yes I do," Walter said, and laughed at the sudden honesty, and she laughed, too.

"I don't mean ordinary showing off; we all do that. I mean all three of those boys at the Koller cabin. You know."

Revenge came at last, full revenge. Letting the boat drift, Walter told her about what Billy and Bob had done to his camp, and she agreed with him that it was a childish trick and that those boys were not really any fun to be with, and then next thing Walter was teaching her how to row, the two of them side by side on the middle seat and he could smell her hair and her lipstick and feel her body next to his and inside he felt as if he would burst from pleasure. But it finally came to an end and he had to drop her off at the Peebles' dock and go home and give his mother her mail before he could go into the woods by himself and feel it, a breathless excitement that lasted all summer, and was there, underlying everything, even though nobody could see it and at times Walter himself forgot it was there until he had a minute or two to himself and realized, remembered, that it was there and had always been there, and would probably never go away.

Of course his age was against him. She could never take him seriously. But on the other hand his age was an advantage, because if she could not take him seriously she would never be afraid of him or bother to measure him against other boys; he would be her little brother, her friend, the one she could talk to, and thus he would have opportunities to be near her that the others would not, could not, have. And nobody (meaning the adults) would suspect a thing, not his mother, not Mrs. Peebles, not even the gang over at the Kollers', whom he now severed from himself and bunched in with the adults. And he was right, and it worked, and he spent more time with her than anybody.

They didn't go anywhere together or even see each other at night because it was too cold, but the days were theirs and they shared them more fully than Walter had ever shared his time with anybody, including his brother. He was her *guide*, her *scout*, her *escort,* as far as anybody else was concerned, and Mrs. Peebles was glad to have her out from under foot and in company less dangerous than the Koller boys, and Mrs. Cannon was pleased that her son had finally found somebody to play with, admitting now she had been worried this first year in the mountains without his brother; and in a way it was all true, they were friends and playmates and she was safe in Walter's hands. They could go hiking or rowing or swimming together and no one disturbed them and they disturbed no one. The Koller boys and Bob Witzger individually and collectively tried to get her alone, away from Walter, but for the first time in his life Walter showed a persistence that no insults or hints could reduce, and finally they gave up, Bob Witzger last, when they realized that she wanted Walter there as much as Walter wanted to be there.

Monday morning he kissed her for the first time. They were high in the rocks behind the Peebles' cabin with nobody else around, fresh from a morning of swimming and up here because the air was hotter this far from the lake, and they lay side by side on their towels and baked in the sun, Walter with his red hat down over his eyes and Marilyn wearing dark sunglasses with white frames. They were both sweating a little and he could smell her and it was making him delirious. Finally he sat up and crossed his legs and looked at her. She opened her eyes and looked at him and smiled and closed her eyes again and without even thinking about it Walter bent over her and kissed her. He felt her arms move up his rib cage and then her fingers on his back and neck as she pulled him gently down closer. After they broke, all Walter could think of to say was "You taste good."

"So do you," she said. They kissed several times more, and Walter's bliss was tempered only by his need to avoid brushing his erection against her. This became a real problem, finally more real than the bliss. Walter was ashamed of the erection, as if it proved he did not love her but only lusted after her, which, he felt, was entirely false. He did love her, and the erection was something that happened to him whether he wanted it to or not. He had had trouble with it before. In school that year he had been having erections every day between third and fourth periods, and he had to walk from class to class with his binder held in front of him until it went away. Now here it was again, and he knew that the kissing and the remarkable feeling he was having was causing it, and so he knew it would persist until they stopped kissing; so he compromised. They did not keep on kissing as long as he wanted to, which he felt would be forever, and he did not stop kissing her right away, to avoid the possibility of discovery, as he knew he really should. When they did stop he turned away from her and sat waiting for it to go down.

"What's the matter?" she asked him.

"Nothing," he said.

After a moment she said, "Oh," in such a way that he was sure she knew, because she did not move until he did, and he didn't move until it was gone. Then he turned and faced her and wanted to start kissing again.

"We have to get back," she said, and she giggled. "They'll catch on if we don't."

"What'll we do this afternoon?" Walter asked her, and they both giggled.

"You know," she said as they were walking back down the slopes, "I first started liking you because I thought this wouldn't happen, but now I'm glad it did."

"Why didn't you want it to happen?" he asked.

"I'll tell you sometime," she said.

Two afternoons later he took her up to what he now thought of as his private lake, on top of Sunset, but instead of climbing the face they went around the back and up the easy trail. They held hands now all the time when nobody was looking, and often stopped to kiss standing up, or, when they were resting in the shade, sitting down. These kisses had nothing of the passionate or desperate about them; they were kisses for the sake of kissing, for the taste of it, and they could break easily and smile and go right on talking about anything they pleased. Walter had not yet told her he loved her. When they got to the shores of the lake she looked around and squeezed his hand and said, "Oh, what a beautiful place," and for once he did not kiss her.

He had a fantasy about this place with her; he had day-dreamed it many times. They would be here, like this, and naturally they would take off their boots and socks and go wading to cool their feet, and even more naturally they would kiss while standing in the water, and then by only a slight effort Walter would make them lose their balance and they would fall over into the water and get their clothes wet. Then laughing they would splash each other and fool around and when the fun was over they would have to take off their clothes, and he would see her naked. That was all he wanted, just to see her naked. Even in his daydream he went no further. But now, standing here, he realized first that he would never do anything so corny as to topple them and pretend it was an accident, nor would he do anything so *adult* as to topple them laughing and on purpose, and even worse, he just now realized that if he saw her naked she would see him naked, and he was not at all prepared for that. The hidden erection would be hidden no longer.

She said, "Oh, let's take off our clothes and go swimming," and he said, "It's not really deep enough to swim in," and she said, "Oh, let's do it anyway," and he avoided looking at her and went to sit in the shade. After a bit she came over and sat by him. He touched her hand and she said, "These mountains are so beautiful. Where I come from everything's so flat. I'll miss California when I go home. I don't see why anybody lives where I do." She went on and on, and Walter listened without really hearing. They had had this conversation before, and he knew she was just making it easy for him. But it was really a question of honor. He did love her, and it was not like that at all, and he knew she was not trying to get him to do anything; she really believed that because he was so young she could take off her clothes and he could take off his and it wouldn't matter. But if she saw that erection she would know better and be disappointed in him, and it would be all over, the company, the fun, the kissing, everything.

"I love you," he said. And then before she could do or say anything, he added desperately, "True love."

Four

Walter was almost asleep when he heard the distant roaring and popping of the car as it came around the spur and then down the dirt road in compression but he was not curious enough to come back fully awake; the noises that did awaken him sometime later were right there in his camp, and he lifted his head up and saw his brother, Teddy, laying out his sleeping bag in the light of the moon. Walter sat up and pulled his own bag around his shoulders.

"Didn't mean to wake you up," Teddy said.

"That's okay. How come you're up here?"

"Man, I been every place else. On my way to Tahoe for a while."

Walter almost said, "Can I go?" but stopped himself, and sat watching while his brother got everything ready, undressed and crawled into his bag.

"Well, what's it been like this year?" Teddy asked. Walter could not see his face, so he lay back down and looked up at the stars and told his brother about the snowstorm and the rockslide.

"Yeah, I read Mom's letter about that stuff. Listen, don't tell *any*body, Clyde or anybody, but me and Tick Snyder went down to *Mexico!* No shit. Tijuana. Man, you wouldn't believe that place!" Teddy talked for almost an hour, telling about the wild border town full of sailors and prostitutes, and then about his trip to the Russian River and running out of money and sleeping under a bridge, and living on stolen food brought to them by girls who lived in cabins, and then said, "Boy, I'm not spending any more full summers up here. This is a good place for when you're a kid and even a good place to cool off for a while, but when you got a car and a little money, there's too much goin' on to hang around the mountains."

Walter liked his brother so much and was so proud of him, especially for having gone to Mexico—even though they couldn't tell anybody about it—that he really didn't stop to think what would happen when he introduced Teddy to the girl he loved. He did know that he couldn't tell his brother what he and Marilyn had been doing. It would have been different if, at the end of the summer, Walter had gone home to Berkeley and found his brother there; then the whole thing would have been over and Walter could have explained it. But with Marilyn right there where Teddy could look at her, no explanation would really work. Teddy would either think Marilyn had been cradle-robbing and be contemptuous of her or he would think Walter was lying. So Walter didn't say anything, and waited for the inevitable meeting.

The only other thing that Walter consciously withheld from Teddy was the killing of the frogs, and he had told nobody about that, especially Marilyn, and he would never in his life tell anyone about it. He had heard about people doing bad things and then forgetting that they had done them, blocking them out of their minds, and he wished this would happen for him, but it hadn't yet, and at moments when he couldn't help himself he would remember and feel sick. He never remembered the whole thing, just parts of it, and that was a blessing, but even then he would have to defend himself from the fragments of memory and think, The snakes would have gotten them, or birds or even fish, and anyway they would have died sooner or later; but the thought would do him no good and he would feel the anguish, the emotions, now, in the memory, that he was strangely without when the thing was happening, and that was the greatest horror of it; that he had felt nothing, not pleasure, not guilt, not anything. He just did it and kept doing it.

After he had pushed the boat into the reeds back of the island in the bay and gotten down with his head in the shade of the rowing seat and his feet sticking out over the end of the boat it had finally gotten too hot for even that posture and he sat up again and was about to push the boat out into the clear water when he saw the first frog, sitting near the tip of a reed. The frog was tiny, only about big enough to cover Walter's thumbnail, and in color it was a brilliant bronze-gold red. It swayed on the tip of the reed and Walter could not help catching it and holding it in the palm of his hand. When he opened his hand to take a look at it, it jumped out into the boat and went down into the water under the floor boards. Walter finally spotted it coming out by the rear seat and he caught it again, holding it tighter, and as he held it between his thumb and forefinger the frog's body seemed to slip up out of its skin, and Walter could see the pale transluscent flesh and the tiny blood vessels. Its skin hung down around its legs and it still kicked and squirmed. He had skinned it alive. He threw it into the water, and looking over the side of the boat he saw that there were a lot of them, frogs, in the water and on the lower stems of the reeds, and they all looked alike. He watched them for a while and then picked up another one and tried it again, and he dropped the living body into the bottom of the boat. The sun was hot on his back but he did not mind. He got another frog, and this time carefully stripped the skin away until the frog was completely skinned and still alive and then with his thumb crushed the body against the side of the boat.

Later when he was finished a great emptiness filled him and he sat with his hands between his legs, looking at nothing. He knew he had to clean out the boat, but he did not want to. But he had to, or somebody would find out. He worked the floor boards loose and put them into the water back of the boat and then started in on the bodies. For some reason he counted them, and not counting the ones he had thrown over the side earlier, or the ones that had washed off the floor boards, there were two hundred and eight dead or dying frogs. He heard the roar of the rockslide just as he was pushing out to get clear water to wash his hands in, and then he put the floor boards back in place and checked the boat over once more, and rowed around the island, not fast, his arms feeling as if they belonged to someone else and his eyes dazzled by the glare of sunlight on the open lake.

Five

The adults came into it while Walter was still sick with rage and caught him off guard, but by the time they, the adults, were finished and Walter's meanest hopes satisfied, he knew he had been acting not out of confusion but spite, and that he could never again give himself the excuse that he was still only a child; that excuse had not worked with the frogs and it did not work for this other, more important, thing. He became one of the adults himself, passing the Kollers and the other children, almost passing his own brother, discarding his youth as if it were an itching skin. This did not change his hatred of the adults, but it did make him cautious about showing the hatred, and this, to him, was perhaps the most obvious proof of the change—that he could smile at them and be polite and hate them and know they were afraid and mistrustful of him. He had no illusions about that. Yet through it all he continued to love her and to love his brother, and to hope.

There was reason for him to hope, if not for a return to the past, at least for a future in which he would not be despised (except by his fellow adults, who understood), because none of the other young people realized that he had done what he had done fully conscious of what it was. They thought, and his brother told him as much, that he had been cornered and forced to tell. They were there and saw it and heard it but they didn't know Walter at all. So he continued to love her, not even hopelessly, for the whole long empty summer.

The morning after his brother arrived the two of them went fishing together and had their catch for breakfast, and then it was time to put on bathing suits and go over to the Kollers' for a swim, and while the older boys were listening to Teddy talk about his adventures Walter walked barefoot over to the Peebles' cabin and knocked on the screen door. He could see Marilyn dimly in the back of the cabin with an apron over her slacks. Mrs. Peebles called to him to come in but he said, "Can Marilyn come out?" and sat on the steps waiting. When she did come out she was wearing her bathing suit and sunglasses and carrying her towel and cap.

"Up this way," Walter said.

"Aren't we going swimming?"

"I have to ask you something," he said.

They went up among the rocks to where they usually sunbathed and she put down her towel and sat on it and he sat next to her and took her hand and kissed her. Afterward, she laughed.

"So soon?"

"Listen," he said, "I have to know something. You told me once you had a reason for picking me. Do you remember?"

She frowned slightly and said, "Yes, I remember."

"Well, could you tell me what it was?"

"Why?"

"I have to know."

"I'd rather not, Walter. We didn't expect *this* to happen but it did and so we should just leave it alone."

"No, I have to know. Please."

She looked away from him and took her hand back. "Well, I didn't *pick* you. What I meant was I didn't want to have dates with boys my age, and you weren't my age and so I thought it would be all right. I *liked* you. But anyway I have a boy friend back home. That was all."

"Oh," he said.

"What's the matter? Why did you have to make me tell you that?"

"My brother's here."

"What's that got to do with it?"

"He's your age."

She got mad at him. "You mean to say you think I'd start dating your brother now that he's here? I'm ashamed of you." She got up and started down among the rocks. Walter followed and took her arm, pulling at her.

"No, wait. I didn't mean that!"

She faced him, angry. "What did you mean?"

"I meant . . ." There was nothing for him to say, and he knew it and she knew it, and he let go of her arm, and single file they went to the Kollers' frontage. No introductions were offered and none were necessary. Obviously the Koller boys and Bob Witzger had been filling Teddy's ear about Marilyn, and about Walter and Marilyn (what little they knew), and so Teddy just smiled and said "Hello, Marilyn," and everybody went swimming. Today's competition was diving for tin cans and of course Clyde Koller kept throwing them farther and farther out in the water, but for once Teddy did not bother to compete; in fact, he was the first one out of the water, and the first to say, "Let's all go up in the hills and get dry."

Billy Koller said in a childish sarcasm, "*They* don't go with us, *they* go someplace by theirselves," but Teddy just laughed and said, "Oh, hell, let's go."

Teddy was not Clyde Koller and he made none of Clyde's blunders. While everybody was sunbathing he did not kid Marilyn or even pay particular attention to her, but when it was time to leave he said to Walter (not Marilyn), "Why don't the three of us go for a ride this afternoon, in the car." There was no way for Walter to refuse, in front of everybody, and Marilyn was cheerful enough about accepting, but when it came right down to it and they were standing beside the little roadster after lunch Walter said stubbornly, "I guess I'd rather stick around here," and looked at Marilyn, not expecting her to say the same, to back out suddenly and for no reason, but demanding that she do so, and when she did not and his brother shrugged and opened the car door for her and she got in and Teddy went around the car winking at Walter he just stood there like a little kid and let them drive off without another word being spoken. He walked around from the pier to the store and saw Lew Matty painting a boat out in front.

"Your brother steal your girl friend?" Lew asked.

"She's not my *girl friend,*" he said.

Lew went on painting while Walter watched. "Someday you'll learn, kiddo," he said.

And that was it. After dinner Teddy went fly-casting alone and Walter walked over to the Peebles' cabin and got Marilyn outside. He did not try to kiss her, once they were alone, but said, "You stay away from my brother!"

"What's the matter with you?" she asked. "You're being mean."

"You just stay away from him."

"I will not. I'll do what I please."

"What about your boy friend back home?"

"I'm not going to talk to you any more." She left him and went back into the cabin, slapping the screen door shut behind her, and Walter had to go home. He met his brother on the trail. "Where you goin'?" he asked.

Teddy said, "Over to get Marilyn. We're goin' for a hike."

"At *night?*"

"Best time," and Teddy was gone. Walter waited up for him at their camp and it was after midnight when Teddy showed up. Walter pretended to be asleep.

Nobody saw much of either Teddy or Marilyn for the next few days, and Walter spent the time alone or with his mother. He did not want to face the boys over at the Kollers' or anybody else. The adults, when they saw him, were particularly irritating. Mrs. Peebles said once, "Well, you've lost your playmate, I see," and his own mother said, "She's such a nice girl, such good manners"—implying that she was happy that Teddy had found such a nice girl friend. In fact, everybody (except the boys at the Kollers') seemed terribly pleased by what Walter felt was none of their business, and now instead of being relieved that nobody suspected what had gone on between himself and Marilyn, he wished somebody *had*, so that they could understand his loss. The worst part was everybody thought he was blue because his brother had finally shown up and now had no time for him.

Walter and Teddy had only one conversation about Marilyn and then Teddy made it clear that the subject was closed. It was late at night again, and this time Walter did not pretend to be asleep when Teddy came in, undressed and climbed into his bag.

"Where you been?" he asked.

"Oh, we drove around for a while."

"Teddy?"

"What?"

"Have you ever screwed a girl?"

Teddy laughed. "Why?"

"I just wanted to know."

"You're too young for that kind of stuff. Wait a couple years and I'll tell you all about it."

"Then you have."

"Just never mind, youngster."

"Clyde never has."

"How do you know?"

"He told me so. He said he'd like to screw Marilyn but he never did it before."

Teddy laughed again. "He sure tried hard. Almost the first night she was up here. Didn't she tell you about that?"

"No."

"God, don't say a word to him. He's not ready for girls. He practically tried to rape her."

"She didn't tell me that."

"Tender young ears. You like her a lot, don't you?"

"Sure, for a girl."

"She likes you, too."

"Do you like her?"

"Sure. She's a nice girl. Pretty, too."

"Are you serious about her?"

"Serious? What do you mean?"

"I mean serious."

"Sure, I guess so. She's nice."

"Teddy."

"What?"

But he could not say it. Instead, he said, "Did you ever feel her up?"

"Okay, kid, now listen. No more of that. You're too young."

"I am not."

"Good night."

Walter was certain from what he knew about Marilyn and his brother that they were doing what Walter had not had the courage or whatever it took to do with her, and he grudgingly admitted to himself that he did not blame her for it; he had been too young, he really had been, and his brother was not. It did not make him feel any better.

On Friday night most of the fathers came up from the Bay area and on Saturday morning Walter's and Teddy's father, without looking either of them in the eye, told them they would have to come to the community council meeting. Nearly all the men were there except for Lew Matty and the others from the store. There were no children younger than Walter. The meeting was called to order by McQueen, the English teacher, who was chairman that year, and everyone went seriously through the business of reading the minutes of the last meeting, going over some old business about running generators during naptime, and then McQueen said, "Now, as to new business, I think Fred Koller wishes the floor. Fred?"

The meeting was being held on McQueen's front porch high above the lake and Walter was sitting with his back against the cabin, hugging his knees, and when Mr. Koller got up and moved over to the rail and leaned against it Walter suddenly thought, The frogs; they found out, and felt his face go hot as he knew, absolutely knew, that he was going to be exposed as a murderer in front of everybody. He wished as hard as he had ever wished for anything that time would flow backward just enough to get him out of there, away, where nobody could find him, but it never happened and even as he wished it he knew miserably that he was caught and would stay caught.

Mr. Koller grinned uncomfortably and rubbed his mouth and said, "Well, several people already know about this, and I guess I don't have to make too much of a preface. We have a nice community here and the problems that come up from time to time are of a nature that we seem to be able to handle them pretty well with a minimum of friction, et cetera. Anyhow, I hope we can handle this problem without any fuss or trouble. It was brought to my attention that some of the young people have been indulging in the sport of nudism, in other words, capering around in the woods with no clothes on. It's a pretty serious matter and I don't think we have to mention any names in particular, but I don't have to tell you that such goings-on can result in trouble of the worst sort, trouble for our children, and hell, most of us come up here for the sake of our children. Well, what

I'm getting at here is that it has to be stopped, and what's the best way to stop it. It seems that one young person in particular is at the bottom of this, and fortunately or unfortunately, depending on how you look at it, this particular young person is *not* one of our children, but a guest. So I propose that the host of this guest be so informed, and be informed that this guest is no longer welcome here. No need to bring up names right here in open meeting, so I guess all we have to do is take a vote on whether this action will be sufficient, and then if you want I'll undertake to tell her."

McQueen stood up and jammed his hands into his hip pockets, turning to face the group. He looked angry. "It's pretty clear to me that there's been some sort of a meeting before this one, because some of us seem to know what this is all about and some don't."

"That's right," Mr. Koller said. "We had a little caucus this morning over to my place."

"Well I'm afraid you're going to have to be a bit more specific before I'll call for a vote on such an important matter."

"Nuts!" Teddy said. He stood up, furious.

"Sit down!" their father ordered. It was almost an impasse between father and son, but McQueen spoke up:

"Take it easy, Teddy. I'm in charge of this meeting and nothing's going to happen to you here."

"Something ought to," Mr. Koller said. "He ought to have that hot rod taken away from him." Teddy's car had been a sore point with Mr. Roller, not because he couldn't afford to buy a car for Clyde but because Mr. Cannon had a way of getting extra gasoline stamps and tires. Right now Cannon said, "That's our family business, Fred," and let it go at that.

"All right," Koller said, "something to go into later on, if at all. You want me to be more specific I will. The ones that were reported to me were Teddy Cannon and that girl Marilyn Pettigrove staying at Peebles' place. Now you see how serious this matter is, I hope. We all know Teddy and we know he's a nice boy, but things have been going on ever since the arrival of that girl that I think would stop if she was politely and firmly told she was no longer welcome and sent away."

"Just a minute," said McQueen. "I don't think this is a council matter at all. If anything it's a matter between the Cannons and Ellen Peebles."

"I disagree," Koller said. "It affects us all, it's a clear-cut matter of juvenile delinquency, and I don't have to tell you that there are plenty of young children around here. What if some of the youngsters saw that. Or *saw something worse?* What about the camp full of little girls across the lake? What if one of those little girls saw something she shouldn't have and went home and told her parents and it got into the newspapers? I tell you this is serious and a matter for the council to decide, and I think the council should see to it that this girl leaves the lake and leaves today!"

Teddy interrupted the sounds of assent that nearly everyone was making: "Listen, you said it was me and Marilyn. You prove it. You tell me who saw us and where."

"Watch your mouth, young man!" Koller said.

"Now listen," Cannon said.

McQueen interrupted again, holding his hands up. "All right, a little orderly procedure. Everybody sit down. Now, Teddy has a good point. You say it was brought to your attention, very well, who brought it to your attention? Who says they saw them?"

Mr. Koller said, "I'd rather not say. This isn't a court of law."

"Indeed it's not. But if you want this council to consider your resolution you'd better be prepared to give us better evidence than a rumor."

"It's no rumor, you can take my word for that!" Herman said.

"His wife told him," Crosstrees said. "That's what he told us this morning. Wasn't it, Fred?"

"That's right, and whoever calls my wife a liar has me to deal with!"

"Nobody's calling Jean a liar," McQueen said. "But was she the one who saw this?"

Fred Koller said, "We don't have to go into that," and he pointed a long finger at Walter. "This boy can tell us all we need to know. Can't you, Walter?"

Walter wanted to disappear. Everybody was looking at him, but he saw only Teddy's strained face.

"Don't look at him," Koller said. "Just answer a few questions for us."

"Dad, are you going to let them do this?" Teddy asked their father. "*Are you?*"

"Be quiet, boy," Cannon said. Walter saw that his face was reddening, that he was very angry and embarrassed.

Teddy said, "Thanks a lot, Dad." He sat down.

"Now, Walter," Koller said. He smiled. "Nothing to be afraid of. We know you're only twelve. You can't be held responsible for anything. But you spent a lot of time with the girl, didn't you? Didn't you?"

"Yes, sir," Walter said. He had to clear his throat to get it out.

"All right then. You spent a lot of time with her. What did the two of you do?"

"Just messed around."

"What do you mean, messed around?"

"Hiking. Fooling around."

"You've heard what we've been talking about here. Did anything like that happen with you?"

Walter could not answer. He knew what he should say, but he did not say it. He sat staring up at Mr. Koller and hugging his knees.

"Can't you answer? Do you know what we're talking about? Taking off all your clothes and the girl taking off all her clothes. Did you ever do that, Walter?"

"No I didn't," he said.

"No you didn't. You didn't. Did she?"

"No, sir."

"Walter, it looks to me as if you were hiding something. Did something else happen?"

"Not exactly."

"What do you mean, not exactly?"

"I don't know."

"Obviously something happened, Walter. Now you have to tell us what it is."

"Well, we talked about it."

"About what?"

"You know."

"About going naked?"

"I guess so."

Mr. Koller looked around at the group. "A twelve-year-old boy! Do you see what I mean?"

Mr. McQueen said, "Walter, are you telling the truth, or are you just trying to get out of this?"

"Well . . ."

Mr. Koller said, "What kind of a question is that?"

McQueen said, "I deal with kids professionally, Fred. The way you were questioning him you could get any answer you wanted."

"I like that!"

To Walter, McQueen said, "All right now. You are not going to be punished. Your brother is not going to be punished. You can tell us the truth. Did the girl actually ask you to take off your clothes? There's nothing much wrong with it, you're not going to be in any trouble.

Obviously, you didn't do it, so there's no reason why you can't tell us."

"What about her?" Walter said. "You're going to send her away." He started crying, he could not help himself. He sat there hugging his knees and crying, and everyone watched him except his brother.

"Yes," McQueen said. "I suppose we are."

Six

Walter did not get to see the fight. His mother restricted him to the cabin area and he had to bring his things down from the camp and set up a cot on the porch and put up with his mother's quizzing, which was far more intensive than the one he had gotten from the men at the council meeting; but he was used to his mother and he lied to her with indignation, consistency and finally with the quiet, open-faced candor that convinced her nothing had really happened. But she did not change her mind about Marilyn, and Walter decided that even though it had been a men-only meeting, the women had been behind it. Marilyn left Monday on the mail truck and Walter's restriction lifted. But by then the fight was over and his brother gone, too.

Walter could not understand his brother. There had been the fight, which he heard about vaguely from Lew Matty, who had not been there, either, that Teddy had gone to Clyde Koller and forced him to fight in front of his brother, Billy, and Bob Witzger and had hit him two or three times before Billy jumped him from behind, crying and saying that he was the one to fight, he was the one who had told, and then Bob Witzger got into it and the three of them beat Teddy up and left him on the ground; and yet when Teddy left for Lake Tahoe that night he took Clyde Koller with him. And then one day Clyde was back and Teddy gone again without even stopping to say hello to his mother and Walter. It was that fall before Walter found out what he wanted to know, or at least what he wanted to believe: that Teddy had not made love to Marilyn and the whole thing had been false. Those three had been out in back of the Koller cabin chopping firewood and making coarse jokes about Teddy and Marilyn when Mrs. Koller came out the back door of the cabin and heard enough to make her ask questions and finally, to stop the questioning and get back at the Cannon boys, Billy, not Clyde, and not even Bob Witzger, said he had seen them running around naked, and under her questioning admitted that although they had been naked they weren't actually running around, and let her draw her own conclusions. Whether it was the truth or a story they all cooked up to protect everybody, he never really wanted to know. Around the lake it was a closed subject, and back home in the fall it was part of the past.

But before that, Walter had the rest of the summer to live through, July and August and a few days of September. It was not easy. On the night of the Fourth of July when they had the big cookout and set off the fireworks from the Cannon float, towed out into the middle of the lake, Walter stayed in the cabin and ate alone, and only walked down to the dark boat landing in front of their place when he could see the fireworks. He watched from there, seeing in the light of the flares and pinwheels the girls across the lake lined up on the shore. He thought about the counselor in the white bathing suit who had waved to him, and felt a wave of loneliness pass through him strong enough to make him shudder, and he wanted to get his flashlight and go over to where the others were; but he knew if he did they would make a fuss over him, perhaps even kid him, and so he went back to the cabin even before the fireworks were over and sat in his favorite wicker chair listening to the hiss of a Coleman lantern until he fell asleep. The next day he was back hanging around with the Koller boys, and spent the rest of the summer doing what they did every summer, only this was the first time he realized it.

1968

III / The Art of the Film

Hollywood Heart

My son comes to me for advice. What can I tell him? What we did is not what they do now. Now it is all business, and the young ones don't even go to the movies or watch their own television shows. No heart. Forty years I fight to keep my studio going and to keep the wolves out, and now I sit in my wheel chair watching television, and you know what? The commercials are better than what my son does. Imagine. It all started when they took away my theaters. That was something. Those New Yorkers come to me and say sweet things, you are forty-five years old, it is time to get out of the business, and all the time behind my back they are saying Max is no good to us any more because they took away his theaters and if he doesn't own the theater who would book his pictures, but they are foolish if they thought I put thirty-three million dollars in some Swiss bank like actors I know about, or maybe they thought I spent most of it for taxes, but they didn't know about a certain amendment to a certain rule, that I get to keep my money. They found out quick enough. Now they are making all the pictures overseas to save money, and the town is going to die. The town will die before I do, and they will have nowhere to come home to. Let them. I could sell my stock tomorrow.

Orchids. It started as a joke. One of the very funny writers I bring in from New York City sends me a pot of orchids with a little sign on it, "Sweets to the Sweet," and naturally I thought he was saying "Orchids to you!"—a nice compliment, but all the writers are laughing and they are laughing at me. Traditionally the writers don't like me, and for a very simple reason. When I made a picture that picture had my name on it, the first thing you see, my name and the name of the studio. So it's my picture, I paid for it. The writers think it is their picture, and the directors think it is their picture, but they all know that it is mine. They hated me because I checked every word of every scene on this lot. I saw every daily and I closeted myself with the editors when I had to. So they hate me when I change their lines. They argue, if Max does not like the way we write, why does he hire us? And I argue back, if you do not like the way I change your lines, why do you keep taking my money? So this writer who I can't even remember his name is mad at me because he has some of his dialogue chopped up, and he sends me orchids. I have the pot on my desk and I look at it. How can such a dumb-looking plant have such a beautiful flower? I ask myself. It's so beautiful it looks fake. But I like it, and I decide that I don't want it to die.

I hear that orchids are tropical plants from such places as Hawaii, and I wonder if my office is too cold for them, so I call a man in the research department to send me a brief on orchids, and then I understand the joke. Orchids, the word comes from the Greek word *orchis*, which means testicle, and nobody had to tell me what that meant. He was telling me, "Nuts to you!" and at the same time, "You are a nut!" A very funny joke from a man who went to Princeton or Harvard. So I get back at him the same way (in those days we had time for jokes) by sending him a vanilla milk shake with a note, "The same to you!" Let him tell everybody I am crazy, he doesn't know the brief on orchids tells me the vanilla plant is really an orchid, too, and I am saying back to him, "May your nuts be ground up for a milk shake!"

So now I have my home and my greenhouse and my television set, and my son has my studio. I am still the boss, but my son has the office. Everybody thinks I am crazy because I don't leave this house. They think I am locked up and there is no wheel chair. I tell you the truth, nobody comes here to see me because I don't want them to. I never had a friend in this business. This is not a business for friends. I am seventy-one years old. Kids I played with on the block are in old people's homes in Brooklyn and The Bronx. Am I so much better off? My son comes to me, thirty-seven years old and crying tears. Mister Nazi around the office and a baby at home, a boy who never had a mother but read a psychology book instead. To tell the truth, if he wasn't my own flesh and blood I wouldn't let him in the house.

When I was his age we worried about things, we worried about money and our personal lives. He worries about his *image*, that's all he's got to worry about. I think he should get married and I say so. "Everybody thinks you're a queer," I tell him, but I'm a Jew and I want grandchildren. I am also a realist and I know I won't have any unless I buy them from an orphanage. He cries because he is masterminding some rotten thing and he gets outsmarted. My son has no nerve. For five years he makes terrible pictures because he is afraid to make my kind of pictures and he is even more afraid to make the kind of pictures everybody at Yale told him were good. The Belknap picture is going to be good. Morgan Cleary is going to be a famous star after this picture comes out, and so my son tries to steal the picture from Belknap because it will improve his *image*. I could tell him. What image? You're my son, that's all the image you got. You could make *Gone With the Wind* and you would still be my son.

He comes in and I am watching a soap opera, my son's soap opera. Television is the only business in the world where my son could earn a dollar. Everything in it is stolen from radio or the comic strips. There is no size, no nerve. That picture fits my son like a glove. So he says to me, "What's that?" He doesn't even recognize the actors. Some producer.

He is not crying yet. The last time I cried I was eight years old and had the shoes stolen off my feet. The Lower

East Side of New York City was no Bel Air to be raised in, but that was the last time I shed any tears. I have heard stories how Louis B. Mayer used to cry over stories, God rest his soul, but I never did. Who was it who came to his funeral to make sure he was dead? God forbid such a thing should happen to me, even though I made enough enemies in my time. Now they are all laughing. Max is crazy, locked up in his house eating orchid flowers. Notice: I am not locked in; you are locked out.

Cigarette commercial. A beautiful Western, good music, a handsome fellow on a horse. Then my son starts crying. He can't sleep. He can't eat. The pressure is killing him. We play our game. I tell him he didn't have to go into the business, and he tells me it is his profession. It is so simple. He is afraid. He shouts at me to turn off the television, and I push the wrong button and the sound goes up. He stamps his foot and leaves me. I am sorry but there is nothing I can do. I know he will spend the whole rest of the evening up in his room. He keeps it in all day and then lets it out in front of me, unloading it on me. This was not always the case. When he was a boy he never said hardly anything to me. Up until the day my legs go out from under me and I fall down the stairs and lay there on the fake marble steps, my legs up and my head down, black specks in front of my eyes, clearing up and me looking up at the green brass letters that spell out my name over the stone arch and hear the wind rushing around, only it is people's voices; that girl, she spent hours sitting waiting to get into the studio and comes out finally from the main entrance just in time to see me fall and comes to me, playing nurse with her knees showing and my head pillowed on her lap, the specks dancing and the needles not yet in my legs, feeling I got a scraped knuckle and wondering what is all the fuss, a man falls down some steps, but now instead of the letters of my name I am looking up into the upside-down face of a beautiful young girl with her mouth open in sympathy and her eyes calculating and frightened and hoping all at once, and I speak to her—this went out over the television news on two stations—"Haven't I seen you someplace before?" When I try to stand up and can't, she is right there, at my side, until the ambulance gets there, by right of accident she is my bodyguard, thinking, How can I tell him my name? and the time slipping by, her big break, the head of the studio falling in her lap, so to speak, and she hasn't got the hardness to take advantage. Some of the cunts in this business would have had a contract signed before the ambulance came, but not this one, so pretty and so young, hard in the face but not in the heart, where it counts, a girl with maybe two commercials to her credit and eating peanut butter until finally it is no use, she is finished and has to go. I was dizzy then. Everything felt bright. I could see all the faces and hear all the whispers. I could have helped her. I could have took her name and got her some work. Maybe I should have. No. I shouldn't have. In all this time no work for her. Instead, I tell her, "You and me, we're finished." I don't know how I knew, but it was like something pulled out of my guts, like a huge splinter, and the blood rushes out but I feel better.

The television shouts at me and I push the button, this time the right one, and it goes off. Blink! I always watch the tiny dot of light. I cross the entry hall under the picture of my wife, God rest her soul, and down the ramp into the greenhouse through the electric doors. It is warm and steamy, with the sun over the ocean low and coming in through the windows. I sit and look at the plants, thinking. The fans turn on and the place cools down. The sun is gone and the lights go on. Long tubes of light that make everything purple and yellow. I know I look like a corpse and so I leave, across the entry hall, back to the television. I have my supper in the library watching television, and I know the servants are in the back of the house having their supper and watching television, and my son is upstairs in his room eating from a tray on his desk, pretending to work. Work? He doesn't know the meaning of the word.

Who could sleep? My son is coming to the crisis of his life, and, to tell the truth, there is nothing I can do about it. The time for me to do is gone. I should have married. But suppose I did? Arlene dies in 1928, and like Hamlet in reverse the birthday cake served up cold becomes the funeral feast. I was forty-one at the time, Arlene was thirty-six. Give me a year or two to get over it, and I marry again at age forty-three. But I don't marry an old person, say a girl of twenty-two. So if she was twenty-two in 1930 she would have been about fifty or so when I fall down the steps, not ready to give up sex. But she could have been a mother to him. I don't know. Maybe now I would have a cracking-up son and a cracking-up wife on my hands. Not one breath of scandal in all that time. It wasn't worth it.

Like walking through a curtain, my mind. All those years fighting and keeping, my mind spread all over the place, from New York to here, keeping track, holding on. It was not money. It stopped being money so long ago I can't remember, still a kid sharking nickels and dimes, it wasn't even the money then. They call it power, some of them. At a dinner party in this very house one of them tells me, "We are men who have gone beyond money, into the deepest part of the water, power." What is power? Power is what you don't know you got until you find out you haven't got enough of it. That's what I told him. He looks at me funny. I don't bother to explain. Another story. My son reaches for it because he does not know it reaches for you. He does not know this because nobody taught him.

New York keeps banging on me, "Get young blood in the executive end, delegate, delegate!" That's easy to say in New York, where they don't understand anything but columns of figures. Come out here and try it. How many men turn out to be generals? I try to tell them, "You don't force it; when good men come along they take the reins themselves," only to be told confidentially that I am like a tyrant who has only kiss-asses around him. I tell this man, "Nonsense, no kiss-asses in my studio, I hate them.

A kiss-ass will cut your throat while you're not looking!" But under the joke I am worried, because it might be true. And true or not, at that time they could have come in here and deposed me with their own bright young men all over the place spying and making trouble. It is hard to believe when you are forty-five years old that people are already thinking of replacing you. They couldn't cheat you or kill you, so they replace you. All your life you fight to make a thing with your own hand, and then they come and tell you, "This thing is permanent and you are not. Delegate!"

Isadore Rapfkin stole my shoes. I cried. A kid of eight. I learn the secret then, delegate. I work hard selling newspapers, steal a little money and buy some shoes. Isadore Rapfkin and his two brothers beat me up and take my shoes. They fit Izzy. I cry, but I think, Anybody bigger than me can take my money. All by myself I learn the secret of delegate and control. I go to Hesh. Hesh has a cap on pulled low to keep the cold wind off, but you can see his little eyes. Dumb Hesh. I offer him five cents to beat up Izzy and get back my shoes. I am scared he will steal the nickel but I have to hold it out, show it to him or he won't believe it. With a boy like Hesh you got to show the money. He doesn't steal the money, I never learn why. In all my life I never really learn why. Me, I would not steal the money because there might be more, but Hesh and those people don't think that way. I never learned how they think. A complicated chain of events, Izzy gets beat up pretty bad, I get my shoes back, Hesh gets beat up by

Izzy's brothers, but for some reason nobody comes to me to get the shoes. For a couple of weeks I duck Hesh, but then I run into him on the roof and he grins, happy. He doesn't blame me Izzy's brothers beat him up. He thinks that's why I offered him the nickel. I meet Izzy and he has respect for me. He doesn't know about the nickel. Later he works for me.

They don't think it's work. Not like selling newspapers is work. I keep that job, but I sell in the poolrooms and see all that money go to the horses. I run errands, I do anything, I make money, and nobody tries to take the money away from me. They know if they do, Hesh will be on them, a dumb kid who don't know when to stop beating. I don't even pay Hesh salary. Piecework. By this time I am sharking, ten cents a day on the dollar, time limit seven days. No extensions. First to kids who are older, teen-agers they call them now, who need money, only kids who work, and then later around the poolrooms to grown men betting the horses or on the billiard games, but then I see the light what a sucker's game I have going for myself.

One day Hesh kills his father and the police come and take him away. I have to hide, because I know people will be after me. I hide in the back of a poolroom on Third Avenue, but a boy named Mordacai Felzer comes in and finds me, but he doesn't want to beat me up, only to ask if I need another muscle man. I hire him on the spot and tell him to forget the money he owes me. He grins and I know he thinks he has put one over on me. But he works for me.

Then my grandfather, God rest his soul, finds out I charge interest to Jews and he reads me out of the family. By then I have enough money not to care, and I don't cry. Not then, not ever again. By the time I am twelve I have five employees, all older kids, and I personally shark money only to family men, mostly garment workers, and the rate of interest has dropped, because I know enough not to press people who are cornered like rats. I didn't know what the rest of the world was like; I thought everybody lived in this kind of misery and was afraid all their lives.

Isadore Rapfkin was the one who went a long way in the sharking, not me. While I was sharking garment workers, he still handled the fifty-cent and dollar gambler and kid trade for me, and nobody was supposed to know he worked for me. After some time, I find out he was buying up markers all over the Lower East Side that nobody else could collect, and collecting them. He really went strong-arm, and before he was twenty I think he had a couple of people killed. I never went that far. By then we are no longer associated and I am out of sharking entirely, but he went on and opened his own poolroom. He was a regular gangster, with cops working for him and everything. He got killed in the 1920's. Some woman got him.

Sex caught me when I was about fourteen and looked maybe twenty. She was a show girl who did an act with her brother, I thought, where he would throw her around to music. It was supposed to be a Spanish act, billed as José and Maria Catalan, but they were Jewish. Previously

I had nothing to do with theaters or vaudeville except to go once in a while if I could get in free, and to tell the truth, the movies they had then didn't impress me very much. At that time they used movies to clear the house after the headliner. Niagara Falls, two people kissing, boxing matches. Feature films came later. People were always coming to me with propositions of how to make lots of money if only they had some to start with, and I got to admit that one out of a thousand really had good propositions, and a few good businesses got started on money I loaned out at six per cent. But the rest were something awful. One fellow I remember wanted me to loan him money to buy life insurance with so he could kill himself in an accident and the widow would pay me back. I never saw such a cold-blooded fellow. I had to turn him down.

There was a stuss parlor on Sixth Avenue where I used to sit from around ten in the morning until about two in the afternoon, and people would come to me there. Everybody except the owners thought I owned the place. Morton Chernig was a man of about thirty with a black suit, a derby and a long mustache, and little else except schemes. He had a father and two brothers working, and that was enough for him. I saw him out of the corner of my eye, hanging around, and as soon as I was alone, he came over and sat down without being asked.

"This is your lucky day," he told me. He reached over and took a cigar out of my pocket and started trimming it with a little gold-plated knife. "I am about to unveil a proposition which is both lucrative and entertaining, especially for a young fellow like yourself." To cut it short, he was offering me a partnership, as much as it broke his heart, because he knew I would not loan him a red cent, even though all he needed to make a cleanup was one hundred dollars for no more than one week. It took him half an hour to get down to what the proposition was about, what with people stopping by and him being nervous, but what it amounted to was he had a friend who just got back from Europe with "a very special reel of motion picture" which was nothing like what anybody had ever seen around here. He needed money to rent a store and some chairs and hire a fellow with a projector.

"What's the nature of this moving picture?" I asked, even though from the way he was carrying on, I had a good guess.

"Women, my boy," he said. "The subject is women. And let me tell you a secret, they ain't got any clothes on, either."

That afternoon he took me to a rooming house and introduced me to Sarah Greenglass, alias Maria Catalan, who was the friend with the movie. This made me a little shy, it being a woman, and they got the film out of its can and told me not to touch it with my fingertips, and pulled it off the spool, their fingers on the edges, and let me look, holding it up to the light. Sure enough, naked women, three of them. You could see the hair and everything, and so I knew they weren't wearing tights, which is what

I had been afraid of. I avoided Sarah's eyes and said, "This looks interesting."

"I would be saving this," she said, "except we ain't been booked in six weeks. A triumphant tour of Europe and now we haven't got to eat. I ask you. This film cost Manny and me fifty dollars American in Paris."

I figured she had stolen it, and later she told me this was correct. But at the time she was trying to sell it outright to me for twenty-five dollars, while what Chernig wanted was for him and me to be partners. This didn't come out right away, not until Sarah told Chernig to go and wait for me at the stuss parlor. He didn't want to leave, seeing his dreams fluttering away, but she made him go, whispering something to him, and then closed the door and we were alone. I didn't know what to expect, being only fourteen although looking twenty.

"Such a handsome young man," she said in Yiddish, making eyes at me and coming up to put her hands on my cheeks. She had no trouble with me at all, and less than an hour later I left the place with the film in a package and memories of her muscles and the things she did to me in my mind. It was quite an experience, and the film only cost me twenty dollars after very little haggling. I went home to my boardinghouse and hid the film under my mattress. The next day I went back to the stuss parlor at my usual time, and Morton Chernig was there, his mustache up on one side and down on the other. His eyes had a worried look but his mouth looked mean. He sat down next to me.

"What happened?"

"The film is mine."

"You bought it from her? For how much?"

"None of your business."

"What's going on here? I thought we were partners."

"What do I need with a partner? Especially a broke one."

This is why he never got anywhere in life. He couldn't believe what I was saying. I purposely made it as tough on him as I could, because I had decided I could use him, not as a partner, but as the fellow who goes around telling the other fellows where the movie can be seen, what it is like, and how much. With such a picture, you don't put up signs.

"So I'm out in the cold," he said. He tipped his derby back and jammed his thumbs down into his vest pockets. "How do you like that?"

"You're entitled to something," I said. "After all, you did the arranging." I offered him a cigar.

The year before that the show people went on strike and a lot of theaters put in projectors and showed exclusively movies, so it was not difficult for me to pick up a used projector for seventy-two dollars and hire a fellow my own age to run it for fifty cents a night. I got the store from a man who owed me money and didn't bother with chairs. The only other expense was to take care of the police, and I let Morton Chernig handle that end of the business.

I was not even slightly tempted to copper my bet by getting Chernig to sign a note; even then I had complete faith in the movies if only they were interesting to the public.

I had seen the movie before we opened for business. Three heavy-looking young tomatoes wearing nothing but ballet shoes and ribbons in their hair. They worked in front of a black curtain and kept disappearing and reappearing, which was trick photography. The film had been hand-tinted and must have been very expensive to make, even in France. I stayed completely away from the place after we opened, and it was not to be known that I owned it. A fellow who worked for me took the money, twenty cents per customer, paid the projectionist and Chernig and brought the rest to me.

In six months I had made a six-hundred-dollar profit and business was beginning to lag. I think every boy and man from the age of nine to twenty-five in the entire island of Manhattan had seen the picture twice by then, and it was time to either close up or find something else. Many people had come to me with propositions regarding the theater business in the meantime, since it was impossible for me to keep it secret that I owned the place. Consequently, at the age of fifteen I opened my second theater, just exactly like the first one, in a store in Brooklyn, and took the movie over there, but before that, I had my first experience as a maker of motion pictures.

I had been visiting Sarah Greenglass on and off for the whole six months, and, frankly, she and her husband were living off the money I gave her. I will confess to the fact that I loved her in a puppy-love way and that it came as a great shock and disappointment to learn that Manny was not her brother but her husband. And a very stupid man. He knew what was going on and he pretended to me that he didn't, and would come and see me at the stuss parlor, and ask me to back him in schemes. Always the heavy-handed hints about his *sister*, and how it would be too bad if they had to go out West to get any bookings. Sarah was much the smarter of the two, yet in retrospect I can say that she was a stupid woman, or she could have cleaned me out. In a sexual way she was quite an experience, and knew a number of tricks that even on the street I hadn't heard about, even though she was only three or four years older than me. Her big trouble was that she had the small-time schemer mind, and could not see past tomorrow. She would consider it an accomplishment to spend two or three days working on a scheme to steal five dollars. She even tried it on me, once. I think it was her idea, and not Manny's. I don't think Manny had enough brains for even such a stupid scheme.

I was in her room with my clothes off one night, about eight o'clock, and she was naked, too, lying on the bed. I was about to join her when Manny breaks into the room and starts shouting about me screwing his wife (I never had let them know I knew about their true relationship) and how he was going to call the law down on me for committing an act of adultery. Then she joins in and starts screaming at him, and he says he has had enough, he is going to call the cops, and she turns to me and says, "For God's sake pay him off, do something, or we'll be exposed!" Then it was supposed to be my turn. This was even then an old racket called "The Badger Game" and why they thought I would go for it is beyond me. I felt like laughing at them. I could have forced the issue by calling a cop myself and having Manny arrested, but already I had decided that it might be interesting to make use of them, and so instead I taught them a small lesson. I took all the money out of my pants pocket, counted it, and gave it to Manny, about thirty-five or forty dollars. You should have seen his eyes light up at the sight of the money. I guess Manny couldn't find a gun to use, because the way the racket is supposed to go, you wave a gun around and threaten to shoot everybody. But I gave the money and left, and then got in touch with an employee of mine and instructed him to get the money back, and be careful not to hurt Manny too much. He brought me the money in less than an hour.

A couple of days later I sent a kid to bring Manny to me at the stuss parlor. He showed up walking kind of stiff, but no marks on his face. He was a handsome fellow, with dark hair and eyes and skin, and just looking at him you would never know he was scared stiff. He just looked thoughtful, as if maybe he had to go to the dentist that afternoon.

"You and Sarah were going to leave town?" I asked him.

"Whatever you say."

"It figures. You needed getaway money, and you thought to take it from me. Why didn't you just ask me? Am I a friend of the *family* or not?"

"Aw, don't rub it in. We make a mistake, that's all."

"A terrible mistake. You should have come to me. As it happens, I have a method for you to earn a considerable amount of money, plenty enough to go as far away as San Francisco or Denver, which, by the way, might not be a bad idea. The South Pole would be even better, but I'll settle for the West."

"What's your proposition?"

"You know, it's a good thing you tried to crook me after all. Now we are all business, and none of this friendship stuff to get in the way. My proposition is simply this: I am going to make a moving picture myself. What I need is a couple actors to play the leading roles. The pay is fifty dollars apiece, and the job lasts one day tops. How does that strike you?"

He couldn't believe it. I think throughout the negotiations he was half sure I would have him beat up again after I paid him. But finally we got down to the crucial part of the conversation, in which I explained to him the nature of the movie I had in mind. "Fellows will pay good money to see some naked women running around," I said. "And you can imagine what they would also pay to see an act of sexual intercourse. Especially one full of tricks. You and Sarah are acrobats as well as Spanish dancers, it ought to be a very interesting movie."

I halfway expected him to look at me with hatred in his eyes, but he didn't. All he said was, "Fifty dollars?"

"Apiece," I stressed. "Your job will be to explain to Sarah."

"We have to get out of town," he said. "I can't stand it around here not working."

"I know just how you feel."

"We could get bookings in Kansas if we could get there," he said.

"Kansas would be fine," I said.

The cameraman was a young fellow no more than thirty who had inherited some money from his family and then spent it all on equipment and making a couple of movies, which he sold outright for less than it cost to make them. His name was Nargosian and he was very intense. He had his studio on a rooftop on Perry Street and that is where we made the movie. It took us half an hour to clear the junk out of his room and set up the black drapes all around, and while we did this Manny and Sarah sat out on the roof huddled together talking. We set it up so the camera was mostly hidden behind the drapes, giving them the appearance of being alone. Nargosian dragged in his own mattress from the next room, and covered it with a sheet and a shawl, and we called in the actors. I explained to them: "You just stand in there beside the mattress and take off your clothes and then lay down and start doing your tricks. Nargosian will be behind the drapes, and when he shouts at you, you do what he says, but don't look at the camera."

Nargosian said, "From time to time I'll ask you to stop, to change film or move the camera. Just stop cold and don't move. Just like the game of freeze, okay?"

"Boy, I don't feel like it," Manny said. He looked cold.

"What does it take to get you in the mood?" I said.

"I knew that would be a problem," Nargosian said.

"That can be part of the act," Sarah said. She didn't look at me at all. "Me getting him hot. How about that?"

They started to work and I went out on the roof. To tell the truth, I didn't feel any too good. I had not quite gotten her out of my system as yet and it made me a little sick to think of what was going on in there. I sat by the edge of the roof, looking five stories down to Perry Street, to all the little people. I could just hear the sound of the horses' hoofs on the pavement, and hear some kids yelling. Pigeons went up from a roof close by and I watched them go up and circle and fly away toward the Hudson River. There was a ledge around the edge of the roof, and I had my hands on top of it, holding on. I felt about a hundred years old. I tried to think about how much money I had in the bank, but I couldn't remember the exact amount. I took the money out of my pocket and counted it a couple of times, feeling pretty foolish. It was quite a sum of money, all I was going to pay for the making of the movie. A couple of hundred dollars, in the big bills like they don't make any more. I folded it double and put it back in my pants pocket. For some reason, I felt nauseous, and before I could stop myself, I puked over the edge of the building. I opened my eyes just in time to see it falling. It didn't land on anybody's head, but I saw some people start sideways, and the black dots showed a spot of white as they looked up toward me. I ducked back and laughed, holding on to my knees. Then I went in and washed my face.

Some days later Nargosian sends for me to come up to his studio. He tries to act calm but his eyes are all lighted up. It is raining and I can hear the sound of it out on the roof while we stand in the dark room watching the final product. The movie lasted about six minutes and was very funny. Also, it was very carnal. I had never before watched people committing acts of sexual intercourse, and I have to admit that to a person my age it was like a tonic. Nargosian pulled back the curtains and let the gray light in.

"What do you think?" he asked me.

"Is that all?"

"Isn't it *enough?*"

"It took you three hours to make five minutes?"

He explained to me that he had to take lots more pictures than ended up in the movie. "A lot of it didn't work," he said.

"I paid for all of it, let me see it," I said, and we spent the rest of the afternoon looking over the stuff he had cut out. He had whole boxes full of it, not on reels, just laying there. Finally I said to him, "Put it together, any whichway, in five-minute reels. Then we have lots of shows."

"But it's just *junk*." He was upset. He ran his hands through his hair and begged me to not make him do it. I convinced him that since I paid for all of it, it was all mine. The upshot was that I had not one five- or six-minute film, but ten of them, some better than others, I'll admit, from an artistic standpoint, but at that time I was not much interested in artistry. I had another scheme. The good one I booked into my own theater, and the other ones I sent on the road with a fellow to sell to other theater owners around the country, realizing a profit of something better than seven hundred dollars net just from that part. The good film showed at my place for three months, and then the old film, the one I sent over to Brooklyn, finally fell apart from too much splicing and burning, and I sent the good one over there, where it suffered the same fate in a few months. We were charging fifty cents to watch this particular movie, and so the audiences were somewhat smaller and older.

Through Nargosian I met a lot of fellows who were making movies. They would come to me naturally for money because even then it was a very expensive proposition to make a movie, although nothing like it is now. I did not think it was a safe proposition to go on making blue movies, and I also did not think there was going to be the money in it that there was in other forms of movies, but that was not really what got me out of the blue-movie business into the legitimate, not then. As a matter of fact, it was a thing we called later "Glamour," where a young fellow like myself could meet show-business people, especially girls. Once I got interested in girls I stayed interested for a long time, and it was always a search for the perfect girl of the moment, one who liked her sex and was beautiful and you could take her out in public. I knew that one way you could influence those girls to be co-operative was to give them gifts, but I was still a very careful person with a dollar, and I thought it would be more in keeping to attract the girls with something more substantial for both of us. I am not talking about putting them in the movies, that came much later on. I am talking about theaters wherein entertainers would perform. At that time, the good acts and the good theaters around the country were locked up by a handful of outfits centered in New York City, and I was young enough to think that with my pitiful amount of capital I could crack the combine. In the back of my mind it was always show girls, and maybe that was what clouded my thinking on this subject. So I wasted a lot of time midtown, which was not a complete waste because I got to know some people who turned out to be very useful to me. I wanted to back a play but I didn't have enough money, and I wanted to break into vaudeville on the ownership side of the fence but this was impossible. It was no wonder then, and I am not taking credit for being a genius, only a desperate young man, that I finally listened to Nargosian and his friends, some of whom being nice fellows were living off loans from me that frankly I never expected to see again.

The proposition was a simple one: we would make a short movie that was actually a play, with a plot and everything. There is a lot of talk in the history books about this idea, not just ours, but that movie about the train robbery and the one about the fire, which all came out at about the same time, but the talk is all about the cutting technique and the use of the close-up shot and other technical matters, which I left up to Nargosian and his friends, while I concentrated on the most important part. They wanted to make a movie like the kind of plays that were popular at that time, the plays of Dion What's-his-name, with the train about to run over the girl and the villain closing down the mortgage, but that was too difficult to do without words, so what we did was a nice short thing called *The Rescue,* where a girl falls off a ferryboat and nobody notices except a fellow on the shore. I must admit the cutting was interesting. They would show the girl and then the people on the boat not noticing and then the girl again, and then the fellow on shore, cutting back and forth until you are jumping out of your seat, and the fellow finally takes a rowboat and goes out and jumps in and saves her. Nargosian was so excited he couldn't stand it, because he didn't know what he had until he developed the pictures and edited them together, and then he went half crazy wondering if anybody else would see it the way he saw it, that is to say, suspenseful and exciting. I did. I was thrilled half to death.

It was expensive, but I had Nargosian make a number of prints, and then I went out on the road. I did not sell the prints, I rented them, and in the space of a year's time, I had made something like twenty-eight thousand dollars net. The picture cost me three hundred to make. There was no question in my mind that there was money in the movies. When I got back to New York Nargosian was gone, off to Europe someplace; I never heard of him again, but I still had many acquaintances in the picture-making business, and I bought outright a number of short feature films, some good, some awful, and went back out on the road. This time I did not rent or sell, I bought. I bought a theater in Portland, Maine, that is to say, I bought a store front, some chairs, equipment, a big sign, ads in the local papers, and opened a theater in direct competition to the existing theatrical enterprises, and mine made money because I had the good movies. Opening night was closed to the public, only the local civic leaders invited, free, and I gave a little speech before the show outlining how my place of business was going to help progress and art. I got a fellow in New York to write the speech for me, for two dollars. It was a good speech. After opening night the place did a fine business, and I hired a manager in the person of a young man recommended by the mayor of the town, and moved on. The same story, or practically, everywhere I went. In a couple of places I found something interesting: the person who owned the one local movie house would have his friends on the city council pass a law there could only be one movie house in town. In the first one, I opened my place in a sort of barn outside the city limits, did my advertising, invited the local nabobs and everything. On the second night the public came, a mean-looking bunch of men, and they tore my place apart. I got beat up, too, but it didn't bother me much, because I was too busy thinking about how to handle the situation. The best way, I decided, was to bypass the place and wait until I got back to New York. Before that I ran into another town with the one-movie-house ordinance, and I didn't even bother to try.

Back in New York I checked around to see where these people got their films. Neither of them had agents in the city. They would write to the film companies and rent their films in that manner. There were only a few companies, and I got a lawyer and signed contracts with them giving me one-year exclusive showing rights, in exchange for a higher percentage of the box-office receipts. These were very complicated agreements and I had to limit them to the two towns in question because the film companies weren't that crazy, but when I went back to these towns nobody objected to my opening my movie houses, because it was no longer a violation of the ordinance. The existing houses, by the time I got there, were showing stuff people had been tired of for years, and they were glad to sell to me. I booked my own pictures, and therefore did not have to lay out a cent on the contracts I had made with the New York companies, except for the fee I paid my lawyer.

I should say that before I went on the road in the first place I changed my name and got completely out of the sharking business. In New York I now lived midtown and never went below Sixteenth Street for anything whatsoever. I might add that with the passage of time, those people who ran the booking combine for vaudeville, who wouldn't let me in on it, or anybody else, for that matter, dried up and blew away. It was of great satisfaction to me.

There is one awful thing that happened in this particular period that made me feel sad. Sarah and Manny Greenglass were doing small towns in the Pacific Northwest when a very bad coincidence occurred. The blue movie they starred in was showed at a policeman and fireman smoker while they were doing their Spanish dancer act in this little town, and they were recognized and arrested. Manny got beat up pretty bad, and I would rather not know what happened to Sarah. The way I found out about it was that Sarah sent me a telegram to my New York office, using my new name, Max Meador, begging for money to get away from that town and buy Manny out of the jail, where he would die if he didn't get treatment. I sent her a thousand dollars care of Western Union, San Francisco, and a hundred dollars care of Western Union in the town she was in. Don't ask me why. And for a long time I expected to hear from one or another of them with a blackmail demand or something of the sort, but I never did. I never heard of them again. I wonder where they are now? Probably dead.

Everything I did somebody else did, either before me or after me. The gold in the movies was easy to see. Some went into production, some went into distribution, and some like me went into exhibiting, with a little producing and distributing on the side. It was easy to see if you made your own pictures and distributed them to yourself and exhibited them yourself, the profits would be immense and the number of middlemen small. I did what I could. So did thousands of other young fellows. The competition was very fierce and there was many a time when I would be lying in a hotel bed without any sleep wishing I could get off the merry-go-round, especially times when I would come into a town where I had a theater and discover my manager had been cheating me and I would have to go to all kinds of trouble not to get ahead but just to stay even.

Here is what a lot of people would not understand, and it is the same thing that knocked off a lot of the competition early in the game. When you got everything you ever wanted, why don't you quit? A lot of fellows are after money, and so when they get together quite a pile of it, they retire from the business. With me I can say honestly that it was money only in the very beginning, and I sometimes wonder if it was money even then. Maybe it was fear even then. The glamour part wasn't what it was supposed to be. Once it was a big thrill to me to be around show-business people who had their names in the paper all the time and wore the beautiful clothes and so forth, but after you start dating show girls you wonder what you are going to do for some conversation, as all they talk about is themselves or show business. Also I know that somewhere down inside of me I wanted to build a family and be in the middle of it, but also I hated my own family and wanted no part of them, which is probably why I married late. It was a long time before I had occasion to meet nice family-type girls. And power. It didn't take me long to find out, for example, that a lot of girls would go to bed with me not because they thought they could get something out of me in the way of a job or cash money, but because they wanted some of my power. I can't find any other way to explain it. This power meant nothing to me, because so far in my life every time somebody pulled a shit trick on me, I pulled one right back on them but only if it was to my advantage to do so.

But underneath it all was the fear. I could not stop. There was something inside me telling me, "You stop now, you end up back on the Lower East Side cutting throats for nickels." I knew it wasn't true, but a person's feelings are not subject to the control of the mind. I used to wonder who I was. Everywhere I went outside New York City people would laugh behind their hands at the way I talked. For a while I tried to fix this up so I talked different, but that didn't work, and so after a while I talked like myself, only more so, and especially when I would be doing business with somebody who didn't like Jews and could not hide his feelings. It got to be a mask I could sit behind. I got to see other things, too, in little towns outside Chicago,

St. Louis, and such places, where there were kids my own age playing baseball without a thought to the future, and green grass and trees on streets with houses on them, where people lived one family to a house. I used to think when I would get mad about this that I could buy and sell most of these people, but it was not a thought that could console me for long. I was hungry for that kind of life even though I knew I could not personally stand it.

So one day I am out in Los Angeles where I had a hand in a company producing pictures. They are shooting scenes on a beach near Malibu, and I am walking along the sand by myself, dressed in a business suit with a vest, feeling the sun and the wind come in off the ocean and wondering why the Pacific doesn't smell like the Atlantic, and I look around and I have gone over a hill of sand and can't see a single human being. I take off my coat and vest and sit down in the sand and watch the water come and go. It hisses in the sand, and I listen to that for a while. I feel at peace. Not a cloud in the sky. I pick up a seashell laying in the sand, and it is one that I recognize. A sand dollar. Even on the beach I am picking up dollars. I feel all black inside, like a man suddenly knows he is going to die. The blackness goes on for quite a while. I see my whole life, and it is ugly. My whole youth is gone scratching for dollars. I have no friends, no family. People laugh at me, but they are afraid. More blackness. I want to write a letter to my grandfather or my mother and beg them to forgive me. But in the blackness I can see that it would do no good.

It would not mean anything to them and it would not mean anything to me. A cry in the dark, that's all. I think about God, and that don't do any good. I can't believe. I see kids kill each other for fifteen cents. More blackness. The face of God I can see in my mind turns away from me, not me from it. The inside of my mouth tastes all coppery, and I think not for the first time of killing myself and letting it all go. But I go past that. It would do no good.

Out of it all, I get a bad sunburn on the forehead and a resolve to get out of the exhibition business. The next day I cancel some meetings with production people and instead have a meeting with Karl M. Brannaman, a man who owns one hundred and sixty theaters. After two weeks of meetings and talks with lawyers we become partners, merging our theater operations under the name MBPC, with Brannaman as president. He handles the theaters, and I oversee the production of pictures. The year is 1915 and I am twenty-eight years old. I think the struggle is over, but of course it is just beginning. Ask my son.

1965

Hollywood Whore

I've been in pictures nearly all my life. I was just barely a freshman at the University of California when the stock market crashed, and within a few months I was told that if I wanted to keep my job on the San Francisco *Chronicle* I would have to come to work full time. I tried it for a while, going to classes in the mornings, studying or sleeping in the afternoons, and taking a ferry across the bay in time to pull a full shift ending at midnight, but it got to be too much for me. I quit school, and within a year I was promoted to reporter. I was still just a kid, and the whole thing fascinated me. Like everybody else on the staff, I wrote a book, but I was lucky and mine got published.

A few months later, when it had all worn off, the two-hundred-and-fifty-dollar advance was gone, and I finally realized that I would not write another book, I received two registered letters, a long-distance phone call, and a telegram, all on the same day. The messages were all the same: Max Meador wanted to see me. Both of the registered letters contained checks for a hundred dollars, to cover my expenses getting down there. After stewing at my desk for a few minutes I got up and walked out of the building, without saying anything to anyone, walked over to Third and Townsend, and tried to get a train. Nothing was leaving for Los Angeles for two hours, and so I had time to go to my room on Pine Street and collect my belongings. I gave my books to the landlady, and she gave me an old red cardboard suitcase. It was too late to get to a bank with the checks, so I left one with her in exchange for twenty dollars cash, and took a cab back to the depot. I did not get any sleep on the train.

The air in Los Angeles was fairly clean in those days, and the weather was warmer than San Francisco's. This calmed me down after the sleepless night and made me feel good. I took a cab directly to the studio, identified myself to the policeman on the gate and was admitted. The policeman even walked around the corner of the building with me and pointed to the entrance I was to use.

"You could leave that suitcase with me," he said. "And maybe the hat." I did.

In those days, if Max Meador sent for somebody it meant that he wanted to talk to him. I waited in the outer office for only a few minutes, and I could hear Max's voice through the open door. I was not used to the thick New York Jew accents and I thought it sounded funny. It had a gutter sound that clashed with the luxury of the office as badly as my clothes seemed to. He was talking into a telephone, using words I had never heard before, and

I had just begun to be frightened when I was taken in by the secretary.

"Good God, is it you?" Max said loudly. He was halfway around his desk, coming toward me to shake my hand furiously. He was shorter than I was, plump, coarse-jowled and blue-eyed, and looked to me like a jolly banker. After the handshaking was over and I admitted that I was me, he took me by the arm and led me to a long couch under his window, and we sat down with two cushions between us. Back of the couch there was an inner ledge to the window, and on it a couple of dozen potted plants with thick dull-green leaves, some of them with flowers I recognized with a start as orchids, but in colors I had never seen before. Max sat sideways, his knees drawn up on the couch, one arm over the top and his fingers laced beneath his chin. It was natural for me to turn toward him and raise one knee onto the couch.

"Ah ah," he said. "You shouldn't wear white socks with a suit. You should wear the calf-length dark hose with the garters."

"I walk a lot," I said. "These are sweat socks."

"Don't be embarrassed. I mention your socks only for your personal benefit. One thing I learned in this business is to treat clothes like costumes. If it's a pirate picture, we dress our people like they were pirates. We have men who look up in books what the old pirates used to wear, and they tell us, and then we dress our pirates like we saw them dressed in another picture. The public has not looked in the books, but they have seen the other pirate movies. Get it?" He laughed and waggled a plump finger at me. "Authentic is what looks right."

"Thank you," I said.

"Don't thank me yet. Thank me when you feel it. Right now you don't want to thank me, you want to kill me for mentioning your socks. Forget those socks. Nobody walks in Hollywood. Except for one star who I know personally, and I bet he don't wear any sweat socks. If I know him he wears silk socks and throws them away after one day. What waste! Hollywood is full of waste. If a talented boy like you came to another studio I could name but won't— make that three studios—you would be wasted tragically. They would give you a room in the writers' building and let you sit there going to pieces, earning big money and wishing you was someplace else. Not me. I pay nobody big money except myself and my stars. I got to pay the stars or they will go away. Don't ever forget one thing about this business: the people go to the movies to see their favorite stars. That's what puts them in line. At home everything is rotten, the baby cries and there is no money, so they want to go to the movies and get away from it all. What makes them go? A good story? Beautiful photography? No. Stars. We waste two minutes in every movie listing credits nobody in the audience reads. We list those credits for the benefit of the people in the business. Do people go to see a Max Meador picture? No. They go to see a Clark Gable picture, and I wish to God he worked for me. So

I pay my stars too much money, and I pay everybody else a living wage, no matter what those God-damn fucking Communists say."

He got up and went behind his desk, opened a drawer and got out a copy of my book. He waved it at me and put it back. "This is a beautiful piece of merchandise, to me. Oh, yes, I read the whole book, not just an outline. Mostly I read just the outlines, but when I decide definitely to buy a property I read it all, even the hard parts." He came back to the couch and sat again. "Some of the books I have had to puzzle through! But not yours. You write a very simple form of the English language, and I thank you for that. Also, you wrote a great story. Don't get me wrong. I think it's a great story because it is going to be so easy to make it into a movie. To me, that is greatness. What do I know from books! I read what the critics of books said about yours. Mostly they didn't say anything at all. Not one of them mentioned that it would make a good movie. Those critics hate the movies. I hope you are not on their side.

"Now, I got you down here because I obviously want to offer you a deal for your book, but I want to do more than that. I think you can write good, and what I want to find out is two things: if you want to write movies and if you *can* write movies. Naturally you are not interested in this talking talking, what you want to hear about are the terms I've decided to offer you, right? Okay. I am willing to pay you five thousand dollars for your book, and good-by. I can have the check ready today, and you can go back to San Francisco and write another book, if that's what you feel like doing. Or, I will pay you an option of one thousand dollars for your book, together with a six-week contract, renewable on a week-to-week basis, paying you two hundred and fifty dollars per week. Your job will be to sit in an office in the writers' building and change your book into a screenplay. You will have help. At the end of six weeks I look at what you have written, and I make a decision, either to buy your screenplay, or let you keep working on it, or fire you and give the job to somebody else.

"If I fire you, you lose twenty-five hundred dollars and you would have been smarter to have taken the five grand and gone home. If I decide to have you keep working on it, you will get another two-fifty a week until I decide to take another look, probably another six weeks. By which time the screenplay should be done. Then maybe I fire you, and you go home, but with an additional fifteen hundred dollars. But, if I like what you are doing and want to use your treatment, I will pay you five thousand dollars cash above and beyond everything you have gotten so far, and in addition to that I will offer you a regular job, a contract calling for a weekly salary of five hundred dollars, and put you right to work on another project. Now, how does all this strike you?"

I was of course dizzy and amazed. I was just a kid, and sitting talking on equal terms to one of the men who had made Hollywood. I did not know who I was, or what

I wanted to be. The whole country seemed to be slowly drying up, and here was a chance at the big money. The suspicions I felt about my own book—that it was cynical, imitative and unreal, a glib performance rather than any kind of honest effort—all washed away under Max's enthusiasm.

"Just a minute," he said. He trotted out into his secretary's office and came back in a moment with an armful of documents. "Naturally you can't make up your mind without looking at your contracts. This one sells me your book outright for five thousand. You can read it if you want. Make no mistake, there are no loopholes. I can make one movie or I can make a hundred movies from your book, and all you get is the five grand. Now this one is an option contract giving me the exclusive right to purchase your book within the next six months. I pay you one grand for the option, and the purchase price is six thousand dollars including the option figure. No loopholes. Are you understanding me? This one here is a contract for your services as a writer, for a sum of two-fifty a week for six weeks, an entirely separate document, with a renewable clause on a week-to-week basis. No loopholes. Everything you write during this time, even letters to your mama, belong exclusively to me. Now, come with me, and bring all your contracts. I want you to sit down and study them carefully, but I need my office to do a little work."

I followed him, at a trot, out through his secretary's office, across the hall, and into the office that was next to his, on the same side of the building. There was a man seated behind the desk—I learned later he was a producer—and Max said to him, "Please go do something, we need your office for this young man to study his contracts," and the man got up and left without saying a word. Max took me by the elbow and maneuvered me behind the desk. "Sit. Read the contracts. Tell my secretary when you're ready to talk. Read them carefully, because you may not know this but a contract that a party has not read is not binding on him. Don't kid yourself about that." He picked up the telephone from the desk and jerked the cord loose from its jack plug in the baseboard. "I need this instrument," he said, and left the room, shutting the door.

I sat for a moment, and Max stuck his head back in the door. "That five hundred a week later on," he said. "That is not in any contract. That is a promise from me to you." He vanished again.

I had nothing else to do, so I read the contracts carefully. There was no question about what I was going to do. When I couldn't stall any longer, I went out and told the secretary that I would like to see Mr. Meador again, and she smiled and invited me to sit down. I held my contracts on my lap and waited. Max's door was shut. After a while, two men came out, and I heard Max's voice calling, "Shut the door after you!" I waited some more, and another man came along and asked to see Max and was ushered in. He came out with Max, and the two of them went off.

"Do you know when he'll be back?" I asked the girl.

"I really couldn't say," she answered. "I have to go to lunch. Do you want me to bring you a sandwich?" I took it that I was not supposed to leave. I said I'd like a sandwich, and she made a telephone call, and pretty soon a younger, rather pretty girl came in and sat at the secretary's desk. I tried to make some conversation with her.

"It must be interesting, working here," I said.

"Oh, you can't imagine," she said. She had brought a boxful of script with her, and set it up on a supporter, and began typing. She typed for a full hour, answering the telephone twice, and then the secretary came back with a waxed-paper-wrapped ham sandwich for me. I ate it, had a drink of water from the cooler, went down the hall to the toilet, washed my hands and face, combed my hair, came back, and waited two more hours.

When Max finally returned he did not look at me, but hooked a finger for me to follow him in. I did. This time he sat behind his desk, and after a moment of hesitation, I sat across from him. I still had my contracts.

"You wouldn't believe this business," he said. "Now you know what it is like to be an actor. Sit and sit, while crazy people run around fixing things. There is a great lady who works for me, or maybe I work for her, and I would not call her a dumb little cunt because that would be disrespectful, but everybody else does, and it makes you wonder. Somebody says something snotty to that little Cuban pimp she has installed in her dressing room, and the whole picture collapses. Highly paid executives running around like chickens with their heads cut off. Are you going to work for me?"

"Yes," I said.

I took a room in a hotel with monthly rates, rode to work on a streetcar, and spent most of my evenings reading or listening to the radio. I did not go see any movies. I figured it would interfere with my style. The office they gave me was in the writers' building—the same one they turned over to television a dozen years later—and had nothing in it but a long table, a chair and a typewriter on a stand. There was one dirty window, high up on the wall, and late in the afternoon a shaft of light would come in through it, land on the floor beside my chair and slowly move across toward the entrance. There were no interior doors in my wing of the writers' building. Down the hall in a wide place there were two secretaries behind desks. They answered the telephone, distributed the flood of memos, typed scripts and helped us with matters of format. They had the water cooler, the supplies and a few reference books. I was told that the girls could answer any of my technical questions, and they could, and did.

I came to work each morning at nine and left each afternoon shortly after six. No one came near me. I had no telephone calls, no memos, nothing. I got quite a lot of work done in the first two weeks, and I was able to turn in a completed sixty-page treatment of how I thought my book should be filmed. That was on a Friday. I took a bus to

Tijuana for the weekend, and at ten on Monday morning a tall man of forty with gray hair and a gray mustache came into my cubicle carrying my treatment.

"I'm Wes Horowitz," he said. "Come on down to my place." I followed him down the corridor into a wing of the building I had never visited before. Here, the offices had doors. His was filled with books, and instead of a table, he had a mahogany desk. The usual couch and a couple of easy chairs completed the furnishings. He got behind his desk and I sat on the couch.

"You look a little sick," he said.

I told him where I had been for the past couple of days, and he smiled, but not very much.

"That's a real pesthole," he said. "I like your treatment. It has a real cinematic feel to it, and it's climactic. The girl is wrong, but that's easy to fix."

"I'm sorry," I said, "but I don't know who you are."

"I'm your collaborator. We're going to do this together. I guess Max didn't say anything to you at all. How much did you get for the book?"

"A thousand dollars," I said. "Option."

"Ah. And how much a week?"

"Two-fifty."

"I'll bet he had the contracts ready. Son, you took a screwing. Not a bad screwing, just a routine, proper, well-executed screwing. Max is a marvelous screwer. I get three thousand dollars a week, and I've never written a novel or a play or anything else but screenplays. You should get at least half that. I don't have to ask you who your agent is, because it's obvious that you don't have one. But we can forget all about that, because you're locked in solid. Let's just go to work. I think you ought to come in here every morning, for a while, until we can get this thing shaped up."

I wanted to talk more about money, but it didn't seem like the proper time. He sat back in his chair and began to discuss my treatment with me. It went on all morning, and at lunchtime we walked to the commissary together, but once inside the big room he said, "See you back at my place," and went to sit with some people at a big round table. I ate alone, as always, and all afternoon we continued with the script. I was making notes, but all he did was lean back in his chair, often with his eyes shut, and talk. He was a good talker, and he had a good voice. By the end of the week I had dozens of pages of notes, and Wes decided that it was time for me to go back to my cubicle and start writing. I didn't ask him what he was going to do.

I didn't see Wes—or much of anybody else—for three weeks. After I completed blocking out the opening scene, I took it over to his office, but no one was there. I put the typescript in the middle of his bare desk top, with a note, and went back to work. A few days later I went back with another scene. The first one was still there, and appeared to be untouched. I put the second scene under it, added a P.S. to the note, and left. At the end of my first option period, I had done a little over half the screenplay, and it was all stacked up on Wes's desk. I went back to my own wing and had one of the secretaries call Max Meador's office and leave a message. That afternoon she came and got me. "You have a telephone call. Congratulations."

It was Max Meador's secretary. She told me that my contract had been renewed and that I was to keep working on the script. She must also have found Wes Horowitz, wherever he was, because the next morning he came and got me.

Back in his office he said, "I read your work this morning, and I must say you're doing nicely. I still don't like the way Maggie is developing, but we can save that for last. And do me one favor, please. Don't call Max. Always talk to me."

"I couldn't find you," I said.

"Make an effort. I'm on the lot every day, all day."

"You're never in here. I wouldn't know where to start looking."

"Don't get salty, kid. We have an excellent story going for us. There's no reason for friction at this point in the game."

I said, "It looks to me as if I'm doing most of the work and you're drawing most of the money."

For the first time since I had known him, he laughed; a good, deep, full laugh. "Kid, you're beginning to understand the workings of capitalism. But let me give you a few hints about the way things are. I say you're doing good work, and you are. But this thing is far from a script.

When you get done writing your full script, then I begin to do the hard work. Let's just say you're an engineer or an architect, and I'm a mechanic or builder. If I'd turned your script—as is—in to Max Meador, you'd be out on your ear, right now. As it is, I'm going to take my script—the one I'm going to build from yours—in to him as if it were a joint effort."

I didn't argue any more. At the end of the second six weeks, I had finished a complete script and turned it in to Wes. That afternoon I came back from lunch and found a termination of employment slip on my desk. I packed my few things and left. One of the secretaries looked up as I went past and said, "See you soon." I wasn't quite so optimistic.

Two months passed, and I was glad I had been saving money. I got no calls or letters from the studio, and my calls and letters didn't seem to get anywhere. My only mail, in fact, was forwarded from San Francisco, including one from a Hollywood agent, saying he thought he could sell my book, and asking me to write him. He couldn't have been much of an agent, or he would have known the property had already been sold. I didn't bother to answer or to call him.

Two months is a long time if you're anxious and lonely. My only hooks into the world were my mail slot and my telephone, and when I left the hotel it was almost always with the optimistic premise that I would return to find something thrilling waiting for me. Even so, it was hard to leave. What if I went up to Hollywood and Vine for a lemon phosphate and Max Meador called? By now of course I knew that I should have an agent to take care of things for me, to receive the telephone calls and make the appointments, to prod the studio into action, but I had decided earlier—once I was certain I had been taken over the bumps—that I would handle this one alone, finish it, and then, if Max offered me another contract, go straight to an agent.

The check for five thousand dollars finally came, and on the following day I was asked to come to Max's office. I felt that I was a changed man, and I had the security of knowing that I had enough money to last me at least a couple of years. I meant to drive my own kind of a bargain.

Max brought me in with an arm on my shoulder, and we sat again on the couch in front of the orchids, but Wes Horowitz was also there, on an easy chair, with his feet on the coffee table. He looked lazily wary, and when I smiled and saluted him, his only response was to point a finger at me and waggle his thumb.

"Well, my friends," Max said, "here we are all in the same room together, poisoned arrows shooting all over the place." He smiled over at me, a merry banker with merry blue eyes. "I see you got rid of the sweat socks. The minute I saw those sweat socks I knew I was dealing with a two-fifty writer. Now you are wearing something a little more appropriate, and I think maybe I am going to have to up the price a little, if I want you to work for me. But first, let me tell you something, with Wes right here in the room. Maybe you have formed some kind of conclusion about the kind of contract we can make on your next project. Is that so?"

I said that it was possible. "What I'd really like," I said, "is to have a look at the final script on the last project."

Wes snorted.

"That isn't necessary," Max said, "because as far as we are concerned here the last project is over. It is presently in the hands of Mr. Curtis Wavell, who will produce it, and who will probably change it around to suit himself. And then the director, whoever that may be, will do some changing and so will the stars. So that project is finished, and we go on to the next project."

"No," I said. "I have to know what I did that was right, and what I did that was wrong. If I sign a contract now, it'll be under the same conditions. I'm still an untried, untested quality." I had to gather myself emotionally without moving my body to make the next remark: "I'd rather wait until this picture comes out. If it makes money, then I'll know that at least part of it was my book, and maybe some more, my script. If there's any of my book or script left in it. If not, then I've failed and I ought to go home. If the movie is essentially mine, and loses money, then I still ought to go home. It wouldn't be fair for me not to."

Max blinked. "Are you dictating terms to me?"

"No, sir. I'm dictating terms to myself."

"I told you," Wes said. His face was tight, and I began to get a hint of what was going on. But I was still so wrapped up in myself that I couldn't believe it.

"Let me tell you something, before you saw off your limb," Max said. "You are thinking that maybe you could go to another studio with your screen credit from me, and make a better deal. But two-fifty writers do not get screen credits around here. The only credit that will appear will be that of Wes Horowitz. If I remember correctly, your contract doesn't even call for the name of your book to appear. My boy, it is not what the contract says that is important, it is what the contract does not say. Yours does not say a great deal. Fortunately, you have my word that if your work was any good I would hire you for another project at five hundred dollars per week. My word is not like a contract. My word is good. So relax." He turned his head casually toward Wes Horowitz and said, "By the way, how much of that script you turned in was this boy's work? I ask you purely for information purposes."

And that was it. Wes couldn't control the reactions of his body. He squirmed, took his feet off the coffee table, put them back, and his right hand, out of control, went to his face, the fingers touching his cheek, his nose, and then tugging at his ear.

"None of it," he said. "I had to throw the kid's script away. He can't write for the screen." He stood up and put his hands in his pockets. "I told you this before, Max. You're embarrassing me."

"I think it is worse than embarrassment," Max said. "You know I am not a complicated man, but where I was brought up you had to know how to handle every kind of human rottenness, and that goes double for the movie business. Now, I don't care about what you are trying to do to this boy, he can look out for himself. But for the past year and a half—yes, right back to that Baghdad picture—I have been watching you and watching you, and seeing you get more careless all the time. But I gave you the benefit of the doubt. But this time, no benefit. I happen to know to the line how much of this script is yours, and for your information, none of it is yours. I know you had it retyped and you destroyed the kid's copy. I know you have all kinds of evidence that the script is yours, and I know the kid has none. So you are going to get your screen credit. But I happen to be going to dinner tonight with some people I don't even have to name, and by tomorrow you won't be able to get work in this town sweeping the streets. Do you understand me? Just between you and I and the gatepost, your career is over. And that is a pity, because you are a good writer. But why did you turn into a thief? I'm not afraid to call you a thief in front of witnesses. I know that you started out by writing an original when you were being paid by me to work on another story, but what were you doing this time? You weren't even on the lot! Certainly I had you followed. Did you think I was a dummy? Did you think I got to be the boss of this studio by being stupid? Get out of here, my neck hurts looking up at you. Go."

Wes turned and walked out the door without saying anything. After a few moments I said, "He gave me a lot of help on the story. Really."

Max got up, went behind his desk, and sat down. He did not look happy. "Sure, I know. He's a good man. But you know what happens? At home he has a wife and nice children and halfway across town he has a girl friend bleeding him dry. Every day he is with the girl friend, and then goes home at night to his wife. I don't see how he does it. It would make a wonderful movie if we made that kind of movie. You wrote a wonderful script, for a first try, and I think the movie will show a nice profit. But don't kid yourself. Wes helped you on it, and maybe you will need help on your next project. But first we will try you alone. I brought you into this little scene today so you would know what things are like, but don't expect any favors from me."

"You look tired, Mr. Meador," I said. "Why don't I come back in a couple of days?"

"With an agent? Is that how things are? I tell you you did a nice piece of work, I give you my word on another contract, and you want to come back at me with an agent? Some bloodsucker to take ten per cent of your life? I would recommend one myself, but you wouldn't believe me. Go get yourself an agent. Where have the old values gone?"

I spent a bad night, but the next day I went up to Sunset, walked in cold on an agent, and within a week Max had sent me—through the agent—three books. I picked one I thought I might like to work on and we made a contract,

HOLLYWOOD WHORE   219

at a thousand dollars a week. I read in the trade papers a few days later that Wes Horowitz had gotten a job at Metro-Goldwyn-Mayer, and then some time later I heard that he had been fired again and had gone to New York. By that time I was occupying his old office.

I made and spent and gave away a lot of money while I was a screenwriter. I built a house in Coldwater Canyon and filled it with the kind of furniture I liked, bought all the books I thought everybody ought to read, subscribed to half a dozen newspapers and a lot of magazines, from *Partisan Review* to *The New Yorker*, hired a Mexican couple to run the place, and entered into the social life of the industry. As a screenwriter, of course, I was nothing. I did no originals, but translated other people's novels, plays and stories into scripts, and the only writers in town who were treated with respect were those with "class." It took me a while to discover what class actually was, and I finally decided that its first requisite was a contempt for Hollywood, a refusal to write for the screen. The second was reputation, or, in lieu of that, notoriety. Writers with class were offered top salaries, thirty-five hundred to five thousand a week, invited to name their own projects and provided with collaborators who could teach them the art of the screenplay. Writers with class were wined, dined and softened with all the sexual resources of the industry, until at last they gave in and signed a contract. From then on, they were treated with contempt. The ones who actually came up with some good writing for the screen could erase the contempt, but they could never regain their class. This was all outside the studio, of course. Inside, the writers, class or not, were treated as well as any of the other technicians.

I was not admitted to the industry's social life because I was a writer, but because it got around that I was Max Meador's protégé, and was headed for far better things than mere writing. The reputation probably began in the studio's mailroom.

The most important Hollywood parties of that time were not given by stars, but by studio executives, and people were invited because they were famous or powerful. These were not large parties, unless they were given for publicity on a picture about to be released or begun, and getting an invitation to one was out of the question. Everybody in the studio knew Max was going to give a party in honor of a member of the House of Morgan, a man named Jules Schofield, and everybody in the mailroom recognized the stiff little buff envelopes the invitations came in. We had fifty writers under contract at the time, and I was the only one to receive one of the envelopes. It was a mystery to everybody in the writers' building except me; I was certain it was a mistake. I thought perhaps some important person somewhere had a name like mine, and the secretary had made a slip. If that was the case, then the executive—whoever he was—would not be amused by hearing that the invitations had gone out and he had not gotten one. I called Max's secretary and told her about the invitation.

"It's for you," she said. "I don't understand it, either. Need a date?" That last was really a joke, not just half a joke, because you did not take dates to such parties. If you and your wife were expected, both would receive an invitation.

The impact was immediate. When I went to the commissary for lunch I was waved at by Saul Prentice and invited—for the first time—to sit at the Writers' Round Table in the far left corner of the room. This is where the formerly class writers and the big single-credit writers ate lunch. I sat down next to Saul, and a man across the table called out, "Let's not be cute. How come?" A few of the others laughed, and one or two looked embarrassed.

"A simple forgery," I said. That seemed to work, it got a laugh, and nobody asked any more questions. I ate quietly and listened to what had been reported as the wittiest conversation west of the Algonquin. The funniest thing I heard was a line attributed to Max Meador: "Sure a movie needs a story, but it doesn't have to be *your* story." The rest of the chatter was mostly about New York, and full of names that didn't mean anything to me at the time. While all this was going on, Saul Prentice was quietly asking me questions about myself and my project. I answered him and left it at that. The next day I didn't go near their table and nobody came over to get me, but on the following day Saul caught me in the lobby, took me by the elbow in the Hollywood grip and escorted me back to the round table.

"You must think we're a bunch of pricks," he said as we sat down.

"I didn't know they came in bunches," a lady writer said.

"No," said another. "They come in boxes."

"Really," Saul said to me, "why didn't you come over yesterday? We all saw you over there sitting by yourself. Good God, man, I admit I wanted to pump you about that invitation you got, but hell, you're a writer, too."

"Maybe he doesn't like us," the lady said. She had fine dark hair and white skin and she was looking directly at me.

"Well," I said, "everybody else here makes at least twice as much money as I do."

"Do you think that makes any difference?" she said.

"Doesn't it?"

A large plump man with honey-colored hair said, "Maybe he thinks we ought to join *him*."

"That's a good idea," she said. "We can go sit at his table, and he can stay here at ours." She stood up. "Anybody who sticks around is a suck-ass." They all got up but me, and went to the other side of the room, the unfashionable side, pushed together a couple of the square tables, and sat. I was alone at the round table, supposedly chastised for having received the invitation to Max's party. Everybody in the room saw what was going on, and when, in a few minutes, another of the round-table set came in and started toward me, they all yelled and he turned and joined them. I could hear their laughter and conversation throughout lunch.

A couple of hours later, Saul Prentice came by my office, knocked and came in.

"I guess we were a little rough," he said. "When I brought you over, I didn't know what Rebecca was going to pull."

"Why did you walk away with them?" I asked. I was still a little angry. "You could have stuck with me. They don't pay your salary, do they?"

He sat down. "Money isn't everything, as you seem to think."

"It is in this business," I said. "Who do you guys think you're kidding?"

"Okay, you're mad. I don't blame you."

"Get the fuck out of my office. I have work to do."

"Now, listen, kid, it doesn't pay to offend too many people around here—"

But by that time I was typing, and he shut up and left. When I got out to the parking lot that evening, I found that somebody had let the air out of my tires. That broke it, and I sat down on the running board and laughed until my face was wet with tears. Then I got up, wiped my face, and started laughing again. I was helpless, and when Rebecca pulled up in her yellow convertible and said, "Get in," I could hardly get the door open.

"Car trouble?" she asked. That started me again, and I laughed all the way to the gas station. She had to give instructions to the attendant about my car, and I had to make an effort to tell the attendant my address, so he could deliver the car. "I'll pay for it," she said, "and I'll take you home. That's Coldwater Canyon, right?"

"You don't have to pay for anything," I said. "That's the first time I've laughed since I've been in Southern California. I should pay *you*."

"I didn't let the air out of your tires. That was Hal Weintraub. He thinks he's a wit. Hollywood makes children out of everybody."

By the time we got to my house I was all right, and I asked her to come in for a drink.

"I'm too old for you," she said. "I'm fifteen years older than you, at least."

"I really want to offer you a drink," I said.

"Now, that's downright insulting. I accept."

I didn't care how old she was. She was no taller than me, well-formed, with beautiful skin. It would have been perfect revenge for me to make love to her, particularly if I just knocked her down and raped her. The only thing I would have to fear would be her witty report to the round table, and I didn't care what those people thought. The patio was in shade and we went out there. Ofelio came out in his white jacket and asked me in English what we wanted to drink, and then in Spanish if the lady would be staying for dinner. Rebecca wanted a double Martini, and so I asked him to make a pitcher of them, and I'd tell him later about dinner.

She said, "What was all the Spanish?"

"Household details."

"You're not used to having servants, are you?"

"No, and in fact, I forgot they were here. I was going to throw you down on the ground and assault you. But if I did, Ofelio and his wife would probably quit."

"That tells me how attractive I am to you. You probably would have succeeded. Does that tell you how attractive you are to me?"

"Not really. How about telling me what all that stuff at the round table was about? I really don't understand."

"First you tell me how you managed to ace Wes Horowitz clear out of the studio."

"Oh, he was one of your friends, is that it?"

I could hear the telephone ringing in the house, and I excused myself and went in. It was a man from *Daily Variety* wanting to know the name of the picture I was working on and what my past credits had been. He wanted a lot of other information but I finally got rid of him. When I went back out, Rebecca was pouring our Martinis.

"I really don't know what any of this is about," I said. "I didn't ace your friend out of the studio, although I was in Meador's office when he got fired."

"You're not kidding, are you?"

"No. Why would I bother?"

"Forget it. I guess I should say I'm sorry about this noon. I am, not for what we did to you, but for what I did to myself. It was one of those good childish opportunities to make a scene. I should have controlled myself better. But I thought you had gotten Wes fired, and we all thought you were snubbing us when you didn't come to the table. It didn't occur to us that maybe somebody wouldn't want to sit with us. Now you be honest: were you snubbing, or did you sit by yourself because you're used to eating alone?"

"So this is Hollywood," I said. "City of glamour and excitement. How about staying for dinner?"

She told me—in effortless Spanish, much cleaner Spanish than my Mission District brand—that she would be delighted if only, *por favor,* she could use the telephone for a few moments.

Later, she said, "I can see that you're used to eating alone. The only time you opened your mouth was to stick some food in it."

"I'm sorry. I guess I do have bad manners. No excuses."

"I take it you've lived alone for most of your short life."

"Not really. Just the last few years."

"Does your family have any money?"

"No."

"That's odd. You haven't told me the price of everything in the house, you haven't taken me through, pointing out which is the bathroom and which is the kitchen. You know, you're being very un-Hollywood. Is it an act?"

"Look, why don't we talk about something else, for a change? I'm not used to talking about myself. I don't think I would like it."

She smiled. "All right. Let's talk about the studio. No? Me? No." She went over to the bookshelves, carrying her third or fourth Martini. "How about James Joyce? Shall we talk about Jimmy Joyce?"

"Oh, balls."

"Do you think *Ulysses* would make a good movie? With Clark Gable as Bloom and Bobby Breen as Stephen? What the hell can we possibly talk about if you won't talk studio politics or get poisonal? We don't even know each other."

"Let's get to know each other. Better."

"You mean sex. But you're only a child. I'm fifteen years older than you."

"No, ten, but why count? Are you going to hide behind your age?"

"I'm afraid I have to hide behind something."

"You really mean that, don't you?"

She sat down on the couch, her face in shadow. "Any female piece of meat you can get into your house is fair game, I suppose. Look, we've been social, I've made my apology for this afternoon, now I'm tired and I think I ought to go home. I know, you're just a nice young man, not at all what we thought. But nice young men like a lot of sex and that's why you're acting the way you are. But I'm not a nice young man. I'm a dirty old woman. I've had all the impersonal sex I can take. No offense, child. But that let's-go-upstairs-and-make-discoveries routine gets a little—tiresome."

"All right. I admit that's what was on my mind. But you can't blame me. You're very pretty."

"For a woman my age."

"You're making me feel like a fool. I can hear you tomorrow, telling all the gang what an eager little beaver I am."

She put a hand to her forehead. "Oh, my God, you didn't think I'd—" Abruptly she stood up, rocking a little. "No wonder. It's my own fault. That's my reputation, and I guess I deserve it. I better go home."

"I want you to stay," I insisted. I came up to her and put my hands on her arms. But no luck. Some more of the same kind of talk, and I finally had to walk her to her car. Mine was not there yet.

"Can you drive?" I asked.

"No."

"Then you better come back in the house. I'll get you some coffee, honest."

"That's the second time you've insulted my femalehood tonight. Okay."

We went back in. Ofelio and his wife had gone home a couple of hours before, and so I went into the kitchen and made coffee. When I was done, I poured a cup for her, got a beer for myself out of the refrigerator, put them on a tray and went into the half-dark living room. She was asleep on the couch, her feet up, her shoes off. I put the tray down on the coffee table, took my beer, and sat in an easy chair. She hadn't had that much to drink.

"Wake up," I said again. She opened one eye. "Sit up and drink your coffee." She did. It was cool enough to drink without sipping, and while she lit a cigarette I went to get her another cupful. When I got back she said:

"That's a myth about coffee, you know. Feed coffee to a drunk, and you've got a wide-awake drunk on your hands."

"Are you married?" I asked.

"Yes and no. My husband left me. A long time ago. We're not divorced yet, don't ask me why. I haven't seen him in a couple of years. Ah, God. He encouraged me to develop my talents as a writer. He moved heaven and earth to get my first play produced. He didn't want one of those wives who just sit home in New Rochelle and quietly go to pieces. He, he, he; God, I won't even use his name. George. Isn't that a perfect name for a husband? George and Becky. My play ran just over a year, and I made a hundred and forty thousand dollars. He helped—*George* helped me invest it. He said, 'You never know, maybe we were just lucky this time,' and invested the money in blue-chip stocks. We weren't sleeping together much, but George was awfully proud of me. He was making seventy dollars a week as a clerk in Wall Street—well, he wasn't exactly a clerk, but something. He never told me about what he really did. I guess men don't. That was when

I got my first offer to come out here. I sent off a very funny telegram and forgot all about Hollywood. Then the stock market went. George was awfully clever about the market, and none of our holdings were on margin accounts. We were just going to ride out the storm, and pretty soon prices would start to rise again. He explained this to me very carefully one night, and then tried to make love to me, but it wouldn't work, and the next day he didn't come home from Wall Street. After a while, I knew he wasn't coming home any more, and so I came out here. He's selling insurance, these days."

She frowned over her coffee. "Put in a penny, out comes the story of my life. Ugh, I hate the taste of copper."

"You have nobody at your house waiting for you?"

"Waiting? No. 'How come a pretty ol' gal like you ain't got a man somewheres?' I wrote that line myself, once. It was practically my sole contribution to the film."

"It's a good line, but I won't use it. Come upstairs. You'll sleep here tonight."

"All right."

She followed me up the stairs and into my bedroom. The drapes were pulled aside and we could see down the canyon into Los Angeles.

"Let's take off our clothes," I said. "Do you need any help?"

"I can manage," she said. She was finished before I was, and she slid open the glass doors and went out onto the terrace, naked. In a minute or two, I followed.

"I like the feel of the air against my skin," she said. "Even though it makes goose bumps."

"I have another bedroom, across the hall. You can use this one by yourself, if you want."

"No, you're right. I need sex just as much as you do. Maybe even more. Just sex, not love. But I wish you hadn't made me say it."

I took her hand and we went back into the bedroom. I slid the glass door shut, and she said, "Let's leave the lights on. I want to look at you."

"You never go out in the sun, do you?" I said.

"Let's stop talking. We can talk any time."

We got on the bed and I kissed her, and felt her go tight, and then relax, and then go tight again.

"What's the matter?"

"Maybe we better turn off the lights."

"Is that better?"

"I hope so."

It took some doing, but she finally relaxed, and we started being together, and playing, and losing ourselves. Not too quickly we made love, but it turned somehow into a struggle between us to get there together and in the end it failed. I was sorry but there was no point in saying so. We lit cigarettes and lay quietly.

"You know," she said, "when you get to be my age, it isn't all that easy. If you get out of practice, it takes a while to get back. It's hard to lose your mind, when that's all that's between you and extinction." She kissed my shoulder. "We should try again, sometime. If you want."

A long time later, she said, "It doesn't mean anything to you, does it? I wish I could be that way. But I can't. I was brought up wrong. To me it always has to mean something. That's what's wrong. I'm not out of practice." She sat up and said, "Oh, I've leaked on your sheets. What will the servants say?"

"Never mind."

"You must be a genuine aristocrat, not to mind what the servants think. Or maybe it's just that you don't care what anybody thinks."

"I care what you think," I said, but she just laughed.

"Do you know the last time I had an orgasm?"

"Do you want to talk about it?"

"Why not? That's another of my favorite lines. 'Why not?' It supplies motivation for devil-may-cares. It was with a call girl. I was at a party at a friend's house, and you know me, four drinks and who shut out the lights? I passed out in a garden chair. When I woke up it was cold and the house was almost dark. I went back in and took the shawl off the piano and sat in the dark, trying to get warm. The house had a playroom downstairs, and the only light was coming from the stairwell. Pretty soon, I saw a shadow coming up the stairs, and then a beautiful light-and-shadow naked girl came into the living room, lit a cigarette and sat down on the piano stool. Her hair was long down the back, and she didn't see me, but sat there humming to herself, and smoking. At first I was going to say something bitter and sarcastic, and then I realized that I didn't know who she was, and so I just said hello. She didn't seem surprised that I was there, and when I asked her what was going on downstairs she told me she was a call girl. I asked her a lot of questions, and she said, 'You talk like a man,' and came over and kissed me. I froze up, of course, and wouldn't talk to her any more. She got dressed and came back into the living room and gave me one of her business cards. 'If you feel like it,' she said, 'it's twenty dollars.' Then she left.

"It was two weeks before I called her. I got good and drunk all by myself. You see, I couldn't forget that kiss. It was so friendly, somehow. And what she said about my talking like a man. As if she knew things about me I hadn't dreamed. More than that. I called her and told her how to find my house, and then I got so dizzy that I took a cold shower and drank coffee, to sober up, to get myself in shape to tell her to go back home. I was going to give her the twenty dollars and cab fare and send her home, you see. But when she got there and came in, and I saw her in the light, it changed. She's such a simple little girl. She has a nice, innocent face, modeled lips and very light blue eyes, auburn hair. She sat down and we talked, and I got us drinks, and then after the drinks she came over and kissed me again, and I kissed her back. We lay in bed kissing for a long time before she started anything, and by then I was just as eager as she was. Afterward I asked her if she was a Lesbian—seems like a silly question—but she said no she wasn't as if she didn't care if she was or not, and I asked her if she thought I was a Lesbian, and she said, 'I thought you were, over at that other place, but I know now you're not, 'cause you're just like me, you like sex,' or something like that. But I came, with her, and I haven't been able to do that with a man since I was first married. Do you see?"

"No," I said.

"I can give myself to her, because it can't lead anywhere. It can be sex without love, without engagement. That's what I needed. Does this bother you?"

"To tell you the truth," I said in the darkness, "it excites me. I don't know about the psychological parts, but the idea of two beautiful women making love to each other, well . . ."

After a moment, Rebecca said, "Why don't I call her to come over here? We could all be together. We might all learn something."

I didn't tell her that for months my only love-making had been with the prostitutes of Tijuana and aside from that I was almost without experience. I just said, "Okay," and told her where the telephone was. While she was calling, I went down to the kitchen and got another bottle of beer. I looked at the clock on the kitchen wall: it was only a little after one. I went back upstairs. Rebecca was sitting on the edge of the bed, the lamp on, her hands in her lap.

"Is she coming?" I asked.

"She'll be here in a little while. The price is fifty dollars."

"Oh. I have some money downstairs."

"No, let me pay for it. It was my idea."

"Oh, come on. My treat."

She laughed. "The perfect host."

Waiting around for the girl was embarrassing, and we didn't talk much. When the doorbell finally rang, I was upstairs in my robe drinking beer, and Rebecca was downstairs naked with the money I had given her. It was another ten minutes before the two of them came into the bedroom. Rebecca's eyes were glittering with excitement, and I suppose mine were, too. The girl was pretty in a conventional Scandinavian way.

"This is Joanne," Rebecca said.

"Joanne, I'm pleased to meet you."

"Don't you have a pool?" she asked me.

"I'm sorry, no. I don't swim very much."

"Oh, it wasn't a social question. But it's going to be harder to get started without a pool."

"Jesus," Rebecca said. "I'm going downstairs." She left the room.

"Is she mad?" I asked.

"I don't think so. Just shy. Are you shy?"

"Just a little. What did she tell you?"

Joanne began undressing quickly. "Let's not talk. Let's just party."

"Are you in a hurry?"

She smiled. "Oh, no. I just love to party, that's all. Do you really want to talk? Sometimes talk gets in the way."

"Let's not, then," I said. She came to me, and, after a while, Rebecca came back into the room and joined us. It went on, in one form or another, until nearly daybreak. After the barriers came down, anything was possible. There was no more shyness, and even when I was out of it for a while I was still part of it, just by being there on the bed with them. Even when I left the room I still felt part of it, and when they brought me back in I was not made to feel like an intruder. They wanted to use me, and I wanted them to. It was really a lot of fun.

I heard the birds starting up outside. Rebecca was asleep, and Joanne was lying next to her, looking at me. She smiled lazily. "I love you both," she said. "You're such sweet people." Her lips were puffed, and mine were, too. I was beyond exhaustion, and nothing seemed quite real. I reached out to touch her on the thigh, just a touch, and felt myself slipping out of consciousness.

When I woke up I was alone. The alarm clock was buzzing. My head hurt, but not as much as I had expected. I wanted to stay in bed, but I knew that Maria would have my breakfast ready in half an hour. I got up and took a cold shower. When I got to my office there was a memo on my desk: "Saw yr car at the gas stn. Pick me up for lunch?" It was signed with a big sprawling R. I got her on the telephone. Her voice was bright, almost brassy, as it had been on the day before. This slowed me down for a moment, because I had been used to hearing her speak in low, almost hesitant tones. "Did what I think happened actually happen?" I asked her.

"I'm glad you called. I have two men in an elevator throwing lines at each other, and they're boring me to death. How did you get to work?"

"I took a cab. I asked you a question."

"I didn't even think. I could have picked you up. I had to go home and shave, or something."

"I guess it did. Do we eat in the commissary?"

"With that pack of wolves? Let's not. Let's see if we can pick up some box lunches and eat out on the lot somewhere."

I made a date to pick her up at one, and got back to my writing. It was difficult to do. Too much was going on in my mind. There were too many unanswered questions. Finally, I gave up and asked for an appointment with Max Meador. His secretary asked me to wait a moment, and then Max's voice came on the line.

"No appointments today," he said. "What can I do for you?"

"Mr. Meador, why did you invite me to your party?"

"Are you nervous? Do you want me to tell you what to wear?"

"I'm just curious, that's all. It doesn't seem . . . well, right."

"Believe me, it's right. What's the matter, are the writers giving you trouble?" Before I could answer, he said, "Never mind those smarty New Yorkers. Let them cry on the way to the bank."

I knew it was wrong, but I said, "Well, can I bring a girl with me?"

"A girl? What girl?"

"Rebecca Stennis," I said.

"I thought you said girl. You let me think about that proposition. Meanwhile brush up on your sweetness and how to keep your mouth shut when you are surprised. Is that all you wanted? Are you wasting my time with social questions?"

When I told Rebecca what I had done, she was angry. We had gotten the box lunches and were eating in a grove of trees just off the Western street, sitting on the ground.

"Max'll think I talked you into asking me," she said. "Don't you know these parties are formal? My God!" She bit into her sandwich, chewed for a moment, and then stopped. She looked at me, her eyes wary. "You didn't do it on purpose, did you?"

"What do you mean?"

"Just exactly twenty-four hours ago I publicly humiliated you with that march across the commissary. This isn't your way of getting back, is it?"

"No. Do you think I could do something like that after last night?"

"I don't know. You're so awfully young. If it's revenge, it's beautiful. But the rules are, we keep our petty jealousy away from the main building."

I spent the rest of the hour trying to convince her that I had made an honest if stupid mistake, and then asked her to come home with me again that night. She refused, saying she had some other things to do. I was a little upset, and we didn't go back to the writers' building together. In the late afternoon Saul Prentice stopped in my doorway, not smiling this time.

"Do you have a minute?" he asked.

I asked him to come in. I wanted to make peace with everybody, if possible. I hadn't been able to get any work done that day at all. He sat on my couch, crossed his long legs, and said:

"Something I ought to explain. There's quite a number of writers in town, I don't know exactly, probably about four thousand, with maybe a quarter working at any given time. When a new one comes along, he pushes an old one out of a job. That simple. You can't just drop into a business as complicated as making movies without stirring up a little mess. It's not like going to work in a filling station. Anyway, I'd like to apologize for all of us, and ask you to join us for lunch at the round table." He held up a hand to stop me, if I had been about to say something. "I know it's not a big honor or anything like that. But you're obviously not just a come-and-go hack, and us writers got to stick together. Believe me, bad feelings don't help. Okay?"

"You know, this is just what you'd say if you were setting up some kind of a joke. I can't tell if you're sincere or not."

"I know this is ridiculous between grown men, but would you shake hands with me?"

We stood and shook hands, and grinned at each other.

"All right," I said. "Even if it's a gag, it'll be worth seeing."

"No gag. The children will behave."

After he left I wondered how a man with three hit Broadway musicals and a string of successful films to his single credit could act so strangely, but of course it all became clearer in the course of time.

Max called me into his office the Monday after his party. I did not get a chance to sit down.

"Why shouldn't I fire you?" he asked me.

I didn't have an answer.

"Your contract has another three weeks to run. I could terminate it out of my pocket without leaving this room. But I have to ask you if you have any excuse. Do you?"

"Not really," I said. "I got scared. My stomach started hurting and I decided it would be better for me if I stayed home."

"Your stomach hurt. Are my parties an ordeal that your stomach should hurt? Young man, if you thought you were being clever not to come you have another think coming. I did not ask you to my party so that you could have fun talking to the most important men in this industry. I invited you for a reason. Do you know what that reason was?"

"No, sir."

"*Business.* Movie business. I just work here. The purse strings are back in New York City, and one of the things those people want to know is who are the bright young men we are grooming to take over when we pass on. Do I have to say more? Mr. Jules Schofield was supposed to go back to New York today and tell his Wall Street friends that he met a very bright young man at the home of Max Meador, and that Max Meador is looking to the future of the company, even if nobody else is. Do you think I want to sit here in this office someday and see a punk kid walk in with a vest and a briefcase and tell me that he has come out from New York to take my job? I *built* this place! I tell you, if it came to a proxy fight this morning I don't know who would win."

"I can't really believe that would be my fault," I said.

"Your fault? What has it got to do with you?"

"Mr. Meador, if you had bothered to tell me any of this before, I probably would have come to the party. I'm sorry I let you down."

"You didn't let me down. In my life you are a cipher. Don't think I sat around worrying about you. I covered myself without any help from you. But I wonder if I didn't make a mistake. I wonder if a young man who gets sick to his stomach is ready for the big time."

"Are you going to fire me?"

"Let me tell you that there are perfectly good reasons to fire you right now and give your picture to somebody else. Oh, I'm not like some around this business, I don't have ten people working on the same story. But life would go on without you around. Go on back to your office, but remember that you have made me a disappointed man in you, and keep that thought in the front of your mind. Well, why don't you leave?"

"Look," I said after a moment, "I'm no sensitive artist, but I don't think I can work with that kind of thing hanging over my head. Maybe it would be better for everybody if I just quit."

He took off his glasses and closed his eyes, raising his eyebrows. "You can't quit. You are under contract. You quit, and you never work in this industry again."

"It doesn't look as if I'm going to, anyway. All you have to do is say the word, and I'm out. It looks to me as if all I have to lose is three weeks' pay, which seems a little strong for failing to go to a party. But if that's the way it is, that's the way it is. I'm sorry I let you down, but I guess I have to quit."

I left his office, walking on needles and seeing little of what was going on around me. I did notice an actor, whom I knew only from having seen his pictures, wave and smile at me, which didn't help. I sat down at my desk, knowing I should begin to clean it out, knowing I should get off the studio property before something took over inside me and made me call Max and beg for my job, but I didn't. I just sat and stared at the wall. I could hear the typewriters clicking all over the building, and I thought about all the men and women busy grinding out the cheap flashy romantic slush Max was so good at making and the public was so interested in watching. When I caught myself envying them, I got up and went down the hall to the toilet and splashed cold water on my face. When I got back my telephone was ringing. It was Max.

"Young man," he said. "You don't have to quit. Don't be foolish. I apologize for calling you on the carpet. It's just you are a lot younger than I thought you were. When I was your age I was much older."

I made some kind of apology and thanks and hung up. At lunch I went to the round table and sat between Rebecca and Saul Prentice and when they asked me how the big party had been, I told them I hadn't gone, and saw the entire tableful of people stop, stare for a moment and then go back to what they had been doing as if they had just seen a human being commit suicide. After a while, Saul said, "I wonder why you weren't barred from the lot this morning. Did Max come in?"

"We had a talk this morning," I said.

Everyone was listening but few of them were looking at me.

"You weren't fired?" Saul asked.

"I guess not."

"Wheels within wheels," Saul said, and under the table I felt Rebecca's hand grip my thigh and squeeze. I looked at her and she smiled and winked. We left the commissary together, and I asked her to have dinner with me.

"All right," she said.

"In fact, let's eat at my place."

"All right."

"Aren't you going to ask me what happened?"

"All right."

"The hell with you, then."

She laughed and took my hand. "You poor little fellow. You poor, poor little fellow. You snapped your fingers under Max's nose and got away with it. What do you need me for?"

That night Rebecca and I tried to make love by ourselves. Joanne, the call girl, had been with us twice since the first time, and our desires and energies revolved around her, but this time we wanted more, we wanted to be together and alone. We were even careful not to drink too much, as if the alcohol had been calling Joanne, and not Rebecca. Neither of us said anything about love or marriage or age, but all three things were on our minds, and so after the servants left and after we had exhausted the subject of Max Meador and studio politics, we went upstairs hand in hand, undressed and climbed into bed. After only a few minutes I knew it was going to be hopeless, at least from my viewpoint. I continued to try, but we were both forcing it and we knew it. I swore and got up out of bed and lit a cigarette.

"What's the matter?" she said.

"I don't know."

"You're so tense."

"Is it just me?"

"You sound bitter. I'm sorry."

I pulled back the drapes and moonlight flooded the room.

"Oh, that's beautiful," she said.

"Maybe it's the full moon," I said.

"You're so young. This is the first time for you, isn't it?"

"What do you mean, first time?"

"The first time you've failed."

Until that moment it had never occurred to me that such a thing could happen, or had happened to other men. I didn't answer her, but sat down in a chair, on top of some of her clothes. I pulled at the cigarette and looked at her, sitting up in the bed, her breasts exposed, her skin pearly in the light. She looked very young and, completely beautiful, but instead of making me feel better, it made me feel worse.

"What do you think it is?" I asked her finally.

"It isn't anything. Nerves. You're tired. We were trying too hard. I wonder why."

"There's something we're not saying."

"Yes. Joanne."

"I didn't mean that. That can't be it."

"Then what?"

"Never mind."

Her voice changed, back to the sharper, louder tones she used around the studio. It sounded odd, coming from the beautiful half-seen girl on the bed. "Listen, how tough are you?"

"What do you mean?"

"I think I know what's bothering you, but I wonder if you're tough enough to hear me say it without hating me."

"Try me. What difference would it make?"

"I think you're frightened. For the first time in your life, you're making pretty big money. You bought this house and a car, probably some stocks or real estate, or whatever you spend your money on, and you're probably in debt. You came into Hollywood on a half-good book and you've been climbing steadily ever since. You don't know why you're in with Max, but today, or maybe the afternoon of that God-damn party, you began to see that it could all disappear. So you acted like a baby; if my job depends on going to a party, the hell with it. Today you almost got yourself fired, almost quit, and saw yourself out on the street again. Fighting for every fifty cents you get. It scared you, it would scare anybody. You found out what I found out years ago, that you can't run your own life, that things can happen to you, and so you're terrified, but you can't show it, even to me, and that's about it."

I defended myself. "That's not it. It's worse than that. We're trying to screw, and what we should be doing is making love. I have to tell you I love you. We haven't done that. But that's it. We have to quit faking."

She laughed. "Yes. All right. I love you. But that won't do any good."

"Not saying it this way, it won't. I admit what you said is probably part of it. I want to marry you."

She was quiet for a long time, and so was I. A breeze came up and I could hear branches knocking against the side of the house. I remembered having paid twelve hundred dollars for full-grown trees, because the garden had looked so new with young ones.

"No," she said.

"Why won't you? You can get a divorce."

"No, you don't want to marry me. I'm too old for you, and you know it."

"Don't try to tell me what I want and don't want. I know what I want. Marry me."

"No."

"Why not?"

"Do you want to have children?"

"No. I want you to marry me."

The argument went on fruitlessly, and what had happened to me, even before it had a chance to happen to her, got obscured in the argument. My body was damp with sweat, and I smoked two or three more cigarettes. It was as if we were having a story conference instead of discussing our most intimate lives. Finally, I gave up.

"Oh, forget it," I said. "You don't love me and I probably don't love you. Call Joanne. At least we can try to fuck."

When she came back upstairs and told me Joanne wasn't at her number, I was relieved. Rebecca could go home now, and I could go to bed and to sleep, and maybe tomorrow everything would be different. But instead of letting it happen that way, I said, "Well, can't you get somebody else?"

"Another call girl?"

"Yes. You must have some more numbers."

This time, when she came back upstairs, she turned on the light. I sat blinking up at her, and she said, "You know, this could be interesting. I had to call a friend and ask for a number, and I got one. The girl will be here in about twenty minutes. Twenty dollars. That must be the standard price. I wonder what she'll do when she finds the two of us. Oh, I guess she must know. Unless she thinks I'm a Lesbian. A Lesbe alone. Her name is Oona. Can you imagine? Let's have drinks."

I drank some whiskey and took a hot shower. The girl was something like forty minutes late, and by then I was drunk. I thought that being drunk would help me forget what had happened earlier, but it didn't. The girl was ordinary-looking and had very small breasts and meaty buttocks, and I just couldn't get interested, until Rebecca and the girl began to be involved with one another and were ignoring me. I took a voyeur's pleasures from the chair across the room, and eventually became excited enough to join them, but it wasn't like it had been with Joanne; it wasn't anything but sweaty sex. Rebecca seemed to be enjoying herself, however, and after a while I left them alone together and went into the spare bedroom and fell asleep on top of the bedspread. When I woke up in the morning my body was covered with welts caused by the tufted spread. Rebecca was gone, the girl was gone, and I was certain that I never wanted to see either of them again.

Three weeks later, after my contract expired and I had turned in my completed treatment, I was given a contract at twenty-five hundred dollars per week for a year, not as a writer, but as script supervisor for the entire studio. That made me everybody's boss, and I no longer ate lunch at the round table. I had continued to eat there because Rebecca's picture had ended and she had gone to New York to try to get her play produced. When she came back I was the boss and she had to come to see me to get an assignment. We never spoke of the evening with Oona, and we didn't date. It was odd, because I continued to see Joanne from time to time, and so did Rebecca.

1965

IV / One of Those
Big-City Girls

Natalie was brought very slowly, drowsily, from the long death of sleep by the sounds of children playing outside, below the bedroom window of her apartment. She recognized first the shrill voice of the little girl from the apartment below, and then those of the narrow-faced Italian boys from across the street. They were arguing about whose turn it was to come to bat, and in a few minutes Natalie was fully awake and slowly pressing the sleep from her eyes with thumb and forefinger. It was Saturday morning and she did not have to go to work. Outside, the argument resolved itself and the morning quiet returned, broken only by infrequent shouts and the distant sounds of the Market Street traffic. Natalie closed her eyes again and turned over in the bed, feeling the warmth of the sheets against the bare flesh of her body. She buried her face in the pillow and smelled the faint remnants of her perfume, and she saw in her mind the face of Jerry Hoeffer, her occasional lover. Lately her memory had been playing tricks on her, and she was trying to remember if Jerry had been with her the night before, or if it had been a dream. She saw his full-lipped ironic smile, the calculated heavy-lidded look of his eyes, as he leaned against the bedroom door, hands folded across his chest, head tilted slightly downward as he watched her undress. That had been the supreme moment, and Natalie remembered her own feelings, which came from doing as he asked and preparing herself for *him,* while he watched her from across the room, fully dressed, as always, waiting until that last moment when she stood before him (her skin now slightly cold, both in the recollection and in reality) and waited for his next words of command. Then he slipped out of the room, as he had before, to undress neatly and privately in the bathroom, always hanging his clothes on the hangers on the back of the door, while Natalie waited for him on the bed.

She knew that the purpose of this elaborate foreplay was to humiliate and degrade her and that it was only in this way that Jerry could bring himself to even the pitifully scanty climax he managed to accomplish. But it did not matter to her, because she was in love with him. She knew also that the size of her love emasculated Jerry, and that he was potent only with cold women (if she could believe the stories of conquest he told). She knew what a complete swine he was, but that did not matter to her; she loved him, and on this Saturday morning she wished he was in the bed beside her so that she could hold him and kiss him. But the fact was, Jerry never stayed the night with her, never had breakfast at her apartment, and, for that matter, almost never took her anywhere.

His habit was to come over late in the evening, "make love" to her and leave. Aside from that, the only times they saw each other were at the office, where a discreet aloofness prevailed so that Jerry's position would not be endangered. Jerry was twenty-five years old and Natalie forty-five, and this alone, Jerry felt, was enough to "screw things up" if it got out that they were lovers.

Most of the time when they were together she was either in misery or in anticipation of it, and the only genuine pleasure she got from him was in remembrance of those rare and subtle moments which were beyond Jerry's power to destroy. She forgave him his need to torture her and she hoped that somehow her love would change him and make a man of him. As for her falling in love with a man twenty years her junior, she almost defiantly refused to question her motives, particularly since she could do nothing about it anyway.

Her throat was beginning to hurt from the aftereffects of yesterday's cigarettes and she was beginning to feel the edges of a headache, caused by staying in bed too long after awakening. Sighing, she got out of bed and moved across the thick carpet to the closet. She opened the door without glancing at herself in the full-length mirror and removed her pink cotton bathrobe. She closed the closet door and this time watched herself as she got into the robe, looking not at her body but at the lines of tiredness around her eyes and the lines that appeared beneath her chin as she reached back with both hands and fluffed her hair out from under the collar of the robe. Her eyes were slightly puffed, too, as if she had been crying. She could not remember having cried the night before, so she attributed the puffiness to oversleep. They had gone to bed at a little after eleven and it was now midmorning. Thank God for those damned kids, she thought, and she immediately smiled at the idea; it was so reminiscent of Jimmy in his prime, Jimmy years and years ago, when they slept all day on the weekends and partied all night. Jimmy had been her husband from 1928 until 1946, and lately she thought of him often, her memory again playing tricks, so that she sometimes remembered things which had not happened, and could not bring into focus things which really had.

She went into the small kitchenette and stood at the blue-and-white-tiled sink, assembling and filling the automatic coffee maker. She was thinking, her mind not quite out of control, but wandering as a mind does in those few endless moments before sleep, of a party she and Jimmy had attended in Berkeley, perhaps in 1929 or 1930. They had promised each other not to get too drunk to make love, and the anticipation of what was to come had given the party an aura of warm sexuality, so that when she had been dancing with a heavy man in a striped blazer she had permitted herself to pretend that the man was Jimmy, and she nestled against him until the man made a natural mistake and put his hand on her breast. She could remember the forward-backward sensation, her impulsive reaction to permit the hand—even encourage it—while at the same time knowing that it was not Jimmy's small hand or Jimmy's body she was pressing against. She broke away, perhaps too abruptly, and saw the quick mask of indifference slip down over the man's round face. She could remember all this very clearly, including the blue and yellow crepe streamers twisting down from the ceiling, the buzzy noise of the orchestra, the slippery waxen feel of the floor, the semidarkness. She could remember seeing Jimmy, dancing with a thin girl dressed in flashing silver, his wink over her shoulder, telling Natalie that he had seen the whole thing and it was all right, that *later* would come and they would be sober enough.

Natalie shook a pinch of salt down into the heaped coffee and placed the lid on the maker, plugging it in on the stove. She got a cup and saucer from the dish dryer and put them on the stove beside the maker. Then she set the oven timer for five minutes, and, shaking her head to shatter the image of Jimmy's winking face over the silver shoulder of a slender, long-forgotten Berkeley girl, she went into the living room and sat down at the table in front of the two wide windows. But the mechanical ritual of preparing the coffee had not worked to rid her mind of the memory.

They had not, after all, stayed sober enough to make love. She owed it to herself to remember *that* part, too.

Because that was more like Jimmy. She should not, she reminded herself, permit her mind to remember only the pleasant, fulfilling isolated moments, but force herself to recall at the same time the aftermaths of those times, when things had not gone so well. They had gotten to bed at last at six or seven in the morning, the sun making the yellow shades bright and garish. Jimmy had vomited twice into the toilet and then passed out, face up, across the bed, with fluttering snores emerging from his mouth. She saw now, with instant clarity across the years, the small fleck of vomit on his thin mustache; she remembered fully her own vertigo as she fell backward across him and passed into a whirling limbo of nightmarish drunken nausea.

Natalie shook her head again and the images vanished. But the traces of nausea remained, and she felt her cheeks grow cold as she stared out the window down Market Street. The nausea caught on now and probed into her belly. She brought her hands together on the white tablecloth, her knuckles edged angry red, her fingers squeezing and washing each other in compulsive anxiety. The nausea was real; it was not just the result of a sickening remembrance. It came from within her, familiarly, from down deep in her belly.

Now she knew she had cried the night before. There was no denying it. Jerry had been unusually cruel to her, unusually vindictive after the few flickering moments of actual love-making. He had been, she now remembered, well above his usual form for cutting her down, for insulting her body, her face, her age, the roots of her hair, the color of her eyes, the way she spoke, the way she walked, the food she ate, the clothing she wore. His dry sour grating voice came to her out of the darkness of the night before, its usual false timbre gone as he told her how much he despised her and despised himself for having anything to do with her. She cried then, turning her face so that he should not hear the crying sounds, hunching herself down over her pillow and feeling the neutral warmth of his body against her back.

A moving cramp passed downward through her belly and at the end of it came a faint, small fluttering. She waited in the stillness of her apartment. The bell went off in the kitchen, indicating that the coffee was done, but Natalie did not move. She sat waiting. Then it came again, just the tiniest *beat*, in nervous muscular thumps, like foetal kicking.

She reached up absently with her left hand and stroked the muscles of her neck until they softened, and then broke herself out of the chair and went into the kitchen, the edges of her cotton robe making soft fluttering noises against the swift movement of her legs, catching and tugging slightly at the invisible day-old growth of hair on her calves. The red light glowed on the chromium coffee maker and Natalie picked up the pot and poured a full cup of coffee, the steam pushing gently against her face as she bent over the cup. She could still feel the faint drumming beat in her belly.

After a few delicate sips of the hot coffee, she went down the carpeted hall to the bathroom, and when she came back to the kitchen she picked the short yellow pencil off the top of the refrigerator and made her daily mark on the calendar; a tiny cross over the number of the date: May 12, 1955. Then, using the tip of the pencil, she counted back to the circled date and discovered what she knew but had forgotten, that her period was seventeen days late. She frowned. She had been thinking that it was only "a few days."

"I've never been that late," she said. She put the pencil back and picked up her coffee cup and took it in to the table. Then she had to go all the way back to the bedroom to get her cigarettes from the bedside table. Usually the routine of awakening included moving the cigarettes from the table to the pocket of her robe. This morning she had forgotten to do this and it irritated her. She drank the first cup of coffee and smoked the first cigarette, waiting for the feeling in her belly to go away. Often now before the first cigarette she felt funny pains, but this time they did not go away. Instead, the nausea returned and she had to put the cigarette out before she was halfway through, her fingers tight, jabbing it down hard into the ashtray, knocking the coal loose and pursuing it with the bent stub. She felt sick and wanted to go into the bathroom, kneel at the toilet, embrace it, be sick into it; but she was afraid, even now, to give in to the admission of her nausea or to permit herself to think of the drumming within as anything but a nervous tick or the freak manifestations of an attack of gas.

She sat quietly waiting for the symptoms to go away, her eyes down on to the white tablecloth, not wandering or unseeing, but fastened to a tiny pale-red spot of tomato juice, the merest fleck, now dried hard into the texture of the cloth, surrounded by an aura of pale pink no larger than a dime. Idly, she reached for the spot and pried loose the scab, depositing it in the ashtray. Then the spot was gone and only the aura remained. But Natalie could not keep her mind on such trivia for long, and with a shake of her head she lit another cigarette, and at that moment heard the rasp and clank of the mail slot below. She rose automatically and walked down the hall and down the carpeted stairs to the street level. She scooped up the single brown envelope and opened the front door, blinking at the brightness of Carson Street. With her free hand she pulled her robe tight around her legs and stooped down and picked up the quart of milk from her box. Coming erect again she saw the little girl who lived below her, seated on the curb across the street. She was alone, dressed in a pair of tiny faded overalls and a bright-yellow blouse, her dark hair in twin braids down past her ears.

"Hi, Natalie," the girl said.

"Hello, Nancy. Where did the boys go?"

Nancy shrugged. "They went away someplace."

Natalie smiled fondly at the little girl. She was a sweet and innocent child, and when Natalie sat with her the few times her parents had enough money to go out to a movie they watched television together, and Natalie always had to keep from laughing aloud at Nancy's intense belief in the action, particularly in the cartoons.

"I'm just sitting here thinking," Nancy said. "Good-by."

"Good-by, Nancy," Natalie said. She went back upstairs with her milk and mail, and put the milk in the refrigerator and took her telephone bill into the living room, opening it with the edge of her thumbnail. The bill was for eight dollars, and included several toll calls to her daughter, Rita, in Walnut Creek. Because of Rita's pregnancy, there had been an increasing number of calls and visits from her daughter, who in a sudden surge of daughterliness was confiding each symptom, every possible variation, twinge, attitude and plan to her mother. Had it not been for her own anxiety about such matters, Natalie might have enjoyed this renewal of her relationship with Rita.

Natalie smiled as she put the telephone bill on her small fold-out desk with the other bills. Rita had an obstetrician, a husband who was making a lot of money (rather than just talking about making a lot of money), a home of her own and everything a woman could want for a child-to-come, and yet she was more anxious about it than Natalie had been about Rita's arrival, in 1930 (when Jimmy, like so many others, was out of work and they were living in a one-room apartment in Oakland). But even with all the modern improvements available to people with money, children still died at birth, and mothers still died bearing their children. They could cut the percentage drastically, but they could not eliminate the possibility of death, and so Rita had some justification for her worry. Statistics, Natalie knew, were utterly meaningless when you were grunting and shoving a living thing out of your belly and the pain was as sharp as knives.

Natalie did not have a daily newspaper delivered to her door. During the week she picked up a *Chronicle* at the streetcar platform at Market and Castro and read part of it during the trip to the business district, finishing it on her morning coffee break. On the weekends she walked around the corner and down the sharp hill to the little grocery on the corner of Nineteenth. It was usually sunny and she enjoyed the walk. It got her out of the apartment. On this particular morning she had dressed, walked down to the store and come halfway back up the hill before she realized the pains in her abdomen were gone and that in fact she felt fine. It was a bright noon and not too hot, and when she got back into her apartment she made herself an unusually large breakfast of tomato juice, toast and poached eggs, with two more cups of coffee. While she ate she read the newspaper from one end to the other, skipping only the sports section and the real-estate and automobile ads. This was all part of her Saturday routine, and it made her feel comfortable. After breakfast she knew she would vacuum the apartment, clean up the kitchen, scrub down the bathroom fixtures and then shower and dress for downtown. During the afternoon she would visit the department stores, looking for some nice maternity clothes for Rita, whom she was going to visit on Sunday. She often spent weekends in Walnut Creek with her daughter and son-in-law, but this time she had a date for Saturday night, and would not go to Walnut Creek until Sunday morning. Having the housework and shopping to do gave a sense of fullness to her day, a sense of purpose. When she was good and busy she did not think about herself.

It was nearly two-thirty and she had just finished making up her face when the telephone rang. She slid the cap down on her lipstick quickly and walked through the apartment to the living room, picking up the instrument and catching herself just in time to avoid an embarrassing eagerness. The cultivated mindlessness of the past few hours dropped away instantly, and she felt swelled with expectancy and an anxious eagerness. But it was not Jerry Hoeffer; it was not even Rita, or her son, Jay. It was Bill Hastings, calling politely to confirm their date for that night. Almost with impatience she agreed to the time and place of their meeting and listened to his small talk.

Natalie admitted to herself the pleasure she got from looking at her freshly washed body in the tall mirror in the bedroom, seeing the firmness of her skin, its color from the light above a pale pearly white. It was a body that had not gone out of fashion in twenty-five years: the hips full but not buxom; the abdomen a mere inch rounder than flat; the breasts neither large nor small, shapely, still firm; the thighs and calves full and sleek.

She turned sideways in front of the mirror, aware of the immodest nature of her actions but secure in her privacy; no longer after these many years afraid to look at herself and feel good from what she saw. The Natalie she could see had lasted all this time and because of the contrary evidence before her eyes, the time might not have passed at all. Of course it was not the body of a *girl,* but that of a *woman.* Yet with so much time having whispered across her skin, there should have been more evidence to see: a swelling here, a sagging there, the skin of this place gone a dead pale white, the legs become fine-ribboned with blue veins. It was impossible, looking at such evidence, to doubt her immortality.

She had not suffered, dieted, watched her weight with more than normal female caution; she wore no beauty aids to bed, nor, with the exception of an accentuating tint, did she dye her hair. It was now as she remembered it from long ago, the dark auburn which summered into copper gold; not yet brittle or stiff, still fine spun-soft gently waving hair. She shook her head, making the hair fly out, its tips brushing the flesh of her shoulders. She could feel its near weightlessness and see it glinting in the light from above; a mantle of auburn around her shadowed oval face.

Her eyes met her eyes in the mirror, and the game of vanity was over. She smiled to herself and then, on sudden impulse, winked. Laughing softly she moved to the vanity table and seated herself before the smaller mirror, feeling the brocade of the cushion against her bath-softened flesh. She began at once to make herself up.

Normally Natalie would have half dressed before going to work on her face and hair, but tonight she was still savoring the pleasure of nakedness, the cool free feeling of the air against her body; and there was really no reason to dress first. She was not going to wear anything that had to be pulled down over her head. She began with her hair, giving it the one hundred brush strokes that were almost a nightly ritual with her; her wrist smoothly manipulating the brush, her mind comfortably vacant. From the living room came the sounds of soft violin music, emerging from the FM radio Rita and Tod had given her last Christmas, and as she brushed she listened to the music, the brush moving in quarter time. That finished, she ran the comb through her hair a few times and was satisfied. Next, her eyes: first the mascara, then the touch of green shadow at the corners, patiently rubbed in the way a painter of the Flemish School might lick the strokes of a detail. Then with her short pencil the careful, almost painful, lining of her eyebrows, retaining the natural arch and drawing them out only a fraction of an inch beyond normal length. The pencil clattered back into the plastic tray in the drawer, and Natalie uncapped her lipstick and touched it to the ball of her little finger, rubbing her cheeks to a soft pink. She applied the lipstick to her lower lip, feeling as always the cool oily sensation, tasting the rich perfumed flavor, rubbing the lips slowly together until the coating was even on both upper and lower lip. It was a grotesque exercise. She took a Kleenex from the plastic dispenser on the table and placed it between her lips; selected a perfume from the dozen bottles, applied it first to her finger tip and then to the cup of her neck, between her breasts, a faint touch on each shoulder, and then, as an after-thought, the merest brushing behind each ear and at the nape of the neck, her finger rubbing it into the soft hairs. Still involved in the ritual of the thing, she touched her scented finger to the hollow of her navel and to her hips, not planning consciously on any such detailed investigation of her body that night, but going through her ritual of these many years, even when its significance was not consciously clear.

This occurred to her as she removed the Kleenex from her lips and happened to look again into the mirror. It was, she thought with some emotion, as if she were expecting Bill Hastings to make love to her that night. She was not dressing for a date; she was getting ready to receive a lover. And tonight she was going out with a young man she had never dated before. For that matter, one whom she hadn't the slightest notion of sleeping with. It was as if she were getting ready for Jerry to come over. She even felt the same way, the same tenseness, the same sad tone of expectancy (for it was all wasted on Jerry, she knew). It even occurred to her that the perverted elaborate foreplay Jerry engaged in—the curtness, the voyeurism, the bragging, the cruelty—was not so very different from this ritual of hers; yet she could not help assigning a great difference in moral value: hers was preparation to receive a lover and to give him the greatest possible pleasure from their lovemaking; his seemed designed to repel rather than attract, and to withdraw as much pleasure from her as possible. She could not help thinking this was bad.

For a moment she was confused. She looked down at the bright smear of crimson on the white tissue in her hand, and somehow this frightened her. No one had ever treated her cruelly before; her beauty had seemed to act as a barrier between herself and all viciousness. But now she was frightened for herself. Jerry treated her horribly and she loved him. Because of it or in spite of it, she did not know. Jimmy had never treated her this way and her love for him had disappeared. But there were good reasons for that. She was not getting ready for Jimmy; he was long gone out of her life. How could she confuse Jimmy with Jerry? For so long she had been his goddess, his very word for her: goddess; he was standing behind her, so unlike Jerry, his face happy and eager, impatient; he was lying on the bed waiting for her. The delusion persisted, and Natalie did not want to turn around and look at the bed.

She *felt* his presence in the room. She could almost smell his cigar. She was having nearly tangible delusions.

A thin trickle of sweat ran down her side. She looked with confusion into the mirror. The face was not hers. It was a woman, but it was not Natalie. Her stomach gurgled with cold reality and the room pulled into focus again. The violin music was still there, and the strange yet familiar face still stared back at her, but she was herself again and she knew where she was and that she was alone. She was sitting in her bedroom, getting dressed, getting ready to go out. She stood up and walked nude into the living room, where she tapped a cigarette out of the red package, lit it with her small silver lighter, and then returned to her vanity table. She decided there was no reason for this confusion or for the slight feverish feeling she was still experiencing. She leaned forward and looked at her eyes, widening them unnaturally. There were no traces of disease, but the irises were expanded and her eyes seemed larger than usual, almost as if they were swelling out of their sockets. She probed her body for other signs of illness but found none, other than the unusual warmth of her skin. Of course it could be the natural raising of surface temperature after taking a bath, but the bath had been some time ago. And, just to get the record straight, she was not getting ready for Jimmy, or even Jerry. It was a boy named Bill. There was nothing to get tense about, and no reason at all to think about Jimmy, long gone out of her life except for their occasional meetings when he was out of money, cold sober, extra polite, vague and almost tragic.

All this would be wasted on Jimmy now, as it was on Jerry, whose only love of her beauty was as a thing of his, not hers, a pretty trinket, like his long blue Jaguar. Of course Jerry treated the Jaguar with almost pathological care, bestowing on the machine the love and respect he claimed he felt for no human other than his mother. And it was wasted, she thought firmly, on Bill, too, because she was not getting ready to make love to him. She took a puff of her cigarette and blew the smoke down among the bottles on the vanity. *Or was she preparing to make love to Bill?* Exorcise Jerry, get him out of her system. Have a lover who will care for her, make her the beloved in the act, go back to that other, unperverted, kind of love.

Natalie knew it was important that Bill make a pass at her, because if he did not it all would have been wasted, whether she accepted the pass or not. If he made a pass at her then she was what she wanted to be, however degrading and embarrassing it was for her to realize this. It was not that she wished, like Circe, to reduce all men to swine through the device of her beauty; she did not think men were beasts. It was something else, something far more difficult to find words for, something about touching and being touched, about human warmth together, yet tinged with the need to be able to accept or refuse, structured into a game of Yes or No. Her violent cry of yes to Jimmy had lasted over fifteen years, and that had begun as the warm bursting love of a child; it was not asked to develop itself into anything more mature, since Jimmy was willing to accept it and turn it in on itself. So until now Natalie had never practiced any of the wiles of courtship on any man, and with Jerry Hoeffer she was of course not permitted to. He held the whip and she danced. Perhaps this is what she intended to do with Bill: play turnabout, so that for once in her life she would have the prerogatives of beauty and be given the chance to exercise her choice.

But she knew she was out of touch with the methods of courtship. She wondered what they did nowadays, if she would be behaving stupidly if she refused Bill. She did not know what girls did these days. If she could believe what she read and heard and saw in the movies, then modern girls simply went to bed with anyone on any excuse (except the dream girls in the romantic movies, who never went to bed with anyone under any circumstances). But she could not believe this, even though Jerry said it was true (implying that it was true in *his* case, at any rate). Her own generation had been the subject of a myth also, and she knew how false the myth was. The Flaming Youth. The Lost Generation. What nonsense! Particularly nonsense when given lip service by people of her own age, who pretended that they had been more than they were at one time, that they had been wild and dangerous and debauched. For that matter, Natalie had read only one honest book about the 1920's, *The Great Gatsby,* by F. Scott Fitzgerald, which by its very tone denied the actuality of the events it recorded. That was what it had been like, as Natalie remembered it. A veneer of fraud obscured the true memory, and the fraud was that they had all been disenchanted, when in fact the dominant emotion Natalie remembered from before the Depression was unbridled optimism and hope, based on nothing more tangible than their youth itself. It was an attitude that Natalie could not expect any of the young today to share; not after 1945. If they, the young, Jerry's generation, made love without discrimination, perhaps it was because they halfway expected the world to disappear before morning.

In 1948 Natalie had come home in the afternoon and found her daughter, Rita, on the living-room floor with her steady boy friend. What Natalie first saw were her daughter's white thighs spread wide, the hand of her boy friend pressed intimately on her belly; the boy's wide-eyed expression as he turned toward the sound of the opening door, the pink smears of lipstick on his cheeks and jaws, the collar of his white shirt bloody with Rita's lipstick. Rita sat up quickly and flipped down her skirt and snapped at her mother, "What are you doing home?" Her eyes were passionately angry, and Natalie was the one to be embarrassed, along with the boy friend. Rita was righteous about the whole thing, and after the boy left told her mother that she was capable of taking care of herself and that it was essentially none of her mother's business what she did with a boy she was almost engaged to.

If Natalie's mother had caught her doing any such thing in 1927, before she married Jimmy, Natalie would not have been defiant, she would have been shamed. But not Rita. Rita's and Jerry's generation made Natalie's look puritanical.

But perhaps she was wrong about this, too. Perhaps her own experience with Jimmy had been atypical. The first time he had kissed her was on their fifth or sixth date, in the year 1927. They had taken the ferryboat across the early-morning bay through swirling summer fog and then driven across the already sunny peninsula to the coast highway, and wound their way down over the cliffs to Half Moon Bay. Natalie and Jimmy were in the back seat of the phaeton automobile, and in the front seat were Jimmy's friend Mickey Ross and his girl. Natalie could not remember what the girl looked like, but she could still see Mickey's thin pale face and his long black hair flying in the wind, his long yellowish crooked teeth behind heavy lips, which spoiled the effect of his expensive clothes. She did not see him in the car, but standing on the beach at Half Moon, looking slightly absurd in his tweed topcoat, tight at the waist, hands in his pockets, cigar in his mouth, his hair down over his eyes.

Jimmy was dressed more appropriately for the occasion, wearing a straw hat, a white shirt with thin orange chains on it and his collar off; wide-bottomed flannel trousers and narrow pointed shoes. But Jimmy was very cold until the fog dissipated and the sun broke out in the sky, turning the beach sand bright yellow, and the bay itself a delicate emerald.

They picked a spot high on the crescent, only a few hundred yards from where the rocks began to edge the high cliff, and Jimmy and Mickey, each carrying a bottle of beer, went up among the rocks looking for driftwood, while Natalie and the girl (not the girl in the silver dress, Natalie remembered suddenly) sat in the now warming sand and watched the boats from the crab fleet ride the soft swell of the bay. The girl talked about the fast launches of the bootleggers, which used this bay to deposit liquor brought in from Canada and Mexico, for the bay area trade. The boys came back with some old gray boards smelling of kelp and built a fire, and not long after that they ate their picnic lunch, and Natalie tried a bottle of the needled beer. After that she and Jimmy went for a walk, down the line of the retreating tide, their shoes and socks in their hands, the seething water running up over their ankles. Natalie looked back once and saw the other two in an indistinct huddle, and she knew they must be kissing. It gave her an almost violent thrill of anticipation and danger. She was seventeen years old, and she had been kissed by boys only twice in her life.

"Look at this place," Jimmy said. His straw hat was tilted back and with his hand he gestured at the flat wooded land between the bay and the hills. "Undeveloped. Twenty miles from San Francisco and nothing here but a few farmers and roadhouses."

Taking her hand he turned, and they began walking back up the beach. Natalie kept her eyes down, on the sand, telling herself she was looking for sea shells, but knowing she was trying to avoid having to look toward Mickey and his girl, wrapped in their blanket in incredible intimacy, kissing.

"Maybe I'm new at this game," Jimmy said, meaning that he didn't think it meant anything, "but it seems to me this would make just one heck of a real-estate development, right here along the beach. They could subdivide into lots with fifty-foot frontage on a little road that winds along the edge of that bluff, and have an easement to each property come right down here on the beach. Be a kind of summer resort."

"It sounds like a good idea," Natalie said. "I wonder why nobody ever thought of it before."

Jimmy snorted. "People got no imagination. People are crazy, that's why. Santa Cruz is thirty miles farther down and people go there for the summer all the time. Drive right by this place and don't even see the possibilities. Hell, this could be a real playground."

"You know," she said. "I like it the way it is. Nobody around. Almost wild."

Jimmy snapped his fingers. "Boy! The thing to do is get an option on the land, and instead of just subdividing, why hire your own contractors and actually build the cottages yourself! Little places, you know, not too big and not too expensive, one, two, three bedrooms, big windows facing the water. Not that crazy expensive crap they have in Florida, but places for people who have to work for a living. You wouldn't even have to landscape; hell, nobody ever landscapes their summer place."

Natalie smiled at Jimmy; she had to, the way his eyes were bright and his hands waving at her as they walked up the beach. By the time they got back to where Mickey and his girl were (they were now sitting up, wrapped together in the blanket, drinking beer) Jimmy was talking excitedly about the big boat pier and the merry-go-round, the concessions, the big restaurant, the rows of sleek white pleasure boats; and he even had a name for his multimillion-dollar development: "Half Moon Bay Estates—San Francisco's Newest Playground." Natalie could tell from his eyes that he could actually see his development—that double-edged trick he had of visualizing—and when he looked down the long yellow strand of beach the cottages were really there, in among the cottonwoods and willows; a long jetty and pier, the boats, the sounds of carnival music. But Natalie could not see it; she could see only the natural land and the sea, and above the valley, a circling hawk.

Jimmy told his idea in outline to Mickey, who was the son of Jimmy's boss and a fellow salesman, and Mickey gave a short sharp laugh and got to his feet, brushing the sand from the back of his overcoat, and Natalie saw, with the blanket unfolded, that his girl's blouse had two open buttons. The girl noticed it, too, and quickly buttoned them, blushing, and then Mickey pulled her to her feet, and the two of them strolled off down the beach, hand in hand.

"Come on," Jimmy said. He had two bottles of beer opened, and he handed one to Natalie. "Let's climb to the top of the cliff; get a better view."

She followed him over the rocks to the trail leading up the back of the grass-covered hill, her eyes on the path, and when they got to the top, stood beside him, looking below them, at the ocean.

"Jesus H. Christ," Jimmy said. "Look at that."

They could see from the top a new bay, much smaller, around the point to the north, edged on both sides by rocks, the sand of the beach a dazzling white, the surf heavy and green. Beyond, to the north again, were the long thin brown fingers of a reef, stretching outward into the blue ocean; and beyond the reef, the infinity of the ocean.

"I'll be God damned," was all Jimmy could say.

They could not resist. They picked their way down the steep incline toward the new beach, and then across the high-piled white sand, both of them hot and happy, to the rim of sand above the surf line. For some time they just stood holding hands, watching and listening to the rattle and crash of the waves, the final electric seething of the white foam as it rose high onto the dry sand and turned it gray.

"*This, is, the, place!*" Jimmy said at last, and he turned to her, close enough that she could almost smell him already. His eyes fairly burned with eagerness and vision. "Half Moon Bay is nothing! This! This place! Cut a road into here, maybe fifteen houses in all, privacy! None of that carnival crap or cheap housing. Big stuff, private stuff!" He grinned at her and said, "And we'll take the best of the lot for ourselves, the very best one, right up here at the end. Our place. Can you see it?"

This time he said it anxiously, pointing toward the south end of the beach, where the cliff rose sharp and dark above rocks in the ocean. "*Can you see it?*"

She could not, but she said yes, she could see it, and he came closer until his body was gently touching hers, and he kissed her on the mouth, not taking her by surprise but fulfilling her tense, half-realized expectations. She was surprised by her own response to the kiss, the way she placed her fingers on the back of his neck, feeling the strong muscles, feeling the quick hotness flushing through her body. After a few moments they pulled apart and opened their eyes and looked at each other, the moments seeming to her sacred with the still-felt pressure on her lips, and through the buzz of her own excitement she heard his vaguely worded apology and felt his cheek just barely touching hers, and then his mouth again and the heavy sweet smell of his breath. He did not whisper that he loved her; but she knew it, and he knew it, and they both knew that he could have taken off her clothes and then his own and she would have made love then and there. They both knew it and they talked about it later, much later, and laughed at the codes of behavior that kept them apart. They loved each other and said nothing about it and did nothing about it.

Natalie felt a twinge of regret now, twenty-eight years later, that they had not after all made love, and then with reality remembered that the first time they did make love it took over two hours and was not very pleasant. For that matter, she remembered ironically, she had also loved the other two boys who kissed her, and if they had been adroit in the least, she might have lost her virginity to either of them.

Love, she thought. What does a seventeen-year-old virgin know about love? Jimmy had been a handsome, fast-talking dapper young man with a lot of money and a bright future in real estate, but that was all she knew about him. She hadn't even known that much, as things turned out. Thinking on it now, she understood that the warm smell of his breath was as influential as anything else, that she had fallen in love with the sound of his voice, the smell of his breath, the texture of the skin of the palms of his hands, the brushing touch of his clothes against hers, and so many other physical, sensual things. She remembered the small delight she got from seeing the way his upper and lower lips met, the firmness and artistry of their construction, like the lips of a beautiful child. She had loved the clean fingernails of his hands and the smallness of his feet, the timbre of his voice when he said certain words. He had a way of saying words that made them more real than themselves, so that you could hear the echo of other words and ideas in them: the ooze in booze, the itch in rich, the honey in money, the dove in love, the whisk and frisky in whiskey; so that the words became the things and had a quick beauty of their own.

She had not fallen in love with a man, but with the isolated fragments of her own sensual perceptions of a man, the things she wanted to have from him, as if they were lost fragments of her own soul, to be gathered back and restored to her.

But she knew, too, as she rolled the hose on to her smooth, fresh-shaven legs that Jimmy had not proposed to the innocent virgin, but to the image of her he saw in his mind, the Natalie she would become under his careful hands. She would have to grant him that; compared to the only other two men she had ever slept with, Jimmy was an artist, a passionate master, a beautiful lover who gave and gave and gave and at the same time took with ardent rapacity. Yet if his voice had once been the rich melody of her life, now it was a rattling in her ears.

She finished hooking her stocking to the garter belt straps and then looked again into the mirror at the fine round line of her belly. She wondered if she should remove the garter belt and put on a panty girdle, to flatten the line. She decided against it. The belly curve was one Jimmy had worshiped; he despised boyish women. She moved to the bureau and slipped on panties and hooked herself into her brassière, feeling her breasts cup and swell and separate. She looked at her bust line in the long closet mirror. Fine, high, full breasts. She watched them move while she gave her hair a final brushing and combing, and then decided to line her eyes a little more strongly, carry the line just a little farther out, to give her face a slightly wanton look. She finished, examined her work, and was satisfied. The beautiful woman. The high-rumped, slim-waisted beauty.

Natalie did not become aware of the quality of her actions of the past hour until, rummaging through her bureau for the black leather purse which went with the dress now covering her body, she found her hand resting on the blue box of sanitary napkins, and before she could check her mind it told her to take one along, in case her period should begin that evening. Then the cascade of remembrance began, and her face went hot from shame at her obscene vanity, and her chest constricted with fear. She went to the bed and sat, her hands folded across her lap. It began while the room darkened around her, the faint drumming in her belly, and she lay back, her eyes seeing the trim around the walls, which made the ceiling of her room look like the inside of the lid of a hatbox, and the room closed in on her while the ripple of pain crossed her spine and traveled deep into her heart.

She saw herself. She saw a painted whore in a gay hatbox, lying on this satin bed where this night this young man would rouse himself to copulate with her. He would see, of course, when the layers of paint and silk and rubber and slimy black mascara were removed, the pregnant old lady with the dyed red hair. He would hear the old lady grunt and smell her rotting breath, and he would be just a little disgusted, but not enough to stop, just enough so that he would hurry, and she would feel his hurry and see his face as he got up to leave.

She burst into frustrated tears at the loss of her youth. If she only had back her youth, everything would be all right. But it was gone; gone forever, and she had nothing to look forward to but disgrace, degradation, and at last, but probably not soon enough to save her from the misery of her lost youth, death itself. The folding wings of death. The gray wings of death. First the hoofbeats and then the arid specter; herself on her knees, eating the black mud of fear, and then the fluttering and the vanishing.

The mood passed quickly. Her eyes destroyed, she went to the bathroom and washed her face, and then with rapid skill made herself up again, taking only a few minutes. She was in a near rage at the duplicity of her mind. Always, at the onset of her period, she began feeling depressed and had funny pains and attacks of hypochondria. It was normal, part of a woman's life. It happens every twenty-eight days. And every twenty-eight days it seemed like a new thing. So she could either wallow in it, like a hog in the mud, or go to dinner with Bill Hastings and have a pleasant evening. Bill seemed like a nice person. Maybe he would pull her out of the fog.

She ate, and she watched Bill Hastings eat. Bill, dressed in a dark-gray well-cut suit, was talking about Beethoven, his warm voice enthusiastic without sounding eager, and she watched his fingers adroitly manipulate the two wooden chopsticks, raise a morsel of dripping food to his mouth, insert it between words; she watched the rhythmic motions of his jaw as he chewed, saw his bobbing Adam's apple as he swallowed, and she wondered, for the first time in her life, why this obscene ritual was undergone in company, surrounded by elegant manners and habits of fond association: the Sunday dinner, etiquette, the customary preliminary gesture of affection on a date; when in fact, and with only a little imagination, *eating* was *filthy*.

She conceived instantly, while Bill talked about the adaptation of Schiller's poem to music, a turnabout society in which people ate privately in tiny closets, obliged to eat by the needs of the body, but necessarily ashamed of it, due to the implications of the act: *the grinding up and swallowing of garbage* (indeed, the plate of heaped vegetables, meats and sauce in front of Bill very much resembled garbage); while in the same society going to the toilet was a public function, to be undergone whenever possible in company, and accompanied with gay conversation, comparison of feces, urine color, et cetera. Her mind raced out of control. In such a society we wear masks over our mouths and kissing is the final act of sensuality; our genitals are exposed, and when a baby sucks its mother's breast it is not the breast we cover but the baby's mouth.

All this time Natalie was eating rapidly, voraciously, as if by filling herself with food she was defying all taboos of a mad society. Bill was saying, "As a matter of fact, I cry nearly every time I hear it." He smiled at her, waiting for her reaction.

"Cry?" she asked. She stopped her fork midway to her mouth. "Cry at what?"

"The Ninth. When I hear something like that, I'm suddenly made aware of a kind of enlargement of the human spirit that makes all the petty meanness and stupidity insignificant. True, we're a civilization that murders children, but we also produce Beethovens. Don't get me wrong," he added quickly. "I don't think Beethoven is worth one murdered child. I don't agree with Faulkner on that. But the Beethovens, the Goyas, the Shakespeares, the Dostoevskys *understand* that we're capable of so much more, that we are so much better than we act, that humanity really does have nobility in it; that we *can't* give up hope. That's what they do; they give us hope in the face of overwhelming evidence. Hitler kills six million Jews, men, women and children alike. Beethoven tells us not to abandon hope in the face of Hitler's insanity; that we can be better than this."

He dabbed at his mouth with the corner of his white napkin.

"Again, let me make myself clear. I don't mean that Beethoven did those murdered Jews any good; nothing could help them. They were in the hands of a madman and a society driven mad by the horrible half of the human spirit. All Beethoven does is tell us that the horrible half isn't the whole animal. Otherwise, suicide would be the only honorable act left."

Natalie asked him what he meant by that, and continued eating. Bill was finished with his meal, and broke the sticks and placed them on his plate.

"You're easy to talk to," he said. "I have to admit that I don't usually talk about such things with women. But here's what I mean about suicide: Hitler begins his slaughter of the Jews, not because he himself originated the idea of the pogrom, but because he was taking political advantage of a situation that already existed. The Jews were the traditional European scapegoats; Hitler just went farther than anyone else. So, we have the Jews being murdered, and everybody in the world knowing it. What did we do? We did nothing. Nasty letters, that kind of thing. 'Oh, well,' we said, 'if Hitler wants to kill a few million Jews, it's none of our business.' So, by extension, we're as guilty as he was. It's like standing by and watching one man beat another man to death, and not interfering. We're accessories before, after and during the act."

"Well, what could we do?" Natalie asked. She was beginning to feel flushed and heavy, and a little irritated at Bill for talking so pleasantly about something so horrible.

"As for me, I could have quit college and joined the British army. I thought about it, and then selfishly I decided that I should finish school first, and then see. So I'm as guilty as Hitler, by extension. The fact that I did enlist after college doesn't help me out; I didn't do it when I knew I must; I waited until it was convenient."

"But what could you have done alone? You're just one man, and one man couldn't have stopped Hitler. I think you're taking too much blame on to yourself."

He laughed. "No. Did you know that when the German commander of Warsaw ordered the Storm Troopers to go into the ghetto and begin machine-gunning down the Jews, that several of the Storm Troopers (and remember, they were picked men, the toughest, meanest brutes alive) revolted and about a dozen of them committed suicide?"

In Natalie's mind, already dizzy from having eaten too much and drunk too much, there was an image of a gigantic brutal Storm Trooper, the shattered bleeding bodies of children strewn at his feet, his Tommy gun in his hands, his eyes large and dulled and terrified. She felt a welling of pity for the poor dumb brute who had just learned that he was a man and that he had gone, beyond recall, past self-justification. She wanted to fold her hands across her breasts and bend her head and cry. But she was in a public restaurant, so she merely looked at Bill, and he saw what was in her eyes.

"I'm sorry," he said. Gently, he began again: "I was trying to say that those Storm Troopers were better men than myself, because I realized what they realized, and I did nothing about it. My last year in college, when the Germans were in France and Holland and Norway, I used to wake up at night in the dorm, and my body would be cold with sweat, and my hands shaking from cold. I was terrified of dying; that's why I didn't enlist right away. I was still terrified when I did enlist, but by then I had no other choice. They were beginning to draft everybody. So I lost my chance for self-respect. But not forever. And I didn't win it back by killing a few sad Japanese soldiers who would have died anyway. I won it back by realizing that it isn't an all-or-nothing battle; that men can do wrong and do wrong and do wrong, and still have a chance to be men. That's the thing about Beethoven's Ninth that makes me cry; it tells me that I am a human being, too, and just because I was a coward once doesn't mean that I have to go on being a coward. If I thought that, I'd have to kill myself. Like a lover killing his beloved for betraying him."

He smiled at her. "Does it make any sense, or have I gone too far for a first-date dinner conversation?"

"You opened up to me," she said. "You're defenseless. Why did you do that?"

"Because I don't give a damn," he said. "No, that's not true. I don't talk this way to women. I guess you just affected me, that's all."

Natalie wanted to reach across the table and take his hand. She wanted to blurt out to him, "I'm sick, I think I'm pregnant, I'm in terrible trouble, help me!" But of course she did not. The waiter came and asked if they wanted anything more to eat, and Bill paid him, and as they were getting up to go, there was a slight commotion at the next table, when a large, red-faced woman wearing a fur coat gave a whoop and fell backward, crashing into another table. In the confusion and suppressed embarrassment, Bill took Natalie's hand and winked at her secretly, and they left the restaurant, laughing all the way down the stairs to Grant Street. Natalie was dizzy and happy, even though her stomach felt distended.

Grant Street was jammed. Cars were stopped and their drivers all looked angry. The sidewalks were crowded with people, most of them tourists. They passed along from window to window, eying the junk tourist merchandise; the oriental curios, furniture, loud silk kimonos on dummies wearing black Chinese caps and red Chinese slippers, samurai-sword letter openers, paper lanterns and parasols, decks of cards with Technicolor nudes on the backs, black velvet-covered racks displaying badly carved bone. Half the stores on the street sold the same things; the other half were divided between bars and the true main-street necessities of the Chinese community: the stinking markets, whose windows displayed flattened brownish-yellow ducks with steel hooks through their gullets, beaks up, eyes glazed; tanks of silvery fish; crates of live white chickens with obscene red combs, the crates stacked against parking meters and blocking the sidewalk; the heaped vegetable racks exuding the odors of compost and earth; the neon-lit supermarket casting its dead blue-white glare out on to the tourists, turning their faces yellow and their lips purple.

Bill and Natalie jostled their way through the crowd, Bill's hand lightly under her elbow. The noise was tremendous, a mingling of high whining Chinese music, hot yellow jazz, the chatter of Chinese voices and the honking of frustrated automobile horns. Shouting in her ear, Bill told Natalie that the Chinese word for din was a pictograph of three women, but she barely heard him. The smells were nauseating her, and she was angry at herself for suddenly becoming too terribly hungry and eating with the greed of a starving dog. She felt somehow angry at the tourists, too, many of them her age and with nothing better to do with their time than wander vacantly around gawking at each other and buying postcards to send home. The women were disgusting; all gone to fat and powder, ugly slit mouths carved into obscene bows with thick blue lipstick, clinging to their sleek stupid husbands while they stored up superlatives for the girls back home. What lives they must lead! What hopeless, desperate stupid lives! They played bridge and they went shopping, and they cooked tasteless dinners for husbands whose minds were still in the office; they got fat and wore girdles and cried to themselves and read the *Reader's Digest* looking for new symptoms, they photographed their grandchildren and interfered with their upbringing, they watched television with blank popping eyes and when something trite enough to burst through the dense gristle of their minds occurred they burbled their appreciation and understanding and clapped their fat pink hands while the dishwasher in the kitchen roared in muffled frustration. Rita had asked Natalie a dozen times to come and live in Walnut Creek, and now she felt so glad she had refused she burst into laughter as they turned the corner into the long dark alley of Adler Place, and she took Bill's arm comfortably into her own, delightfully free.

There were darkened entryways lined with garbage cans on the one narrow sidewalk, and one pale light high on the brick wall, and from behind it came the faint sounds of the interior of a bar, and by the time they were halfway down the alley the band in the bar started another set of incredibly loud pulsing two-beat jazz. They got to Henri's, on the corner, the place they had met, and Bill said, "Not in here, it's too noisy. How about across the street?"

He looked down at her, knowing he had sensed her mood properly, and without waiting for an answer, took her arm again, and they crossed in the middle of the block, between the slow cars on Columbus, and went into an Italian bar.

The pale high-domed room, with its paintings of scenes from great operas and its long dark-wood bar, had the correct degree of stolid warm comfort to wash away the hectic past ten minutes from their ears, and when they were seated in a red leather-covered booth in the back they smiled pleasantly at each other, aware that their minds were in perfect synchronization. Bill ordered drinks for them, and when the old waiter went away Natalie said, "Thank you."

"You're welcome."

She looked at his long thin face and felt, meaninglessly, a sharp clear pleasure at being with him. He was so utterly different from Jerry; he was nice to her, he behaved well, he spoke to her intelligently, he revealed himself to her without self-pity. He was a gentleman in a time when the word was an irony. She reached out and touched the back of his hand lightly, and watched his eyes follow her finger tips and then return to hers. He looked right into her eyes, and she felt the electric sensual tension begin to build up between them. "Electric" is only a metaphor for this feeling, perhaps the most accurate way of saying what it is like. The tension was not a bad, nervous kind, but related to the kind of tension built up in a good joke, when one knows the gate is soon going to open and laughter and surprise burst out. Boys and girls in love can look at each other and in a few moments build up enough of this tension to cause them to start giggling, reducing the pressure that must be cut away or build to an embrace. In Natalie it was not so quick or so difficult to control; but she did not want to control it. She had not felt like this in a long time: free, release and expansion, a slender silver wire of joy between them.

She touched his hand again. His only outward reaction was to fold his fingers around hers and squeeze, lightly.

"I like you very much," he said.

Now that the barrier of tension was gone, Natalie felt the change in atmosphere, from sexual tension to tenderness. She understood why he had only needed to use the mild expression "I like you very much," to convey what stronger, more melodramatic words would only have muddied. She felt utterly relaxed, as she would not have if she had thought she was falling in love. It was not Bill himself who made her feel good; in effect, there was nothing personal about it. But Bill wanted her and she knew it, and this radiating desire cleared the sickness from her body and mind, and she was grateful to Bill. She had to respond to his desire, because it was the only human thing to do.

There was no hurry. They could continue to sit in the back of the Italian bar, talking idly about music, because it was still early and there was no need to rush to bed like a pair of star-crossed lovers, copulate nervously and part with furtive speed. They could sit here and talk, and as they talked they could drink, and because of the contagion of their mood, they could drink for an hour without really getting drunk.

"Let's get out of here," Bill said at last. The bar was beginning to be crowded and the hum of conversation obscured the music. He stood up and took Natalie's hand, and she rose to him, their bodies almost touching. It was the moment for Bill to say, "Shall we go home?" and for Natalie to nod, but instead, knowing that there was no hurry and they had all night, Bill suggested that they go to another bar, and Natalie agreed, her eyes confirming to Bill that she knew why he was putting it off; that the warm conversation and the being together in public was prelude.

They went to the place where Jimmy worked, up around the corner on Broadway. It was a long dark bar with a few tables against the left-hand wall, red leather-covered stools and a shining chromium railing. In the back there was a baby-grand piano with a dark-blue plush shawl thrown over it, and tonight there was a couple seated on the bench, drinking and talking in low voices. There were no other customers in the bar, and Jimmy was in the center, in his white mess jacket, bent over the cutting board quartering limes. He looked up when Bill and Natalie came in, glanced at her perfunctorily and smiled at Bill. He had wiped his hands and was standing in front of them by the time they were seated at the bar, where it curved around near the entrance.

Bill ordered Gibsons and Jimmy nodded and moved over to the mixing stand and began on the drinks. After he had placed the drinks on napkins on the bar in front of them he moved back to the cutting board and picked up a whole lime and the short-bladed knife and went back to work. Without looking up he said, "How are you tonight, folks?"

"Aren't you going to roll me for the drinks, Jimmy?" Bill asked.

"Sure thing." Jimmy turned around and got the dice cups and put them on the bar. Then he looked steadily at Bill.

Compared to Bill, Jimmy was a small man. He had an almost round face. His thin mustache was pure white now, and his lips thinner than Natalie remembered. His hair was white, too, and receding back from his forehead, giving him an almost intellectual expression; and his nose, small as it was, dominated his face because of the burst capillaries beneath its surface, which mottled the skin with bright crimson spots and blue lines. He had the nose of a drunk and the pale complexion of the habitual night owl. But his white jacket was fresh and stiff with starch and his hair combed into a high pompadour, and he looked almost dapper.

Bill picked up one of the dice cups and Jimmy the other, and they played Liar's Dice for the drinks.

Natalie watched them. The wicked little idea of coming here and showing Bill off in front of Jimmy had lost its savor, in just that flickering glance between them. Somehow everything had got twisted, and the implication to Natalie was that there was nothing difficult in picking up young men when you had *that* to offer them. And Jimmy of course knew her exact age and was not fooled by her appearance. He was still a handsome little man, but he looked—*harmless*. Whatever it was he once had, the thing that had attracted Natalie so strongly, was gone. He was nearly, but not quite, an old man.

It was three months since she had seen him last, before Jerry even, on the occasion of the last act of the comedy he played every time he hit a big one at Bay Meadows. This time Natalie had been down around the corner at the Laundromat, putting a load of clothing through the machines. She remembered everything about it clearly, for no good reason except that there had been a very young Mexican boy in the Laundromat with his sister, and the boy had been talking gently to the little girl, sitting on the long bench at the front of the room by the window. He could not have been more than ten, and the sister no more than three or four, but they spoke quietly in Spanish, seriously, their heads close together, and Natalie leaned against her machine and watched them from behind, wondering what the serious thing they were talking about could possibly be. She had been touched by their seeming lack of childishness, two beautiful children who already seemed to know so much about life that there was nothing in them but the seriousness of life, the need to control their emotions and present a dignified face to the world. But as Natalie thought about it, pulling the hard wet clothing out of the machine and transferring it into the tall, still-hot dryer, she decided that one thing all children possessed was dignity, that even crying from a spill on the sidewalk or from a skinned knee, children had a quality of self-possession and self-understanding that older people try so hard for but never quite achieve. Take the matter of clothes; it was almost impossible for an adult to retain his dignity without his clothes, unless that adult was beautiful, and conformed in that beauty to the standards of the viewer. A naked man is usually pretty silly-looking; a naked child, never. Nothing could be done to a naked child to make him appear absurd, and little could be done with the adult to *keep* him from appearing absurd. Only that conformance to a standard of beauty, which would keep the observer from noticing the absurdity while contemplating the beauty. But what had happened to the dignity? At what precise moment and from what cause did the dignity disappear?

When Natalie turned around, the two serious Mexican children were gone, and Jimmy was standing outside the steamy window, his hands tucked into the pockets of his coat, a small cigar jutting from the corner of his mouth. He was turned three-quarters away from Natalie but she would have recognized him even if his back had been to her. There was the square set of his shoulders, the angle of his hat, the way he carried himself, importantly, seriously, yet without dignity. Almost a popinjay. She went outside and felt the suddenly fresh air cold on her face and wet hands. She went up to Jimmy and he turned his head toward her and raised his eyebrows in greeting. His eyes looked tired.

"What do you want?" she said.

He did not bother to look hurt. "Hi, Nat. How about having dinner with me? I got to be a little lonely."

"Oh, Jimmy," she said.

He laughed. "No, I mean it. I was just sitting there in my room and I thought I'd come and have a little supper with you. I got some things I'd like to tell you about; ask your advice maybe."

"Come on in," she said. "I have to get some clothes out of the dryer." He followed her inside and sat on the bench, his hat tipped back, the perpetual cigar pointed at her as she worked.

Finally the voice spoke to her, flattened slightly by the steam in the room: "Let's try it again, honey. I'm so lonely without you."

Natalie turned toward him angrily. "Don't talk about that any more. Please. You'll get your money."

He shrugged and smiled faintly at her. She returned to work, and when she had the dried clothes all folded and packed into her wire cart he volunteered to wheel it up the hill to her apartment.

"No," she said. "I think you ought to go now." She knew he had come to borrow money from her, that he had been drinking for days, perhaps a couple of weeks, that he had lost his job and was broke because he had caught a winner at the track and gone off on a spree. He did not look it, but she knew it; he never came to see her in any other circumstances. He needed money now to tide him over until he got another bartending job. She knew he would not spend the money he got from her on drinking, because Natalie was his last ace, his holecard, and when he had borrowed from her once, it was all over; she would not lend him any more and neither would anyone else. They had played this scene half a dozen times in the last few years.

"I can lend you twenty dollars," she said. She opened her purse, not looking at Jimmy.

"I didn't come here to borrow money; I wanted to take you to dinner, Nat."

"Here."

Jimmy took the bill with a show of reluctance, folded it lengthwise, then double, and tucked it into a vest pocket. "I'll pay you back as soon as I get a job."

"Yes, Jimmy. I have to go now."

He insisted on wheeling the cart up the hill for her, and when they were on Carson Street in front of her apartment, he tried again: "Do you think I'm kidding you just for the money? I really want to try again. Really."

She made it sound harsher than she felt: "But I'm not, Jimmy. Please; I'll see you later." And she went inside.

Bill paid double for the drinks and Jimmy took the dice cups and went back to quartering limes, moving only a few feet down the bar, but, like a good bartender, seeming to have moved out of the customers' circle of intimacy, to blend into the bar furnishings.

Bill leaned lazily on one elbow and sipped at his drink. "It's a cliché," he said, "but did you ever stop to think of how bartenders see things? They're the real existentialists. They see life a moment at a time. They stand back of the bar and watch and listen, not to a cross-section of society, but to a special segment, society in its moments of letdown. But none of it makes any difference to them. The customers ask their advice, tell them their most intimate troubles and lies, and they listen and nod and come up with the right cliché." Bill frowned slightly. "But I don't think they're like Camus's uninvolved man. Did you read *The Stranger*?"

"No," she said. "What's an uninvolved man?"

"It doesn't matter. Ha ha, very Camus-like. Nothing matters, and so, of course, everything matters equally. If you're like me, everything matters very much. He said someplace that if all lives are meaningless, the moral life is no more meaningless than any other kind."

He looked at her, waiting for her comment. But she made none, smiling at him to show that her silence had no ominous meanings, but that she was merely waiting for him to keep talking.

"Don't you have some little tidbit of philosophy to tell me?" he asked her. "Aren't you going to tell me this is true, or this is true, *but?*"

"No," she said. "I feel so comfortable." It was true; she had forgotten all about Jimmy—until Bill reminded her by saying, "I don't suppose Jimmy's at all like my romantic image of him. He probably has a nice sordid life somewhere; a wife and children he despises, a few friends he dislikes, a lawn to mow and a car to pay for. But hell, when he's here behind the bar in that nice stiff white coat, he seems removed from it all, apart, distant. Everybody on *this* side of the bar is in serious trouble and comes here to drink it away, or to drink it closer, or anyway, to drink, and he stands back there and watches and mixes and listens and every so often pops out a cliché on demand. But he's not really involved in the struggle." Bill laughed. "My imagination again. His feet probably hurt. But then, that's a pretty existential thing to be thinking about. The world's going to be blown to smithereens, and my feet hurt."

Natalie wished he would stop talking about Jimmy; it bothered her to think about him. She had too much else on her mind, and for the past few hours she had been able, somehow, to forget herself, and now this talk about her ex-husband was forcibly reminding her that she, too, had a nest of troubles.

But Bill continued: "But of those two ideas, which is the more important? Which can he do anything about?

Hell, he can't do anything about either of them. His feet hurt because he's working on his feet half the night, and he has to work to stay alive and pay for his television set, so that when they come to blow the world to flinders, he'll be alive and waiting, and able to see the destruction of Detroit live. 'There goes the Buick plant, folks, and now a word from our sponsor: Plymouth.' "

Natalie laughed. "You're drunk."

"You're drunk yourself."

"Are you saying that I'm as drunk as you are?"

"Dear heaven, lady, of course not." He leaned back and looked around the bar. There were a few more customers, and Jimmy was back by the piano. "You know, I like this place, even if the bartender's feet do hurt. If they didn't he'd be dead, anyway. Quiet place, not much action. God, you see a lot of screwy things in a bar. That's what I mean. He stands back there and watches the human race go through all the screwy, horrible rotten things, and even the slushy romantic nonsense, and maybe even some beautiful things, but right offhand I can't think of any beautiful things I ever saw in a bar. I saw a man kill himself in a bar, once. Sitting all by himself in the corner, nursing a beer. All of a sudden, when nobody was looking at him, he took out a razor blade and sliced both wrists, held his hands up and let the blood pour into the beer." Bill shuddered. "What a mess!"

Bill told her how they carried the man out and took him to the emergency hospital, but the man had died anyway.

"I saw an awful thing once," Natalie said. Jimmy was still at the other end of the room, and she leaned toward Bill until their elbows were touching. "These two men were standing at the bar, arguing. They were big men with red faces and deep loud voices. I think they were arguing about which one of them would go call on some woman. They were so loud and so big that everyone else in the place was listening to them, but nobody would get up and tell them to be quiet. But then this boy—he couldn't have been much over eighteen—"

Natalie saw the boy's face. Thin, delicate arched girlish eyebrows, large dark eyes. The boy stepped between the men, obviously drunk himself, too drunk to keep himself from doing what he was doing; getting between the men and telling them in a high, sad, silly voice that they mustn't argue, that they must be friends. The two men looked surprised that anyone would presume to speak to them without being spoken to, and taking the boy's arms they led him outside between them, almost as if it had been rehearsed. As they left the bar Natalie saw the hip holster on one of the men, and the bulge in the same place under the coat of the other, and she saw that they both wore the dark-blue trousers and black shoes of the Oakland police. They were off-duty policemen. The boy was thin and sagging between them, his voice trailing off as the bar doors shut behind him. It was quiet in the bar for a few minutes and then conversations began again; low, embarrassed murmuring; distant, self-conscious talk.

"When we came out about an hour later, the boy was sitting on the curb about half a block away, holding his face. He looked awful." Natalie's eyes darkened with pain at the remembrance of the boy's raw beaten face. "We took him down to the hospital. All the way in the car he tried to talk, but he was crying and all that came out of his mouth were sobbing noises. When the doctor got through with him he told us that one of them had held his arms and the other one had hit him in the face and stomach and then left him on the ground. They broke his jaw in two places and he had to stay at the hospital and get his jaw wired up in the morning."

Natalie laughed nervously, looking at Bill's intent, frightened face. She continued without thinking: "The last thing he said to us was that he was terribly afraid of dentists."

They drank quietly for a moment. Then Bill said distantly, "Where did this happen?"

For half a second Natalie thought that it had been Bill himself, from his reaction, that this was one of those freak meetings you hear about. But of course on second thought she knew that it was impossible. Bill was in his middle thirties and this had all happened in 1929. Bill had been about nine years old at the time. Natalie looked at him strangely. "Oh, in Oakland, a long time ago. Before you were born."

Bill grinned at what he knew had been a forced joke. "I thought so," he said. "Nowadays it's the kids who beat up the adults." He told a story he had heard about two Lesbians who had tried to hold up a Greek grocer, late one night the year before. The grocer was about sixty years old, and the two women, dressed as men, crowded behind the counter of the store with the Greek and ordered him to give them the money or they would beat him up. The Greek did not hesitate a moment, but picked up a large can of Van Camp's Pork & Beans and hit one of the women in the face. She fell back screeching and he quickly hit the other one in the stomach. Brandishing the bent can, he lifted the telephone and loudly asked the dial tone to call the police. The women ran from the place and were caught a few hours later, after the old man actually did call the police. He was very happy about the whole thing.

Natalie giggled. "That's really an awful story." It sounded to her as if she had said, "Thass." "Oh oh," she said. "I'm beginning to feel woozy."

"Would you folks care for another?" Jimmy asked from behind the bar. His manicured flat fingers were poised on the lip of the bar, and he leaned toward them without seeming to look at them, the usual blank smile on his face. It seemed to Natalie that he had been there all the time. Of course he could authenticate the story about the boy and the two policemen, since he had been there.

"Jimmy," Bill said, "do you think most men lead lives of quiet desperation?"

"Not around here," Jimmy said. "Not quiet." He waited patiently for the order.

Bill laughed with delight. "Two more and that's all, you old existentialist, you."

"No loud swearing, please," Jimmy said. He went off to mix the drinks. The bar was getting quite crowded now, and a couple came in, saw Bill and came over to them. They were in their middle forties and quite well dressed. The man was an executive for the insurance company that employed Bill, and after a few moments of conversation, he and the woman with him went toward the back of the bar and sat at one of the small tables. Natalie watched them sit down and saw the man take the woman's hands between his, lean toward her, and speak urgently into her ear. The woman seemed pleasant, rather homely, with heavy cheeks and a mouth a trifle too painted, eyebrows arched just a little bit too high.

"She's not his wife," Bill said to her. "He's been shacking up with her for about twenty years. He isn't married. He's a good-looking man, isn't he? Distinguished. But she won't marry him. Their arrangement is temporary. Got him right where she wants him. He can't move, can't take out any other women, can't do a damn thing. She knows. She's smart. Marry him and the first thing he starts going out the back door. He's really hung up on her. Twenty God-damn years."

"How do you happen to know all this about them?" Natalie asked him. It seemed unlike Bill to gossip. But his reply to her went unheard; for some reason her mind was occupied with wondering if men had ever worn such things as striped red- and-white blazers, or if that had been a false memory. The man at the dance, fat, sweating, sausage fingers on her bare back; but there was no doubt about the silver lamé dresses—she had owned one herself—but a blazer seemed so outrageously Hollywood for any fat little men in Berkeley, even twenty-five years ago. It was absurd, like raccoon coats and beanies, something out of a bad movie about a generation that hadn't existed.

"How can people do such things to each other in the name of love?" Bill asked sadly. "He's one of the nicest guys in the world, and he ought to have the things he craves, a home and children and a God-damn garden and all of it; but instead he lives in a little three-room apartment and that woman lives in a hotel room. Twenty years! I'll bet he thinks about leaving her every day. Over six thousand days, the same thought impelling to action; but never any resolution."

Jimmy was shaking dice at the other end of the bar, and Natalie watched him, sipping her drink. Sex isn't everything, she thought. Think about the companionship, and, of course, the grandchildren to come. So soon! Trellis, sunlight, rocking chair. But she knew better. Of course he wanted to come back to her, and of course he was sorry about everything, but he really doesn't care anything about the children, he never has, except when they were young and cute and fun to play with for five minutes before supper. She knew what would happen if the impossible reunion took place: Jimmy would die. He would move in with her, and no longer pressed by the need to earn a living he would stay at home with the racing form and a bottle of brown whiskey and drink himself stupid every day, until the final bursting moment when he would have to be dragged screaming from the apartment and taken to the white confines of the hospital, where he would die from the lack of booze just as surely and quickly as if he had been poisoned. The cells of his body could stand the accumulation of only so much more alcohol, but it could not stand the complete withdrawal at all, and between these things, Jimmy would die. And if by some miracle he did not die of drinking he would turn into a vegetable anyway, and Natalie would have to share her evenings with a silent man who sipped himself into sleep seven nights a week.

But even in her present half-drunk condition she knew there was something beneath her rationale, pushing upward for recognition: she was in love with Jerry Hoeffer, whose arrogant face had not been in her mind for hours, and the thought of him now was like sharp fingernails cutting into the back of her neck. This was the axis of her life, and no matter how she tried to break free, there it was, in the center of things, pulling her down into the completely inexplicable need to have him. It could not have been anything so simple as the need for sexual gratification, for Jerry had never given her that, and her love for Jimmy had persisted long past the time when he could no longer come to bed with her; even then it seemed to have died of attrition, rather than there having been one particular moment when she could have said, I no longer love him.

They were leaving the bar, Bill's hand on her elbow, and Jimmy's last words to them, "Be careful, you two," repeated themselves in her mind as she bled the last thoughts of Jerry Hoeffer from existence, leaving only the heavy-fingered hand of Bill Hastings to anchor her to the earth and reality. She let the fingers tug at her and she soared easily through the peopled streets, and found herself in the corner of a leathery taxicab seat with the hot breath of Bill Hastings flooding her face. At last the warmth was there, the sexual warmth from within her, at last, the thing she knew must happen again, in spite of everything. It did not matter who he was any more; he was a man and his body was pressing against hers. She was blind and dizzy, and let the motion of the cab press her hips into his. She felt his mouth strike hers and she wanted so very much to scream with delight.

1960

About the Author

Don Carpenter (1931–1995) gained immediate critical recognition with his first book, *Hard Rain Falling*, which was hailed as one of the notable novels of 1966. He went on to write many novels, novellas, screenplays, and short stories, including *The Murder of the Frogs and Other Stories*, over the course of a twenty-two-year career. Carpenter was born in Berkeley, California, and grew up in the Bay Area and Portland, Oregon. After serving in the US Air Force during the Korean War, he was discharged in 1955. He wrote about marginal characters like himself, a self-described hustler and punk: pool sharks, prisoners, drug dealers, struggling actors, and movie moguls. Facing a mounting series of debilitating illnesses, including tuberculosis, diabetes, and glaucoma, Carpenter committed suicide.